HOOK, LINE AND BLINKER

JANA DELEON

J&R Publishing

INTRODUCTION

If you've never read a Miss Fortune mystery, you can start with LOUISIANA LONGSHOT, the first book in the series. If you prefer to start with this book, here are a few things you need to know.

Fortune Redding – a CIA assassin with a price on her head from one of the world's most deadly arms dealers. Because her boss suspects that a leak at the CIA blew her cover, he sends her to hide out in Sinful, Louisiana, posing as his niece, a librarian and ex–beauty queen named Sandy-Sue Morrow.

Ida Belle and Gertie – served in the military in Vietnam as spies, but no one in the town is aware of that fact except Fortune and Deputy LeBlanc.

Sinful Ladies Society – local group founded by Ida Belle, Gertie, and deceased member Marge. In order to gain membership, women must never have married or if widowed, their husband must have been deceased for at least ten years.

Sinful Ladies Cough Syrup − sold as an herbal medicine in Sinful, which is dry, but it's actually moonshine manufactured by the Sinful Ladies Society.

CHAPTER ONE

"I think it's ready," Gertie said, and dipped a ladle into the huge pot on her stove. The fumes alone had made my eyes water so badly that I'd finally put on the goggles Ida Belle gave me when I arrived twenty minutes ago.

Despite the potentially explosive fumes, the aroma was actually quite nice. "It has a sort of cinnamon smell to it," I said.

This was the first time I'd been present for an official tasting of Sinful Ladies Cough Syrup. Ida Belle and Gertie had been working on a new flavor, and they claimed their taste buds were officially numb. They said that at this point, they wouldn't be able to tell the difference between their brew and a real bottle of cough syrup. So I was the official taste tester. Payment was all the Sinful Ladies brew I could handle, a pot roast, and a container of freshly baked chocolate chip cookies. It was a darn fine gig if you could get it.

"It should have a bit of cinnamon taste to it as well," Ida Belle said.

"We thought the cinnamon would make it festive," Gertie said. "Maybe release it as a holiday offering."

Gertie poured some of the liquid out of the ladle and into a glass, then handed it to me. "Give it a bit to cool. It will be better room temperature."

"Or maybe even chilled," Ida Belle said.

"Oh," Gertie said. "I like that idea."

They both watched me as I blew on the whiskey until the steam stopped coming off it.

"Go for it," Ida Belle said.

"Not just a sip," Gertie said. "You need enough to give us good feedback, but not so much that you get choked and it doesn't go down smoothly."

"Will you shut up and let the woman drink?" Ida Belle asked.

I held the glass up. "Here's to the last four days in Sinful. No murders. No explosions. No undercover outfits."

"Hear! Hear!" Gertie chanted.

I put the glass to my lips and took a big swig. Almost immediately, my eyes watered and then crossed, and I yanked off the goggles. I swallowed and thought my throat was going to explode. I opened my mouth to talk, but nothing would come out.

Ida Belle and Gertie watched me closely, and I wasn't sure whether to feel comforted or worried that neither had flung me onto the floor and attempted CPR. It was probably only seconds, but felt like much longer, when my eyes went back into focus and I sucked in a breath. It burned coming in and smelled of cinnamon coming out. A flush swept through my entire body, and the soreness I'd had in my neck since I'd gotten out of bed vanished completely.

"Holy crap!" I said. "That was both frightening and awesome."

Ida Belle grinned. "We're calling it the Widow Maker."

"Is Sinful Ladies membership down?" I asked.

"Well," Gertie said, "there have been some deaths and several relocations the last couple years—"

I held up my hand. "I was joking." And if Gertie thought the cough syrup would result in a potential membership increase for the Sinful Ladies Society, I didn't want to know about it.

"So is it a thumbs-up?" Ida Belle asked.

I nodded. "As long as you put a warning on the bottle that it could cause loss of eyesight and limit lung capacity, then you're good."

"Excellent," Ida Belle said. "We'll work up a marketing plan and start moving it through our network."

"Just how much of this stuff do you make?" I asked.

"We have five active stills among the membership," Ida Belle said. "A group is assigned to each one. Every summer, each group submits a new brew for testing at a group meeting and we decide if we'll add something new to the line."

"But I only know of one flavor," I said.

"That's because we've never liked any of the others," Gertie said. "But I think this one is a winner."

"There has been a lot of call lately for something with more punch," Ida Belle explained. "A lot of women in town are worried about the calories."

"Ah," I said, "so if they can get the same effect with less...uh, dosage, then that would keep them in the market."

Gertie shook her head. "It's a ridiculous thing to worry about. How many calories can possibly be in a swig of that stuff?"

"Ridiculous or not," Ida Belle said, "it's something people are starting to think about more often. In choir practice last week, Maisey Jackson's breath was so bad I thought she'd swallowed a skunk, so I passed her a breath mint. She Googled the calories on her phone before she'd eat it."

"Wow," I said.

"But that's not even the most ridiculous part," Ida Belle said. "Pastor Don's mother insisted we bless the mint before she put it in her mouth, claiming it was food."

"I saw her open a protein shake in the General Store last week," I said, "and she didn't pray before she took a drink."

"If you're not chewing, it's not food," Gertie said.

"Where does it say that in the Bible?" I asked. "I'm a little sketchy on the passage concerning breath mints as well."

Ida Belle waved her hand in dismissal. "People have been making up religious rules forever, and Sinful has the market cornered on it. No matter what you do, there's someone in this world that has a problem with it."

"Maybe if Maisey started wearing clothes while she was boating," I said, "she wouldn't have to worry so much about her weight."

"Got that right," Gertie said.

My phone rang and I checked the display. "It's Carter."

"What did you do?" Gertie asked.

"Why do you always think I've done something?" I asked. "Never mind."

It was true that over half of my past interactions with Carter had been over my less-than-legal transgressions that put me smack in the middle of police matters, but now that we were in an official relationship, things were strictly personal more often.

"She's blushing again," Gertie said. "And she still won't tell us about those nights she won't answer her phone."

"I don't think she needs to tell us," Ida Belle said. "It doesn't take a detective to know what's going on there."

Gertie sighed. "I'd still like details. I really miss the details."

"Stop!" I said, and answered the call.

"Are you still at Gertie's house?" Carter asked.

"Yeah, why?" His voice sounded tense, and that was never a good thing. As far as I knew, none of us had meddled in police business since the poacher case, but with Gertie, you never could be certain what else might have transpired when Ida Belle and I weren't around to reel her in.

"The auditors have finalized the election count," he said. "They're announcing the results in thirty minutes."

I clenched my phone. "Where?"

4

"Downtown in front of the sheriff's department. A camera crew will be here. Marie and Celia have already been notified."

"Holy crap, that's huge."

"I would tell you to make those two stay put because things could get ugly, but without handcuffing them, I know you can't."

"No way. We want to be there."

"Please try to keep things under control."

"Yeah, control depends on how this turns out."

I hung up the phone. Ida Belle and Gertie had ceased all conversation and were staring at me, worried expressions on their faces. They knew my serious voice, so they knew something was up. Of all the things they might expect to hear, the election results were probably low on the list.

During the last mayoral election, Ida Belle's nemesis and the first lady of horrible, Celia Arceneaux, ran against Ida Belle and Gertie's friend Marie. Celia won, but Marie asked for a recount based on rumors of ballot tampering. The audit had started weeks ago, and at the rate they were moving, we'd decided it would be time for a new election before they announced the results. In the meantime, Celia held Sinful hostage, making Carter's life miserable and using her position to bully everyone else into doing her bidding. If Celia maintained her position as mayor, I predicted an exodus from Sinful equivalent to that of Moses leading his people out of Egypt.

"The election results are in," I said. "They're making the announcement downtown in front of the sheriff's department in thirty minutes."

"Holy crap."

"Mother of God."

They both spoke at once, and Gertie reached over and grabbed Ida Belle's arm.

"Well," Ida Belle said, "this is it. I guess we best get down there and see what the future holds."

She didn't have to spell it out. So much was riding on this election.

Ida Belle and Gertie had already said they'd seriously consider moving if Celia stayed in office, and even if Carter was allowed to keep his position, he had already stated that he didn't feel he could work for Celia. I was Celia's number one target for takedown, so my plans for future residency definitely depended on what everyone else decided. I really liked Sinful, but without Carter, Ida Belle, and Gertie, it would just be another small town. I could find one of those anywhere.

Gertie let go of Ida Belle, took my hand in hers, and squeezed. "Don't worry. I have a good feeling about this."

I hoped she was right. "Maybe we should take a bottle of the new stuff...just in case."

———

THE SCENE DOWNTOWN looked like geriatric Woodstock. Women milled around the street in random states of dress, some without shoes, many with rollers in their hair, one wearing a green paste on her face, and one still stirring something in a mixing bowl. Some of the men wore muddy boots and were holding rifles, which would be alarming anywhere but Sinful, but here was quite common. Other men stood beside coolers that reeked of fish, and as we approached the crowd, one man ran from behind the buildings where the bayou was located, clutching a rod with a fish still on the line. Apparently, everyone was anxious to be front and center for the big announcement.

I made a note of where live fish guy was standing in case I needed to borrow the fish and slap anyone with it. I'd done it accidentally once, and I'd been itching to do it on purpose ever since.

We weaved in and out of the crowd and finally spotted Marie near the front of the sheriff's department. She wore a pretty blue dress and looked kinda pale. We pushed our way through the crowd and managed to squeeze in beside her.

Gertie took her hand. "Are you all right? You look a little peaked."

"I think I'm going to pass out," Marie said. "It feels like we've been waiting on this forever and now that it's here, I'm afraid. What if the recount is still in Celia's favor?"

"A lot of homes will go on the market," Ida Belle said. "If we had a revote, you can bet things would be a lot different. A lot of people who voted for Celia have her number now."

"If only they'd had a lick of sense before," Gertie said. "Maybe there should be an IQ test to vote."

"There should be an IQ test for a lot of things," Ida Belle grumbled.

The door to the sheriff's department opened and Carter walked out, followed by three men and one woman all wearing black suits and white shirts. It was either the Secret Service, the men in black, or the auditors. I was going with auditors, but I reserved the right to change my selection. This was Sinful.

Carter scanned the crowd and locked in on me. I started to do the ole raised eyebrow thing or a slight hands up, but the strained look on his face told me everything I needed to know. Either Celia was still in charge or he didn't know yet and was as worried as the rest of us. He raised his hands and waved at the crowd of people.

"Can I have your attention please?" he yelled. "We don't have audio equipment, so I need everyone to be quiet."

The noise level dropped, but only by half, as people continued to move about and talk in low voices. Ida Belle stuck her fingers in the sides of her mouth and whistled. An ear-shattering, glass-breaking whistle. My hands flew involuntarily over my ears and as I glared at her, I noticed Gertie pulling some cotton out of her ears.

"She does it every time," Gertie said.

"A little warning would have been nice," I said.

Gertie gave me an apologetic shrug, and I turned back around to see Carter waving at one of the suits.

"This is Bryant Wilkinson," Carter said. "He is the audit manager and will announce the findings."

I watched as the suit moved closer to the crowd.

Midfifties. A hundred and eighty pounds, twenty of it potbelly. Skin that hadn't seen the sun in years. Delicate hands. Only dangerous if he was auditing you and you were a tax evader.

Wilkinson cleared his throat and said, "Before I announce the results, I'd like to introduce my team, who worked diligently to conduct this audit."

"Nobody cares!" a man shouted.

"You got paid!" a woman threw in. "You're supposed to work diligently."

"Get on with it!" another man shouted. "I'm holding a live bass and it's not going to keep in this heat."

Given that his skin was almost glowing white, I didn't think it was possible, but Wilkinson scanned the crowd and appeared to pale a little. He'd probably finally clued in to the array of firearms.

"Uh, okay," Wilkinson stammered. "Our findings show that the winner of the mayoral election is Marie Chicoron."

A huge cheer went up in the crowd, so loud that I couldn't even hear when he said Marie's last name. Gertie screamed and hugged me so hard I would probably bruise. Ida Belle was grinning so big, I was afraid her face might break, as it rarely worked out that hard. Almost everyone was cheering and bouncing and hugging.

And then Celia walked up to Marie and started yelling.

"Who did you pay off?" Celia yelled. "No way you beat me."

"Look around," Ida Belle said. "No one wants you."

"There's plenty of people that want me," Celia said. "This is all some setup job. I know how you operate, Ida Belle, and you've gotten a million times worse since the Yankee whore showed up. Don't think you're fooling anyone."

"Why am I always the whore?" I asked Gertie.

Gertie shrugged. "Just lucky, I guess. I never get to be the whore."

"This isn't the end," Celia said. "I'm going to crawl up your butts with a microscope."

"Are you going to buy me dinner first?" I asked. "Because even whores have standards."

Celia's face turned red and I swear, for a moment, I thought she was going to attempt to hit me. But then she must have had a burst of reality check, and she just glared. "There's something off about you," Celia said to me. "I've known it from the beginning and I'm going to get to the bottom of it. Nothing bad ever happened in this town until you showed up."

"That's enough," Carter said. "The auditors have completed their job. Marie is the new mayor of Sinful. I want everyone to clear out of here and go on with your lives. Including you, Celia."

"I want another audit!" Celia yelled at Carter. "And this time, I want a firm from another state. One that can't be bought."

"If you want to contest the audit," Carter said, "you need to file the appropriate paperwork, but in the meantime, I need to collect the keys to government buildings that are in your possession."

If Celia had been capable of it, I swear her head would have spun around on her neck just like in *The Exorcist*. She sputtered several times, then pulled a set of keys out of her purse. I was waiting for her to fling them in Carter's face, but then Celia did something entirely unexpected.

She took off running.

Shoving people to the side, Celia bolted away from the crowd and in between the buildings, screaming that she would throw the keys in the bayou before she turned them over to lying, cheating trash. Everyone was so stunned that it took at least a couple seconds before anyone reacted.

Then the chase was on.

Gertie was the closest of our group to the edge of the crowd so she got out first, but Ida Belle and I were close behind. The guy with the fish was the farthest out, as the crowd had forced him to stand some ways back before the announcement came. He was lumbering toward Celia at a pace much faster than I would have given him credit for, especially as he was still clutching the rod and the fish.

I passed Gertie as we rounded the building and saw Celia about thirty feet ahead, not too far from the bayou. She flung her arm back, the keys still clutched in her hand, and I knew she was about to throw them.

"Hell, no!" the guy with the fish yelled, and then tossed the enormous bass at Celia, as though he were skipping stones on the water.

The fish hit the ground before it reached her but slid under her foot as she raced forward. Her leg shot out from under her and she fell backward, flinging the keys up in the air. I dodged to the right and snagged the keys. Gertie did not have time to put on the brakes and ran right over Celia, treading in the middle of her chest before falling forward onto the fish.

Gertie's weight on the slimy fish didn't slow it down one bit. It continued its forward progress down the bank and deposited both of them in the water. As Gertie struggled to stand up, the guy with the rod started reeling the fish back in. When Gertie came dripping wet up the bank, Celia sat up and pointed a finger at her.

"I want her arrested for assault," Celia said.

Carter, who was standing in between Celia and the bank, raised his eyebrows. I could tell he was struggling not to smile.

"She ruined my dress," Celia continued to rant, "and probably broke a rib."

"I wish I'd broken a rib," Gertie said. "Then you wouldn't be able to gasbag around town the way you do. The fact that your mouth is open is a sure sign nothing is bruised."

"Except maybe her ego," Ida Belle said.

"Nice," I said.

"Then arrest that man for assaulting me with a fish," Celia said. "He made me fall. I could have been seriously injured."

"We're not that lucky," the fish dude said. "And besides, it wasn't intentional. I dropped the fish while I was running."

Carter looked around at the crowd that had gathered. "Did anyone see this man throw the fish?"

The entire crowd took on innocent expressions with lots of head shaking. Carter looked over at me, Gertie, and Ida Belle, and we shrugged.

"Did you see him throw the fish?" Carter asked Celia.

"Of course I didn't see him throw the fish," Celia said. "He was behind me. But it couldn't have gotten under my feet unless he threw it."

"Or he dropped it while running and kicked it under you," Ida Belle said. "Not like you were breaking any land speed records there. A slimy fish could easily outrun you."

"I believe you wanted these." I turned to Carter and handed him the keys, then looked down at Celia. "You should really consider a better wardrobe. That dress is coming apart and your forty-year-old bra is showing."

Celia looked down at the white bra peeking out of her torn dress and shrieked. She jumped up from the ground, clutching her chest as if she were having a heart attack, and glared at me.

"This is war," she said to Ida Belle.

Ida Belle smiled. "Bring it on."

CHAPTER TWO

After the bowling-with-fish excitement, Gertie headed home for a shower and change of clothes, and Ida Belle and I decided that all the running and sarcasm had made us hungry. We walked over to the café, where Ally managed to squeeze us into our regular table at the back of the restaurant.

"I heard Aunt Celia got attacked with a fish," Ally said.

"Yeah," Ida Belle said, "but her legs and mouth continued working, so we're still not safe."

Ally shook her head. "She's not going to let this go. I heard her talking on the sidewalk yesterday to one of her minions. She's really lost it, blaming Fortune for everything that has gone wrong with her life lately."

"That's bullshit and she knows it," Ida Belle said. "Everything wrong with Celia's life is directly tied to Celia's choices. She just refuses to own up to it."

"I know that," Ally said. "But I'm afraid of what she might do."

"What can she do?" Ida Belle asked. "Fortune hasn't done anything wrong. And now that Marie is mayor, Celia's control of the sheriff's department is over. Unless she goes completely psycho and shoots Fortune or burns her house down, what else does she have left?"

Ally frowned. "I don't know, but I still worry. She's always managed to cause trouble. Her entire life is a master's class in creating chaos and unhappiness. I hope you're right."

Ally headed off to get our drinks, and I blew out a breath. Ida Belle looked at me and narrowed her eyes.

"You don't think that bag of hot air can cause trouble, do you?" Ida Belle asked.

"If I weren't here pretending to be an entirely different person, I would say absolutely not. I've come up against five-year-olds who were smarter and deadlier than Celia. But if she starts looking into Sandy-Sue, I don't know how well my cover will hold."

"The CIA put it in place, didn't they? If they can't provide a solid cover, then I'm not sure who can."

"Even the CIA can't prevent Celia from tracking down colleagues or a neighbor or the guy at the coffee shop around the corner—any of whom might have a picture of Sandy-Sue or whom she might have told she was going to Europe for the summer and not Sinful."

Ida Belle's expression shifted slightly, and I could see the glimmer of worry in her eyes, but she was trying not to let it show.

"Well, there's no point in worrying about it until we need to," she said. "Even if we tried, there's no way to predict what Celia might do. She's always been a loose cannon, and ever since the situations with Pansy and Maxwell, she's gone even further over into the crazy zone."

Celia's husband had disappeared some twenty years ago and had long been presumed dead by everyone. He'd made a miraculous appearance last month and had brought a trail of trouble along with him. His reign of terror was over now, but before it ended, he'd managed to bring to light some things Celia would have rather left in the closet. Celia's daughter, Pansy, was a whole other can of worms, apparently taking after the man she'd thought was her father in the "bringing trouble with you" game. Both situations had ended badly for Celia's family.

So yes, Celia had definitely lived through some stress lately, but she'd picked her husband and she'd raised her daughter, and needed to take some responsibility on both counts. Blaming me, when she'd only met me two months before, hardly seemed fair or logical. But then, I was pretty sure Celia had never been accused of being either. I just hoped she kept a bit of a lid on the crazy long enough for my situation with Ahmad to resolve itself.

"Have you heard from Harrison lately?" Ida Belle asked.

"You must have been reading my mind," I said. "But no. I haven't heard from him in a while. I need to check in, but I have a feeling I already know what he's going to say."

My undercover gig in Sinful was all due to the price on my head by arms dealer Ahmad. Unfortunately, all of the CIA'a attempts to locate Ahmad and put him out of commission had met with failure. They'd come close once in New Orleans, and my boss, Director Morrow, had worried my cover was blown. But Ahmad turned out to be in New Orleans for an entirely different reason, and although the sting to take him down was unsuccessful, my cover remained intact.

"They'll find him," Ida Belle said.

"Maybe. He's a hard man to find even when he's not hiding. So many layers of protection. Body doubles. He doesn't take many chances."

"But he *does* take them. Sooner or later, he'll take a chance that winds up on the CIA's radar. And then all this will be over."

"I really hope so." Because if the summer passed without the CIA finding Ahmad, my future looked pretty grim. The real Sandy-Sue was a librarian with the school district. I was expected to be long gone by the time school started. Sticking around would raise more than a couple of eyebrows. Not to mention that the real Sandy-Sue probably wanted to liquidate the house and her aunt's belongings for the cash.

The bottom line—I couldn't maintain cover in Sinful forever.

———

CARTER CALLED LATE THAT EVENING, saying he planned on grilling that night and wanted to know if I was interested in a burgers-and-beer celebration. I was definitely up for celebrating the end of the reign of Celia the Antichrist, and I couldn't think of a time I'd passed on burgers and beer. Besides, I'd spent the afternoon testing moonshine with Ida Belle and Gertie and was already half lit. Food seemed like a good idea, and sitting in a chair doing nothing sounded even better.

But when Carter's quitting time at the sheriff's department came and went without so much as text, I knew something was wrong. Had Celia figured out a way to cause trouble already? I sent Carter a text asking him to let me know if we were still on for tonight and watched the phone for a bit, but the text didn't even show as read. Whatever he was doing, he wasn't looking at his phone.

The whole thing with Celia and her threat had bothered me more than I expected. I'd been used to blowing off her blustering, but for some reason, this time it felt real. I was afraid she'd finally reached that point where she had nothing to lose and was going to launch full force into her attack on me.

Since Carter was MIA and I was starving, I headed into the kitchen to grab a piece of cobbler and my laptop. I sat at the kitchen table and went through my whole secure-access, bouncing-around-servers thing, and then sent an email to Harrison.

To: hotdudeinNE
From: farmgirl433

Things are back to normal here since the storm. Same ole drama, but I don't expect that to change any time soon. Still, I'm getting kind of tired of dealing with some of the more frustrating people around me, especially one busybody neighbor who is constantly trying to get into my personal business. I might need to get away for a while. Maybe I'll come visit you if you're not too busy with work. Is it still hot there?

I HIT Send and shoved a huge bite of cobbler in my mouth. My email was cryptic, but I knew Harrison would understand exactly what I was trying to convey. Someone might look closely enough at me to compromise my cover, and I needed an extraction plan in place in case it happened. I figured Harrison and Morrow already had a couple of things in mind, and I was more than certain that I wouldn't like any of them.

I had hated the idea of coming to Sinful. Had protested with all of my being and had been so dead set against it that I was ready to risk an assassination just to avoid it. But I'd been wrong. Coming to Sinful and becoming friends with Ida Belle and Gertie was one of the best things that had ever happened to me. The other was Carter. Meeting them and seeing how life could be had made me question everything about my past choices to the point that I'd finally decided I'd gotten most everything wrong.

I'd already decided to leave the CIA when this nightmare was over, but what I still wasn't completely sure about was what I would do afterward. Ida Belle and Gertie had been pushing me toward getting my private investigator license, and I'll admit, it was an intriguing idea, but I knew it would put a strain on my relationship with Carter. He was still coming to terms with who I really was and all the lies I'd told to keep it a secret. He'd had a relationship with a Special Forces woman in the past that had ended tragically, and he'd sworn he'd never get involved with a woman who took those sorts of risks again. I knew that PIs normally didn't have the kind of risk associated with their work that Special Forces or federal agents did, but Sinful had proved to be a hotbed of criminal activity with a lot of violence associated.

I took a drink of soda and slumped back in my seat. None of it mattered if Celia managed to find what she was looking for. If she blew my cover, I'd be whisked away to a new location and unable to talk to anyone in Sinful until Ahmad was in custody or dead. That could be weeks or months or God forbid, even years. It was a bleak thought. Anything could happen over a long period of time. Ida Belle and Gertie weren't getting any younger. They could get ill or even worse. Carter could decide he'd made a mistake getting involved with me and start dating a nice, pretty girl who'd never been shot at and hadn't been paid to kill people for a living.

Basically, I could be forgotten. Replaced.

I blew out a breath and my computer beeped, signaling an incoming email. I was a bit surprised that Harrison had responded so quickly, but popped upright in my chair and clicked on the message.

To: farmgirl433

From: hotdudeinNE

I tried to tell you to be nice to nosy old ladies. If you're nice, they bring baked goods and try to set you up with their grandsons, but if you're remotely off-putting, they see it as a challenge. The weather cooled a bit here for a while, but it's right back up into the stratosphere. I would love to have you for a visit, but I wouldn't have time to even share a cup of coffee at the moment. I'm bringing on some additional help the next couple days. Let me see how that works and I'll let you know if it frees me up any.

Looking forward to seeing you again. Avoid the neighbor. She sounds exhausting.

MY PULSE TICKED up a notch as I read the email. The weather cooling meant the CIA had no luck locating Ahmad, but if things were heating up into the stratosphere now, then they had a hot tip. So hot they were bringing in more agents to work it—hence Harrison's comment about additional help. I was especially excited to read that he thought he'd know more in a couple of days. That meant that whatever tip they were working, the job was already under way.

If the CIA could set me free soon, I would be the happiest person in the world.

With a ton of decisions to make very quickly.

A knock on my door brought me out of my thoughts, and I logged off and closed my laptop, figuring it was Carter. He knew my real identity and had met my partner, Harrison, but I didn't feel like sharing this with him just yet. I didn't want him getting his hopes up. Mine were already up enough for both of us.

I hurried to the front door and was surprised to see Ida Belle and Gertie standing there. Ida Belle looked worried. Gertie looked confused. Neither gave me a warm, fuzzy feeling. I waved them in and closed and locked the door behind them. I'd gotten lax the last couple of weeks with locks during the day and was trying to correct that bad habit. It might be all right for other residents of Sinful to take such a risk, but it was a foolish one for me to indulge in.

"Sorry," Ida Belle said. "I forgot my key."

"And I didn't have a chance to grab my purse," Gertie said. "Ida Belle dragged me out of my house so fast, I didn't even have time to put on shoes."

I looked down at her bare feet with lime-green polish.

Ida Belle waved a hand in dismissal. "No one's going to see you but Fortune, and she's seen a lot worse of you than green toes."

"What if Carter shows up?" Gertie said.

"He's seen worse too," Ida Belle said. "I've got an emergency. Kitchen?"

"Of course," I said, and we started back to the kitchen, our usual room for plotting, gossiping, and brainstorming. Whatever was going on was serious. Ida Belle wasn't one for drama, and even if she hadn't stated it was an emergency, I could see the strain on her face. I hoped nothing had happened with Celia and the election. If anyone could figure out a way to mess things up, it would be Celia.

Whatever it was, clearly Gertie hadn't heard about it yet, which meant that Ida Belle had gotten the information directly from Marie or from one of her Sinful Ladies, who reported everything of interest to Ida Belle so that she was always aware of what was going on in Sinful. Ida Belle and Gertie took a seat at the table, and I pulled some sodas out of the refrigerator and passed them around. I reserved the right to move to the harder stuff depending on what Ida Belle had to say.

"What's going on?" Gertie asked. "Is something wrong with Marie? Did Celia figure out a way to screw things up for her?"

"No," Ida Belle said. "It has nothing to do with Marie."

"Thank God," Gertie said, looking as relieved as I felt.

"There was an incident at Hot Rod's shop," Ida Belle said.

Hot Rod Hank was a local guy who turned regular vehicles into lightning on wheels. Ida Belle had recently purchased a Blazer from him that went so fast it made you younger.

"What kind of incident?" I asked, wondering which one of his souped-up vehicles he'd been in when the incident occurred and what level of warp speed he'd been operating it at.

"There was a break-in," Ida Belle said. "Someone cracked him over the head with a tire iron. He's in the hospital and hasn't regained consciousness."

"Oh no!"

"That's horrible!"

Gertie and I expressed our dismay at the same time.

"Was it robbery?" I asked. "They probably figured no one would be there on a Sunday night."

"I'm not sure," Ida Belle said. "One of the Sinful Ladies has a niece who works as a nurse at the hospital. She said Hot Rod was in critical condition, and the paramedics said it looked like some vehicles might be missing, but no one can be certain until Hot Rod wakes up or the police can check the vehicles in his shop against inventory."

"That must be why Carter bailed on grill night and isn't answering his phone," I said.

Ida Belle nodded. "I'm sure he's there trying to figure out what happened."

"I hope Hot Rod is all right," Gertie said. "I figured his fascination with speed would eventually get him into trouble, but I never imagined this sort."

"Is there anything we can do?" I asked.

"Not that I can think of," Ida Belle said. "His father died in a boating accident when he was ten. His mother passed away a couple years ago. Massive heart failure."

"She was riding with Hot Rod when it happened," Gertie said.

I stared. "He gave his own mother a heart attack?"

"No," Gertie said. "That's not what I meant. He was driving normal, taking her to get groceries, and she had a heart attack on the way. I'm pretty sure he broke some records getting her to the hospital, but not even Hot Rod's car was fast enough. The doctors think she died within minutes."

"Does he have any other family?" I asked.

"Not that I know of," Ida Belle said. "I've never known any to visit, and I can't think of a time that Hot Rod has left town for more than a day, and that was always to look at a car."

I frowned. While what had happened to Hot Rod was horrifying and I hoped he pulled through it all right, I hadn't figured out what the emergency part of the story was. This was definitely a police matter. No way could I get involved in something like this, or Carter would arrest me and throw me in jail, dating or no.

"Okay," I said. "This entire thing sucks, but explain why it's an emergency. Clearly, I'm missing something."

Ida Belle blew out a breath. "I talked to the paramedics who brought Hot Rod in. They said he was still conscious when they found him, but just barely. He kept repeating 'gotta warn Ida Belle' until he passed completely out."

"Okay, that's not cool," I said.

"Maybe he was loopy," Gertie said. "I mean, he'd been hit so hard he blacked out."

"Maybe," Ida Belle said, "but if he really thought I was in some sort of danger, it would have to be because of the Blazer. We don't have anything else in common."

Gertie nodded. "And if other vehicles were missing...maybe they were SUVs."

"Hold up," I said. "While I agree that we need to take this seriously until we can figure out what's going on, the reality is we are speculating as to cause. For all we know, Hot Rod remembered something he intended to tell Ida Belle about the Blazer and before he got a chance to call, somebody took him out."

"That's true," Ida Belle said, "but it feels like there's more to it, you know?"

Ida Belle wasn't a fanciful person. She had written the book on practical, so when she said something didn't feel right, I paid attention. Those same instincts had saved my life on more than one occasion. Smart people were in tune with them and didn't ignore them.

"Maybe Fortune can find out more from Carter," Gertie said.

"I wouldn't count on it," I said. "He's been very careful not to mention any of his casework to me."

"But that was when Celia was watching him like a hawk, looking for a reason to fire him," Gertie said. "Surely things are different now."

"His job is no longer in jeopardy," I said, "but it's about more than the job. Carter won't admit it, but he doesn't want me doing things that put me at risk."

"No one wants their loved ones at risk," Gertie said, "but when you fall for a woman like you, then you have to fish or cut bait."

"I think Carter is firmly in the fishing camp," Ida Belle said, "but remember, Fortune's situation is bigger than the things happening in Sinful. If she's wrapped up in a crime here that puts her in a position to have to testify, or that makes national headlines, she's in serious crap."

Gertie sighed. "I keep forgetting about that. I wish the whole thing with Ahmad was over so you could stop pretending and do whatever the hell you feel like doing."

"You and me both," I said.

"Have you had any news from Harrison?" Ida Belle asked.

I hadn't intended to tell anyone just yet, but Ida Belle and Gertie were my best friends and biggest supporters. They wouldn't leak it to Carter, and they would probably be able to throttle high hopes.

"I heard from him just a bit ago," I said, and described our exchange.

Gertie's eyes widened, and I could tell she was excited by the news. Even Ida Belle looked pleased.

"When I get home," Gertie said, "I'm going to put on my lucky underwear, find my rabbit's foot, pray harder than I ever have before, and keep my fingers crossed for as long as it takes."

"You have lucky underwear?" I asked.

Gertie nodded. "I've had them for a while. Ida Belle and I took this weekend trip to New Orleans and I met this hottie in one of those strip bars. We hit it off right away and I had a night to remember. That pair of undies has been my lucky pair ever since."

Ida Belle stared at Gertie in dismay. "Good Lord, woman.

Those things should have dry-rotted by now. Dinosaurs still roamed the earth when we took that trip."

I grinned. "What happened to the hottie?"

"He probably went home to his wife," Ida Belle said.

"He did not!" Gertie said. "He was on military leave. He went back to fight."

"The Civil War," Ida Belle said.

Gertie shot the finger at Ida Belle, and I couldn't help but laugh.

More than anything in the world, I wanted to figure out a way that moments like this could continue forever. I just needed one bad guy to die.

It wasn't too much to ask.

CHAPTER THREE

It was almost 9:00 p.m. before I got a call from Carter. I'd gotten a brief text earlier that evening letting me know he had to work late and would reschedule our grill night for later this week. He started apologizing as soon as I answered.

"I'm so sorry," he said. "I was on something serious and couldn't call."

"You don't have to apologize to me. You're doing your job. Of all people, I get that."

"Yeah, I know, but all those manners my mom taught me won't go away."

He sounded exhausted, and I wondered just how bad things were. Surely if Hot Rod had taken a turn for the worse, Ida Belle would have gotten word of it.

"Have you eaten anything?" I asked. "I have some leftover roast beef. I could make you a sandwich with chips and toss in some of Ally's peanut butter cookies. Maybe even a beer unless it would put you facedown on the kitchen table."

"That sounds perfect, but I don't want to be rude and eat and run. And I'm afraid I won't be very good company."

"I don't mind the eat-and-run or the bad company. I get the job, Carter. I might be the only person in this town who does."

There were several seconds of silence and finally he said, "I'll be there in a couple of minutes."

I headed into the kitchen and started making up a sandwich. A couple minutes later, I heard a knock on the front door and went to let Carter in. He looked as tired as he'd sounded.

"I just put everything on the table," I said. "Come and get it while it's cold."

He followed me back to the kitchen and sat in front of the plate of food. He pulled the cap off the beer and took a long drink, then blew out a breath.

"I've got the harder stuff if you prefer," I said.

"No thanks. It will just make my headache worse."

I pulled a bottle of aspirin out of the cabinet and sat it on the table next to his plate before taking a seat next to him.

"Long day, huh?" I said. "The whole election announcement and Celia acting like, well, Celia. Then I guess you caught a bad one this afternoon."

He took a bite of the sandwich and nodded.

"Hot Rod?" I asked.

"How the heck did you know that? The only people at the shop were cops, and I asked everyone to keep their mouths shut."

"One of the Sinful Ladies has a niece who works at the hospital. She said Hot Rod was unconscious and had been hit pretty hard. We're hoping he's going to be okay. Have you heard anything?"

"I talked to the nurse in charge on my way over here. He's stable but there's no change."

"That sucks. I don't get it. Why would someone want to hurt Hot Rod? I mean, he's sorta crazy but seemed harmless. He's into his cars, and I didn't get the impression he was into anything else."

"You know I can't talk about an open investigation," Carter

said. "And I need the three of you to stay out of this. I'm pretty sure whoever popped Hot Rod thought they'd killed him. Whatever is going on, this perp is not playing around."

"Did they steal cars?"

Carter gave me the look. The "I refuse to talk about it" look.

"At least tell me if they got the DeLorean."

Carter's mouth opened a bit and he stared at me, clearly dismayed. "Do not tell me you were considering buying that car."

"Okay. I won't tell you."

"Seriously?"

"Well, they look cool and even though it's old, Hot Rod said by the time he was done with it, Enzo Ferrari would be jealous."

"Enzo Ferrari is dead."

I nodded. "I know. It was going to be that good."

Carter shook his head. "As much as I hate to admit it, the DeLorean is still there, but it doesn't look like Hot Rod has started working on it yet."

"Then we'll just have to hope he gets better and can get back to doing what he loves."

"Something we can both agree on."

Carter switched the conversation to Celia and her never-dull brand of crazy, and we chatted about her and the takedown by fish guy until he finished eating. As soon as he polished off the last of the cookies, he rose from the table and stretched.

"I hate to eat and run," he said, "but I'm beat and I've got to get started early tomorrow."

"Of course," I said, and followed him to the front door.

He turned around and wrapped his arms around me, kissing me soundly. I relaxed into his rock-hard chest and thought about just how good he looked when his shirt was off. The rest of him wasn't too shabby, either.

He broke off the kiss and opened the door. "I'll call you tomorrow and let you know how things look for rescheduling our grilling."

"No worries. I never run out of people supplying me with food. Just catch the guy who did that to Hot Rod."

"Bet on it."

I closed the door and pulled the dead bolt, then headed into the kitchen to put the dishes in the dishwasher. I hadn't expected Carter to cough up any dirt on the case, but I figured that I'd still get some information out of him, even if he hadn't intended for me to. In this case, the information I'd gained wasn't what I'd wanted to hear. I'd hoped someone had conked Hot Rod just to get him out of the way long enough to steal a car. But the force of the blow had Carter believing the intent was to kill Hot Rod, not just disable. That was a whole different ball game.

It made no sense to kill someone over grand theft auto. That meant turning a non–death penalty crime into a death penalty crime, and Louisiana wasn't scared to hand out lethal injections if they thought the crime was suitably horrific. Hot Rod had some cool stuff in his shop, but I hadn't seen anything worth killing over.

There had to be something else going on. I'd believed Ida Belle before when she said something didn't add up. Now I felt the same way, which wasn't good for Ida Belle, me, or Carter, because I was about to do what I'd just sworn I wouldn't do.

I was going to stick my nose in it.

———

I WOKE up early the next morning after a long night of tossing and turning and a couple of really odd dreams. In one of them, I'd been a real librarian and Celia was in the library insisting that I'd stolen the book she wanted to borrow. Every time I went to the shelf to retrieve the book, it was gone. It was like being in some awful loop of horror from which there was no escape.

I'd also had a dream about facing down Ahmad. In that one, no matter how many times I squeezed the trigger of my pistol, the gun wouldn't fire. I'd had that dream on several occasions, and it never failed to unnerve me. Living undercover in Sinful didn't exactly allow for me to keep in top assassin shape. Sure, I could go to the range and fire off some rounds, but it wasn't nearly the same as the military training I went through with the CIA when I was in between missions.

I headed downstairs to put on some coffee and fix breakfast. While I was frying eggs, I sent Ida Belle and Gertie a text asking them to come over as soon as they could. I had just polished off my eggs and toast when I heard a key in the front door, and Ida Belle called out a second later as the front door squeaked open.

"In the kitchen," I said.

They walked in, Gertie shaking her head.

"The fact that you're in the kitchen doesn't really need saying, you know," Gertie said.

"Are you trying to tell me I'm fat?" I asked.

Ida Belle gave me a critical look. "You are starting to lose a little tone in your arms and shoulders. You should add some push-ups after your morning run."

"What morning run?" Gertie asked. "Half the time, we're sitting right here stuffing our faces in the morning and lately, she's spending the other half sneaking out of Carter's house before daylight." Gertie winked at me.

"I'll have you know," I said, completely ignoring the wink, "that I have only gained five pounds since I've been here, and given what I've eaten, that's a miracle."

"It's probably from all the running you've done from people shooting at you," Ida Belle said. "I mean, a lot of it was anaerobic, but you had some longer bursts in there that probably burned off a pot roast or two."

"Are you kidding me?" I asked. "Just trying to figure out what the heck is wrong with Celia has probably burned more calories than I consume in any given day. But anyway, I didn't call you over here to assess my weight, muscle tone, or dietary and exercise habits."

"Or your predawn activities," Gertie said.

"Or those. I called you over here to talk about Hot Rod. Have you heard anything else about his condition?"

Ida Belle nodded. "He's been in and out of consciousness all night, but he's only in for short amounts of time and doesn't seem to know what's going on. According to my source, Deputy Breaux was at the hospital all night, but Hot Rod was never lucid enough for him to get any information out of him."

"At least he's starting to regain consciousness," Gertie said. "That's good news."

"Excellent news," I said. "Maybe we'll find out what he was wanting to warn Ida Belle about."

"I guess that means you didn't get anything from Carter," Gertie said. "We really need to work on your womanly charms game."

Ida Belle waved a hand in dismissal. "Carter is not silly enough to be fooled by womanly charms."

"Even if he's hot for the woman doing the charming?" Gertie asked.

"Even if he's on fire," Ida Belle said.

"I have to agree with her," I said. "Carter's not going to tell me anything because he doesn't want me in police business. But I did get one thing out of him."

They both perked up.

"He thinks whoever cracked Hot Rod on the head meant to kill him and likely thought he was dead when he left."

Ida Belle frowned. "Why would he think that?"

"Because of the severity of the blow and the fact that Hot Rod was completely unconscious," I said. "At least, that's what he told me."

"You don't believe him?" Gertie asked.

"Yes, but I think there's more to it than what he said," I said.

"I think whatever is going on is serious business, and he's trying to warn us off."

Ida Belle nodded. "He knows more but he's not telling you. That makes sense on Carter's part. He's trying to protect you and us. But it doesn't make sense overall. Who kills someone to steal cars? Why add murder to the charges?"

"That's exactly what I thought," I said. "But when I asked Carter who would want to hurt Hot Rod, he just told me to stay out of it."

"Did he tell you what cars were stolen?" Gertie asked.

I shook my head. "He didn't admit to any of the cars being stolen. I tried to sneak some info out of him by claiming I was interested in buying the DeLorean and hoping it wasn't one of the ones stolen, but all I got out of him was a lot of dismay that I was interested in the car and that it didn't look like Hot Rod had started working on it yet."

"The DeLorean isn't really worth a lot of money," Ida Belle said. "He's got a Ferrari in there that would bring a good haul but nothing else even close to a hundred thousand."

"Small-time car thieves," I suggested, "but mean as hell?"

"Maybe," Ida Belle said. "People are getting meaner, but still, seems like a lot of risk for a small amount. If I'm looking at the death penalty, it would be for something bigger than one exotic." She shook her head. "I don't like it. It all feels wrong."

"What can we do?" Gertie asked. "Until Hot Rod wakes up and has any kind of decent recall, we won't know what happened or if his cryptic statement about warning Ida Belle had anything to do with this or was about something else completely."

"We need to know what was stolen," I said. "If we knew what the thief or thieves were after, we'd know where to start tracking them. This level of violence doesn't happen in a vacuum."

"You think he's done it before," Gertie said.

I nodded. "And car thieves usually have a particular type of car they work. Knowing what he took could help us track down other thefts of similar nature."

"I agree," Ida Belle said, "but how do you propose we do that? Carter changed all his computer passwords, and so far, Myrtle hasn't been able to figure them out. He's started making all his notes on the computer, so no handy pad of paper with case information lying around, and once he assembles a paper file, he's locking active cases in a safe in his office."

"I think he's officially gotten our number," Gertie said.

"Yeah, I think our days of data gathering with a simple break-in at the sheriff's department are over," Ida Belle said.

Even though I had yet to be present for one of those "simple" break-ins, I didn't bother to argue. The end result was the same. None of us thought it was worth the risk to try again. We'd barely gotten away with it before.

"Well," Gertie said, "since we can't get to Carter's files, I guess we'll just have to break into Hot Rod's shop and check the cars there against his inventory."

There were so many things wrong with Gertie's plan that I wasn't sure where to begin, but I took a deep breath and made a stab at it.

"The shop is now a crime scene," I said. "We'd be breaking a million laws just stepping past the tape. And I'd bet money that Carter called for backup and someone armed is sitting guard there until he figures out what's going on. Then there's the huge assumption that Hot Rod even keeps an inventory that we could check stock against."

"You're right on all the first statements," Ida Belle said, "but I'm not so sure on the last. I signed a bill of sale and all the other pertinent paperwork when I bought my Blazer, and Hot Rod gave me an envelope with copies of everything, including all the receipts for parts and anything he subbed out. I know he doesn't come across as highly organized, but I bet he's got folders on every car that moves through his shop."

"Cool," Gertie said. "So if he has a file with receipts and stuff for every vehicle, then the ones that have been sold would have a bill of sale in them, right? Anything that didn't we would assume should be in the shop."

"Or out to a sub for other work," I said.

"But he'd probably have an estimate in the file if that was the case," Ida Belle said.

"Then it's settled," Gertie said. "We break into Hot Rod's shop."

"Wait a minute," I said. "Nothing about this is settled. Did you miss all the beginning of my statement about crime scene and armed guards and all that? Do you plan on strolling up and asking politely to go inside?"

"Of course not," Gertie said. "I said 'break in.' I thought that was clear."

"Okay, I may be crazy here," I said, "but I'm clearly not the most insane. When I went to Hot Rod's with Ida Belle, I noticed it was at the end of a dead-end road. One road in. One road out. Short of going on foot or dropping in by plane, we can't get there without being seen."

"The plane idea is interesting," Gertie said, "but I was thinking more of an invasion by water."

"She's right," Ida Belle said. "There's a bayou about a hundred feet behind the shop. Unless someone's watching the back, we could probably get in and out without being seen."

"And leave our DNA all over a crime scene," I said.

"Technically," Ida Belle said to me, "our DNA is already there. Gertie's is the only one missing."

Gertie huffed. "Which means I get stuck playing lookout again. I always get stuck playing lookout."

"And I always get stuck playing the floozy," I said.

"I keep offering to play the floozy," Gertie pointed out.

"The point of undercover work is to go unnoticed," Ida Belle said. "You're a good century past your prime floozy time."

"Okay, all talk of floozies aside, we can't do this," I said. "Carter would arrest us all if he found out, and you know what that would do to my cover. Morrow would yank me out of here so fast, I'd get whiplash."

"Then what else are we supposed to do?" Gertie asked. "You can't get anything from Carter. Myrtle can't get into his files. Unless Hot Rod wakes up and has something to help, we're stuck with nothing."

Ida Belle's phone rang, and she looked at the display. "It's my hospital source."

She answered the phone and Gertie and I both leaned across the table, eagerly listening to the one-sided conversation. If you could call single-word responses a conversation.

"Thanks," Ida Belle said after about a minute. "If you get anything else, call me right away."

She put the phone down, and I could tell that whatever she'd heard wasn't good. "The niece checked in. Hot Rod had a decent bout of consciousness. He told the nurse I was in danger and started yelling for the cops. Before the officer standing guard could get a statement, Hot Rod went into cardiac arrest."

Gertie's hands flew over her mouth.

"Oh no!" I cried.

"They got him stabilized," Ida Belle said, "but there's no way to know when he'll regain consciousness again." She sighed. "Or even if he will. I don't want to sound all doom and gloom, but I'm afraid it's serious for our friend."

"And serious for you," Gertie said. "Whatever Hot Rod is worried about was enough to send him into heart attack zone, and with his family history…"

I didn't want to agree with Gertie, because agreeing left me only one option, and that was breaking and entering into what could turn out to be the scene of a capital murder. But if Ida Belle was in jeopardy, we needed to know why, and the answer was probably somewhere in Hot Rod's shop. Maybe it was as simple as him remembering something he had left undone on her SUV. Something he thought might cause a wreck. If so, then he'd have a note in those files Ida Belle insisted he kept.

Whatever it was, it probably had nothing to do with why someone had attacked Hot Rod.

At least, that's what I was going to keep telling myself.

Even though I didn't believe it for a minute.

CHAPTER FOUR

"How come I never get to drive?" Gertie groused as I tossed a backpack of breaking-and-entering supplies into the bottom of my airboat.

Ida Belle stared. "You're seriously asking that question? How many boats have you sunk this year? Because any number over zero is too many."

I'd only arrived at Sinful at the beginning of the summer, but based on my limited exposure to Gertie and boating, I was betting that number hovered somewhere over five and maybe below ten. But then, I was probably being optimistic.

"Ida Belle drives the boat," I said. "She's the best driver. And before you ask, you can't sit in the other chair. That chair is for lookout and I have perfect vision."

Gertie threw her hands in the air, stepped into the boat, then flopped down on the bottom in front of the bench. "Perfect driving, perfect vision. You two are always cramping my style with all your rules."

"Limiting one's chance of death is not cramping your style," Ida Belle said. "It's keeping us all available for future projects."

"You're a perfect cook," I said.

"I suppose that's something," Gertie said, slightly mollified.

"What's the Carter update?" Ida Belle asked.

I shook my head. "He just texted me a good morning and thanks for the sandwich last night. He didn't give me any other clues."

Ida Belle frowned. "He didn't tell Myrtle where he was going either. Just checked in with the office and headed back out."

"You need to put that 'find iPhone' thing on his phone," Gertie said. "That way, we'd always know where he was."

"Yeah, because he wouldn't notice that," I said. "And because that tracking thing always works so well in the swamp."

"Maybe we should GPS his truck," Ida Belle said. "Anyway, it's something to consider for later on."

I stared. "You two know that private detectives don't have the legal right to break and enter and stalk law enforcement officers, right?"

"Veronica Mars does it all the time," Gertie said.

"That's a television show," I said, "and she's a minor. She won't go to prison."

Gertie shrugged. "There's a downside to everything."

I shook my head and untied the boat from the bank. As long as I was in a relationship with Carter, Ida Belle and Gertie were never going to take my being arrested seriously. But Carter couldn't protect me from everything. If the Feds were involved, then I was open game. In fact, being involved with a law enforcement officer would make me an even juicier target.

Not that I was some sort of stickler for the law. CIA assassins didn't exactly care what laws they were breaking when they were on a mission, especially since we usually weren't citizens of the countries we were operating within. Our jobs were all about the success of the mission and not so much about how we accomplished it. But if I was going to make a go at honest civilian employment, then the legal system was something I needed to start taking a bit more seriously.

After we found out why Ida Belle was in danger, of course. Because my friend's safety trumped laws.

Ida Belle climbed into the driver's seat, and I pushed the boat from the bank and jumped inside. My butt had barely graced the seat when Ida Belle took off like a shot. I clutched the armrests as if my life depended on it, and that wasn't too far from the truth. I loved the airboat more than I'd ever thought I'd be devoted to a piece of machinery, and I knew that Ida Belle was a top-notch driver, but there was still that inkling of what-if every time I climbed into the passenger's seat.

But given my personality, that was also part of the attraction.

The ride took about twenty minutes and probably should have taken thirty. Ida Belle had utilized a shortcut for airboats that shaved off some time, meaning, she'd skipped the boat over a patch of land to cut the distance. Given the height Gertie flew up from the bottom of the boat, and the dirty look she gave Ida Belle after we landed back in the water, I guessed we probably wouldn't hear any complaining about having to sit in the bottom again, because if Gertie had been on the bench, she would be sitting on that patch of land.

Ida Belle cut the engine as we approached a long stretch of bank lined with cypress trees. We'd gone under the highway at some point in the blurred ride, so I figured we must have reached our destination. Ida Belle scanned the bank and looked down at Gertie.

"What do you think?" Ida Belle asked.

Gertie nodded. "I think this is about right."

That was my cue, so I grabbed the rope and did a leap onto the bank, then pulled the boat over to the landmass and tied it off. Ida Belle tossed me the backpack of breaking-and-entering equipment, then Gertie handed me her purse. It was heavier than the backpack, which was already cause for alarm, but I knew better than to look inside or even ask. It would just make me worry more, and I needed to concentrate.

I hefted the backpack onto my shoulder, and Ida Belle pointed to the tree line. "If we head straight back, we should hit the back side of Hot Rod's property."

"How far?" I asked.

"Quarter mile, maybe?" Ida Belle said.

A quarter mile was nothing walking upright and carrying a light backpack. I'd crawled farther and with heavier equipment. "Let's get this over with," I said.

There was no sign of a trail, so we picked the least dense opening and stepped into the woods, then continued to pick our way through the trees and brush, attempting to maintain a direct line from the boat to Hot Rod's place. Several minutes later, I saw a break in the trees, and the woods opened up to a clearing of swamp grass. Hot Rod's warehouse was about fifty yards to our right.

"We're not directly behind it," Ida Belle said. "I think we got off a bit trying to find a decent path through the woods."

"Close enough," I said, and pulled binoculars from the backpack. "Let's see if we can spot any movement."

"There's a car out front that looks like a cop," Ida Belle said.

Our side view afforded us a look at a piece of the parking lot in front of the building, and sure enough, right there in the middle of a Camry and an Accord was a sheriff's department vehicle.

"It's not local," I said. "It says 'Mudbug' on it."

"Carter needed some assistance and didn't want the state police in his business," Ida Belle said.

I nodded. "It's twenty yards from the tree line to the back of the building, and it won't take but ten seconds or so to jimmy one of those windows."

"Then let's move directly behind the building and get going," Ida Belle said.

I started to move, but Gertie grabbed my arm.

"Wait," Gertie said, and pointed at the horse and rider coming around the building.

Sheriff Lee.

"Crap," I said. "We can't get into the building with Sheriff Lee and some spare deputy circling it like flies."

Ida Belle frowned. "We could still outrun Lee. Even with the horse."

Given that the horse was as ancient as Sheriff Lee, she was probably right, except for one thing.

"The problem is," I said, "we can't outrun a bullet. And if he sees someone breaking in, he's not going to mosey up close to see if it's just the friendly Sinful busybodies, nosing into a crime scene. He's going to whip out that gun at his hip John Wayne–style and start firing. I've seen him shoot before. It's not something I care to be in the vicinity of again."

"He needs to get glasses," Gertie said. "He can't see squat."

Ida Belle and I stared at Gertie for a moment. Given that we'd been yelling all summer for her to get her own prescription updated, it seemed an odd comment, if not ridiculously hypocritical.

"What?" Gertie asked. "I'll have you know I have an appointment next week. Then you two won't have anything else to complain about."

Ida Belle raised an eyebrow. "You're handling all two hundred things on my list of things to complain about at your eye doctor next week? That's one talented doctor."

Gertie shot her a dirty look, then pointed at Sheriff Lee. "You can keep insulting me or figure out what to do about that."

"What can we do?" I asked. "It doesn't look like he's going anywhere, and that means neither are we."

"We need a distraction," Ida Belle said. "Something that will draw Sheriff Lee into the woods. That way, we could sneak in."

"We could step out of the tree line naked and he still wouldn't see us," I said.

"What about noise?" Gertie asked. "His hearing's still decent. Decent enough, anyway."

"Decent enough to hear what?" I asked, already worried about the answer. "Because if it involves guns or explosives, I'm already voting no."

"What if it involves tiny explosives?" Gertie asked. She reached into her handbag and pulled out a package of firecrackers.

"It sounds too much like gunfire," I said. "He'll come charging this way, ready to shoot."

"Charging is a bit of a stretch," Ida Belle said. "It might work. If you threw one, then moved farther into the brush. He wouldn't be able to move quickly through the brush, with the horse or without. Gertie could draw him away far enough to allow us to get inside, then do it again so we can get out."

"What about the deputy?" I asked. "We haven't even seen him. What if he's a lot younger and quicker than Sheriff Lee?"

"Everyone's a lot younger than Sheriff Lee," Ida Belle said, "but I see your point. Maybe Gertie and I should split the firecrackers and once we have their attention, head off in different directions. That should confuse them enough to give you a window."

As misdirection went, it wasn't that bad of a plan, except for the part where I was the one assessing Hot Rod's inventory. Aside from the DeLorean and the Ferrari, I hadn't paid attention to anything else in his warehouse. If we couldn't come up with some sort of inventory listing, I wouldn't have any idea what was missing. But Ida Belle might.

"What if I work the distraction with Gertie," I said to Ida Belle, "and you do the inventory assessment?"

I explained my reasoning and Ida Belle nodded.

"Hot Rod and I chatted about several of his cars after the test drive," Ida Belle said. "I probably can't remember them all, but I definitely recall several of them."

"Good," I said. "Will you have any problem with the window?"

"Please," Ida Belle said. "I could jimmy a window before you were even born."

"Okay," I said, not about to ask why Ida Belle had perfected window jimmying in her past life. "Then you move into position directly behind the window on the far corner of the building. When you're there, Gertie and I will start the distraction maneuver."

I pulled out my cell phone and checked the service. "We have decent cell reception here. Ida Belle, when you're ready to leave the shop, send us a text and we'll start up the fireworks again."

Ida Belle nodded, grabbed the backpack of tools, and headed off through the woods. Gertie broke the package of firecrackers in half and handed some to me.

"Lighter?" I asked.

She pulled a couple packets of matches from her purse and handed me one. "I'm old-school."

I took the matches, wishing I had a lighter but considering the source, we were probably better off with Gertie going old-school. I didn't want to think about the combination of a leaky lighter and whatever else she had in that handbag.

"When Ida Belle is in place," I said, "we'll set off one firework to draw attention. When they come this way, then you and I will split off in two directions, lighting new fireworks about every ten yards. You go back toward the bayou so you'll be closer to the boat. I'll go north and work my way back around."

"Okay, but I want to throw the first firecracker."

"Of course. It's your stash."

Gertie grinned. "I knew these things would come in handy when I bought them."

"Let's just hope all this handiness yields us some answers, and that neither the deputy nor Sheriff Lee gets too ambitious and hurries. I really don't want to get shot at again. It's getting old."

"That seems a strange complaint given your chosen profession."

"Then maybe *I'm* getting old."

"You're not getting old," Gertie said. "You've just got more to lose."

I frowned. It was a valid point and one I might have to think about later...when I wasn't worried about being shot at again. I lifted the binoculars and scanned the tree line, then spotted Ida Belle inching up to the edge of the woods directly behind the window she was going to enter through. She gave me a thumbs-up. I dropped the binoculars and watched as Sheriff Lee made his way around the corner of the building and started walking our direction.

"Wait until Sheriff Lee gets to the middle of the building, then set one off," I said.

Gertie ripped a firecracker off her pack and readied her match, grinning like a five-year-old at a birthday party. We watched as Sheriff Lee's horse plodded along, then finally he reached the halfway point.

Gertie lit the firecracker, then tossed it. It set off a good pop and Sheriff Lee stopped the horse for a second, scanning the woods. Gertie lit a second one and threw it, and Sheriff Lee zeroed in on the sound and started toward us at a faster clip. The deputy came around the building from the front, and Sheriff Lee pointed to the woods where we were hiding.

"One more," I said.

Gertie stuck the match and lit her firecracker, then tossed it. We waited for the impending explosion, but nothing happened.

"Must have been a dud," I said. "Try again."

Gertie nodded, lit another firecracker and threw.

And that's when everything went horribly wrong, as only Gertie could manage.

"You threw the match," I said, starting to panic. "Where is the firecracker?"

Gertie jumped back, looking down at the ground. "I dropped it."

I spied her open handbag and heard a fizzling sound.

"Abort!" I yelled and shoved Gertie in the direction of the boat.

I took off down the tree line toward Ida Belle, in case she didn't hear me. Barreling through the brush, arms in front of my face, I didn't even take a second to find the easiest path. All I had time to do was pray that Gertie was giving it her best and was out of range for whatever was coming next.

A second later, all hell broke loose.

CHAPTER FIVE

The explosion was definitely not caused by firecrackers. Whatever Gertie had in that handbag caused such a blast that it could probably be heard back in Sinful. I rushed to the edge of the woods, praying that neither Sheriff Lee nor the deputy was near the handbag, and peered out just in time to see Sheriff Lee's horse tender his one-second notice.

The startled animal whirled around so fast, I'm surprised he didn't break his ancient legs, then he set off at a dead run directly at the deputy. The deputy leaped to the side but the horse still clipped him in the shoulder and sent him slamming into the turf. Sheriff Lee had completely given up on the reins and was leaned forward over the saddle, his arms wrapped around the horse's neck. If he remained seated, it would be a miracle. If the horse didn't have a heart attack, it would be a miracle.

Given the determination and rate of speed that the four-legged law enforcement officer was moving, he probably wouldn't slow until he reached his stall or keeled over. I just hoped Sheriff Lee survived to tell the tale. I whirled around and continued running for the spot where I thought Ida Belle had been waiting but saw movement out of the corner of my eye and slid to a stop in horror as I saw Ida Belle's legs disappear over the window ledge of Hot Rod's shop.

I yanked out my phone and sent her a text.

Get the hell out of there. The deputy has probably already called in the armed forces.

I watched the window, waiting for her to swing her legs back out, but no movement was forthcoming. I waited another extremely long ten seconds, then when I heard sirens in the distance, texted again.

5-o on the way. Have to find Gertie and get out of here.

Just when I was getting ready to go through the window and haul her out myself, she poked her head out and did a flip-roll over the sill and onto the ground. If I hadn't been so anxious to get away, I might have taken a second to be impressed, but we didn't have that kind of time. We'd have to high-five over it later. Hopefully, not in a police lineup. I stepped out of the woods and motioned to Ida Belle to hurry, and she ran for the tree line.

"What happened?" she asked as she stepped into the brush.

"Gertie," I said.

That's all the explanation she needed. She nodded and we set off in what I hoped was a diagonal path straight to the boat. The brush was thicker going than coming, and with one arm clutching the binoculars that I still wore around my neck, that left only one arm to block my face. I knew my forearms and hands were going to show signs of a foliage attack. If it had been winter, and I hadn't been shedding my clothes in front of the local law enforcement, it might not have been a problem, but since neither of those was the case, I was going to have to invent a story for the scratches. One that didn't involve Hot Rod, automobiles, or my being anywhere but my own backyard.

A bead of sweat fell into my left eye and I reached up to swipe it, which just happened to be the same time the woods ended and the bank began. I shot off the edge of the bank, which was about two feet above the water line, and hit the water, making a splash like an orca. I came right back out as fast as I went in. It probably looked like video on reverse. No way was I spending time in any murky water in Sinful. Some gator craving a casserole might settle for a lean CIA agent.

Ida Belle paused long enough to watch me run on water, then pointed down the bank where Gertie was limping toward the boat. We had missed the mark by about twenty yards, which wasn't bad considering we were in panicked flight, had no path, and were trying to keep from being eaten alive by the brush. I grabbed the binoculars, which hadn't fallen off during my free fall, and we took off again.

We hoofed it down the bank and Ida Belle jumped into the boat, narrowly missing Gertie, who was already in place at the bottom. I untied the line and jumped in, then leaped into my seat and grabbed the armrests as Ida Belle launched us away from the bank. About two seconds later, I started breathing again and realized I'd been holding my breath since I'd gone into the water.

Ida Belle glanced over at me and frowned, probably wondering why I was gasping for air now when it was flowing across my face at a good forty miles per hour. She pointed at the highway up ahead and I lifted the binoculars, thankful they were military grade and could take a dunking. I could hear the sirens, but with all the water and flat land surrounding us, it was difficult to pin down the direction of the noise. I hoped it was coming from the east, which meant we were in the clear to pass under the highway.

But we were never that lucky.

I spotted Carter's truck speeding down the highway straight toward us. I hit Ida Belle's arm and tapped the top of my head with my left hand and pointed toward Sinful. It was the motorcycle rider's signal meaning law enforcement was ahead. Since Ida Belle had taught me that signal herself, I knew she'd get it.

She scanned the bank, looking for a hiding place, but on both sides, the trees had disappeared and made way for long stretches of marsh grass, which provided no hiding place at all. I lifted the binoculars and checked again and waved my hands, gesturing her to the bridge. If we turned around, Carter would see us. Our only chance was to make it under the bridge before he got close enough to notice us.

Ida Belle nodded and gave the boat that last bit of juice she'd been holding in reserve, and we flew toward the bridge. I could see Carter's truck without the binoculars now but it was still a tiny blip. No way he'd be able to identify us yet, and we were almost to the bridge. There was just the small problem of stopping.

Usually stopping involved coasting to a dock or bank or occasionally, running up a bank, if the situation called for it. It wasn't as if the boat came equipped with brakes. But even though we were drawing dangerously close to the bridge, Ida Belle showed no signs of slowing. Gertie looked back at me, her eyes wide, and I shrugged. At the rate we were moving, we were going to shoot out of from under the bridge just in time for Carter to get an excellent look at us.

I shouldn't have underestimated Ida Belle.

When we were ten feet from the bridge, she cut the boat hard to the right, and it was all I could do to hang on to my seat. We went sliding across the top of the water sideways, and Ida Belle killed the engine just seconds before the side of the boat slammed into the bank below the bridge.

My hip crashed into the armrest and I knew I was going to have a good bruise tomorrow, but Gertie was probably going to be in worse shape than me. She slid across the bottom of the boat and banged into the side. I sucked in a breath, waiting for some indication from her that she was alive, and finally it came. In the form of a middle finger.

I heard Carter's truck approaching and several seconds later, it roared over the bridge above us. Ida Belle waited until we couldn't hear the engine any longer, then told me to grab the pole and push us around. I hopped off my seat and grabbed the long pole we kept in the boat for maneuvering and managed to get us turned back into the right direction. Once the pole was secured and I was back in place, we were ready to leave.

And then Ida Belle's phone rang.

"It's Myrtle," she said, and answered.

She couldn't have heard much, but she shoved the phone back in her pocket, fired up the boat, and floored it.

"Deputy Breaux is on the way to your house," Ida Belle yelled as we barreled down the bayou.

Crap. I should have known we'd be first on the list of suspects for the blast. There was rarely an explosion or fire or even gunshots that didn't involve one of us. The only plus was that Deputy Breaux was a lot easier to fool than Carter. I think it was because he was young and slightly afraid of all of us. And he had that whole Southern-raising, respect-your-elders thing going on with Gertie and Ida Belle.

Still, we needed to get to my house before Deputy Breaux did. If he spotted us in the boat, then Carter would assume the explosion was us and we'd be in hot water. And I might have to go back to sleeping alone some nights. Which would suck because for the first time in my life, I was actually enjoying sharing my space. Not all the time, which is why I was glad we had separate places, but sometimes it was nice.

Ida Belle knew the score, and she used every trick in her airboat sleeve to get us to my house as quickly as possible. I didn't see any sign of Deputy Breaux when we approached my back yard which was a good thing. Ida Belle cut her speed a little but still launched the boat halfway up the bank. I jumped out of my seat and hauled Gertie up from the bottom before we'd even slid to a stop, and all of us ran away from the bank as fast as our legs would carry us.

Then I remembered I was soaking wet and stopped.

"I'm wet," I said. "And we have scratches all over us from

running through the woods. Deputy Breaux isn't clever, but he's not blind."

"I got this," Gertie said, and ran for my shed. "Turn on the water hose, Ida Belle!"

Apparently, Ida Belle understood what was going on because she ran for the hose and starting unreeling it, tossing it all into the yard. Gertie came running back with a shovel, hedge clippers, and pruning shears and handed me the clippers.

"Chop those bushes," she said, "from behind."

I grabbed the clippers and squeezed in between the bushes, their prickly branches scratching my arms all over again. And that's when it all clicked. Gertie started with the pruning shears on the front side and Ida Belle watered the beds to the side of us. I hacked a bunch of small limbs off the back of the bushes and flung them around so that it looked like a lot of work had already occurred.

Not a minute later, I heard Deputy Breaux calling out for me.

"In the backyard," Ida Belle yelled.

When I saw Deputy Breaux round the corner, I stepped out of the bushes. He looked at us, then at the bushes, and frowned.

"Why are you trimming those in the middle of the summer?" he asked.

"They're growing too close to the house," Gertie said. "I kept offering to do it for Marge in the winter, but you know how stubborn she could be about accepting help. They're scratching the paint off the siding."

Deputy Breaux nodded and focused in on me. "Why are you wet?"

"I had a bit of a time with the hose," Ida Belle said, "and Fortune got the worst of it."

I shrugged. "Probably did me a favor. It's hot as heck. What can we do for you? I assume you didn't come by to see our riveting morning of bush trimming."

"No, ma'am," Deputy Breaux said, and blushed. "There was, uh, a situation at Hot Rod's place a bit earlier."

"Hot Rod's still in the hospital, right?" I asked.

"Yes, ma'am," Deputy Breaux said. "It didn't involve him. But there was gunfire and an explosion in the woods near his shop."

My expression immediately morphed into my incredulous look. "An explosion? Of what? For what purpose?"

"Was anyone hurt?" Gertie asked.

"Was the shop hurt?" Ida Belle asked. "All those cars..."

"No one was hurt," Deputy Breaux said. "That we're aware of, anyway, and the shop wasn't damaged. We don't know what caused the explosion or why it was set off."

A wave of relief rolled through me when I heard that no one was injured. I'd been worried about the sheriff and his horse ever since I'd seen them pull their racehorse maneuver.

"That's good that no one was hurt," I said, "but what can we do for you?"

He shuffled his feet and stared down at the ground. "Deputy LeBlanc suggested I see what you ladies were up to."

"I see," I said. "Something happened that Carter has to deal with, and he automatically assumed it was us. If an explosion were out of the ordinary for Sinful, I could see where he might be upset, but there's been an awful lot of that sort of thing recently."

Deputy Breaux nodded. "Mostly since you came to town."

I held in a smile. The deputy wasn't the sharpest tack in the box, but he was far from stupid. He knew Ida Belle, Gertie, and I got up to all sorts of things we had no business being in the middle of, but he was too polite to come right out and accuse me of anything.

"That's fair enough," I said, letting him off the hook. "But this time, it wasn't us. We've been right here hacking bushes all morning."

"I'll let Deputy LeBlanc know," he said. "Good luck with your gardening."

We waited until Deputy Breaux rounded the corner before smiling. "Nice work," I said to Gertie.

"I have my moments," Gertie said.

"Oh, you definitely have your moments," I said. "Like that handbag explosion. What the heck was in that handbag? And please tell me there was nothing in it that could identify you, assuming there's anything left that's not in a million tiny pieces."

"I would never carry my license in my handbag," Gertie said. "I'm not even sure I know where it is."

I narrowed my eyes at her. "You failed the eye test and your license expired."

"That's why you made an eye doctor appointment," Ida Belle said.

"Whatever," Gertie said, and Ida Belle and I both smiled.

"So anyone want to head into the air-conditioning for a beer and a recap of the morning's events?" I asked.

"We can't," Gertie said. "We have to chop up these bushes some more. You know Carter will check, and this isn't ten minutes worth of work."

Ida Belle sighed. "I hate when she's right about things that involve lawn work in hundred-degree heat and eighty percent humidity, but she's right. Get to hacking. I'll turn some of the dirt over with the shovel. We can update as we work. You can start by telling me how Gertie's handbag ended up being an incendiary device."

I relayed the situation to Ida Belle, who stopped digging and shook her head at Gertie. "That handbag is going to get us all killed one day."

"Technically speaking," I said, "*that* handbag won't."

"I've got backup," Gertie said.

"Of course you do," I said. "So what kind of explosive were you carrying in that bag? And don't tell me more fireworks, because I kinda know the difference."

"There might have been a stick of dynamite in it," Gertie said.

"What the heck?"

"Have you lost your mind?"

Ida Belle and I both yelled at once.

"I shouldn't even bother asking why," Ida Belle said, "but why in the world did you have a stick of dynamite in your purse?"

"I must have forgotten it in there from the last time I went fishing," Gertie said.

"You fish with dynamite?" I asked.

Ida Belle shook her head. "That's why you've had such big hauls lately. If Carter catches you, he's going to put you under the jail."

"Given that her current pastime is blowing up the bayou for a slab of trout," I said, "it's not the worst idea I've heard today. And that's saying a lot."

"Everybody fishes with dynamite," Gertie said. "It's too hot to sit out there all day."

I stared. "If everyone fishes with dynamite then I'm moving back to DC this afternoon."

"Everyone does *not* fish with dynamite," Ida Belle said. "Only a few do."

"A few? What's a few?" Two sounded like too many to me, especially when one of them was Gertie. "And where is everyone getting this dynamite? It's not like you can pick up some sticks at the General Store."

"There's a guy who works construction who sells it on the side," Gertie said.

"Good God." I was positive that construction guy was lifting dynamite from his job. What was even more disconcerting was that the foreman hadn't noticed the missing sticks. Lord only knew how many other people were boating around with sticks of explosive fun.

"Anyway, that's not the point," Gertie said. "There was an accident and I lost a perfectly good handbag and a couple other items, but we're here in one piece and that's all that matters."

I opened my mouth to reply, but there was no use. At this point, it was all over but the lying. I took the clippers to a group of branches and peered through the brush at Ida Belle.

"I know you didn't have time to find anything," I said, "but maybe Hot Rod will be okay and he'll be able to talk to you soon."

"I don't need to talk to Hot Rod," Ida Belle said. "I think I know what he was going to warn me about."

"How?" I asked. "You weren't in the shop a minute."

"It was long enough to pick out what was missing," Ida Belle said.

"So there *were* vehicles missing?" I asked.

Ida Belle nodded. "All three black SUVs are gone."

My heart dropped. No way Hot Rod had sold every black SUV in his shop in the last week.

"Someone's targeting black SUVs," I said.

"But why?" Gertie asked.

"My guess is he's looking for something," I said. "Something hidden in a vehicle, and our car thief doesn't know the exact one."

"So he stole them all?" Gertie asked. "That doesn't sound like something one person could manage very easily."

"No. It doesn't," I said.

"Whatever they're looking for, they don't know where it is, either," Ida Belle said. "If they did, they wouldn't have had to take the vehicles. It would have been quicker to search them there."

I nodded. "So they took the cars somewhere that they could take their time searching through everything. That's an awful lot of heat to draw, especially when you add attempted murder to the rap. Whatever they're looking for must be worth a lot of money."

"Or could implicate them in something worse," Ida Belle said.

I didn't want to think about the big crimes that could be associated with something like this. It was too much like *The Sopranos*, and I wanted small-town problems, like fishing with dynamite. But I couldn't ignore the facts. Three similar cars had disappeared from a remote location in a reasonably short amount of time, and a man had been struck so hard he might die. It didn't sound like amateurs.

Which led to the even bigger problem.

"You need to hide your SUV," I told Ida Belle. "If they took the vehicles, you can bet they took the records of any recent sales. If they don't find what they're looking for in what they stole, they'll come after your vehicle."

"I know," Ida Belle said, and I realized she'd probably put everything together in those seconds she'd been in Hot Rod's shop.

"So we find a place to stash the SUV," I said, "and you stay with me."

"And just how are we supposed to explain that?" Ida Belle asked. "You're cozied up with Carter. Having a long-term sleep-over doesn't sound like normal behavior for someone just kicking up their relationship a notch."

"Say your hot water is out," Gertie suggested.

"It's a million degrees," Ida Belle said. "Everyone is taking cold showers."

"That's true," I said.

"No water?" Gertie suggested.

"I suppose I could have a leak," Ida Belle said, "but all this will accomplish is moving the party from one house to another. Even someone who's not connected to Sinful could easily find out who my friends are."

"Yeah, but there's strength in numbers," I said.

Gertie nodded. "Especially when Fortune is one of the numbers. And she couldn't stay at your house and lie about something being broken here because Carter would get all manly and try to help her by fixing it."

"Okay," Ida Belle agreed. "Then I have a plumbing leak. I'll turn off water to my house just in case someone checks, and say I have a friend in New Orleans who can look at it for free in a couple of days."

"That takes care of Ida Belle," Gertie said. "But what about the SUV?"

"We can't just leave it anywhere," I said, "because then we're potentially putting someone else at risk, but we need it close by so we can go through it ourselves."

"I know a place," Gertie said. "Plenty of room for us to work, no one can see it when they're driving by, and the best security in a hundred-mile radius."

I stared at her for a minute, rolling over the possibilities in my mind that fit everything she'd just described.

"Oh no," I said when it hit me.

"Why not?" Gertie asked.

"For once," Ida Belle said, "I'm the one that's lost."

"She wants us to hide your SUV at Big and Little's storage facility," I said.

"It's perfect," Gertie said. "Everyone knows who owns that facility, and no one is going to break into it unless they have a death wish."

"Have you forgotten the part where Big and Little Hebert *are* organized crime?" I asked. "For all we know, it was one of their people who took those vehicles."

"Do you really think that?" Gertie asked.

I didn't, but I couldn't give her a solid reason why. Any sane person would tell me I was crazy to trust the father-and-son Mafia team, and it wasn't as if I trusted them explicitly. But the truth was, they had helped me in a couple situations. And the airboat had been a gift from them for agreeing to help get a drug dealer out of Sinful.

Maybe I was getting soft, but I didn't think that was it. I'd had my suspicions about the Heberts since our last bit of business, but I had no proof. Just gut instinct. The question was, could I risk our safety on that alone?

If the answer was yes, then Gertie was right—it was the perfect hiding place. If people pulled one over on Big and Little, they paid the price for even attempting it. I looked at Ida Belle and Gertie and thought about the risks. Could I still trust my gut?

"I want to go talk to them first," I said. "Feel them out before we just drive up with the SUV."

"That's a good idea," Gertie said. "They might even know what's going on."

"They might already have three black SUVs in their storage facility," Ida Belle said drily.

"If you don't want to run the risk," I said to Ida Belle, "I won't do it. If it feels wrong to any of us, then it's got to be a no-go."

Ida Belle shook her head. "For whatever reason, I doubt they're involved. Don't get me wrong, I'm certain they're involved in plenty, and I'm certain they've bashed a head or two. Or ordered the bashing. But I can't see them coming down on Hot Rod that way. He did the work on that Hummer of theirs. It's completely bulletproof. All they would have had to do was ask to go through the SUVs and Hot Rod would have let them."

That perked me up considerably. If Big and Little had done business with Hot Rod and were happy with his work, then they might take personal offense to what happened to him. When Big and Little took personal offense, it was usually a very good thing for us and a very bad thing for the offender.

"Okay," I said. "Then let me clean up and we'll head out to the storage facility for a chat."

I headed upstairs for a quick shower, wondering what it said about my life when requesting favors from known Mafia members was probably going to be the least dangerous part of my day.

CHAPTER SIX

Big and Little ran their business in an old warehouse not far from the storage facility. The building was huge and well protected with high-tech security and any number of beefy, trigger-happy guys who did the Heberts' bidding. The storage facility that they owned was off the highway between Sinful and New Orleans a couple miles before the warehouse. Both were located off the same highway where everything outside of Sinful proper was, except the Swamp Bar. Because it was the only passage in and out of Sinful, passing Carter on the highway was a medium-to high-level threat, so we needed a solid reason for heading that way.

Ida Belle suggested that since Hot Rod had no family around, we go to the hospital and pass off a few bucks to the nurses to keep a closer watch on him and check in with him more than the usual schedule called for. It was, she insisted, something that any Southern woman worth her salt would do for a close friend or family. Gertie agreed, so we headed out, planning on stopping at the storage facility first to set up everything with Big and Little, then continuing on to the hospital to check on Hot Rod and grease palms.

We tucked Ida Belle's SUV in my garage before heading out, figuring if the bad guys came around, they'd be looking at Ida Belle's house first and it might take them some time to work their way around to mine. If Big and Little okayed our storage plan, then we'd take it at night to help avoid being seen. It all sounded good as long as Big and Little agreed to help and we didn't suspect they were involved in the other car thefts.

The drive to the warehouse went quickly and quietly. We were probably all assessing our personal risk factor for coming here in the first place. I parked near the front door and we walked into the lobby. The place was quiet, but with several cars out front, including Big's and Little's Hummer and Mercedes, I figured we were under surveillance and eventually, someone would come out to see what we wanted.

After a short wait, the hidden door on the back wall of the lobby swung open and Mannie, Big and Little's right-hand man, stepped out, smiling at us.

"Ladies," he said. "It's been a while. What can we do for you?"

"We've got a situation," I said. "And we'd like to ask a favor of Big and Little."

Mannie grinned. "A situation, huh? I just bet you do. Come on back. Big has been in a lousy mood lately, but you three always entertain him. You'd be doing the rest of us a favor."

Only Big Hebert would find circumventing federal agents and trying to avoid death entertainment, but I appreciated his viewpoint. The three of us did have a certain flair that made even the most mundane of nefarious activities more colorful.

We followed Mannie through the secret door and onto the elevator, then down the hallway and into Big and Little's office. Big, so named because of his enormous size, sat in his usual position on a park bench behind the massive desk. His son Little, so named for being the exact opposite in size from his father, was perched on a chair to the side of the bench and wore an exasperated expression.

"You have to wait to click," Little said, pointing at the computer screen. "You've closed the entire window."

Big shot him a dirty look and turned his attention to us. "To what do I owe the pleasure? Please, sit. Mannie, get us all a drink. The good whiskey. We haven't had visitors in a while, at least, not the voluntary kind. It's a cause for celebration."

Little rose from his chair, always the consummate gentleman, and nodded, his face shifting from frustrated to relieved. It appeared we'd interrupted a computer training session between father and son. Little was probably praying that Mannie made that drink a stiff one.

"Ladies," Little said, taking his seat again after we slid into chairs in front of Big's desk. "Nice to see you looking so well."

I was pretty sure we looked like hell. Gertie and I had narrowly escaped death by handbag, and the run through the woods had left us all a bit worse for the wear, but if Little wanted to deal out compliments, who was I to argue?

"Thank you," I said. "We really appreciate you seeing us."

Big chuckled. "I must confess, I'm always happy to see you because no matter the reason, it's going to be more interesting than anything else I've got going on. So what is it this time? Arms dealers hiding weapons in the baptismal font? Drug runners stashing product in alligators?"

"Those are some interesting thoughts," I said, "and now that you've thrown them out, I will probably check the baptismal font this Sunday, just to be safe. But I'm afraid our situation isn't that creative. It's just plain ole auto theft."

The smile vanished from Big's face and he looked over at Little, whose expression was grim. "You're talking about Hot Rod," Big said. "We were very sorry to hear what happened. He's a good man and does solid work. It's hard to find someone with his skill set who doesn't bother you with needless questions. Rest assured, my son and I have our people looking into it."

I watched him as he talked, but he showed no signs of lying.

Granted, Big was a professional criminal and one who had managed to avoid incarceration, but I would have bet money he was telling the truth. Which was really good for us, because that meant he'd probably agree to hide the SUV. Unfortunately, it also meant he hadn't found the bad guys yet. For what they'd done to Hot Rod, the Old Testament part of me sorta hoped the Heberts caught them before Carter did.

"I'm glad to hear your men are on it," I said. "But I guess that means you don't have any idea yet. No word on the street?"

Big shook his head. "I've checked with the family in other cities, but no one is aware of any new car theft ring operating in their territory, and none of the existing rings have this MO. Professionals don't try to kill people."

"People never even see professionals," Little agreed. "They take the car and are gone before anyone even notices."

I looked over at Ida Belle and Gertie, who both nodded, giving me the go-ahead to present our theory.

"We have an idea about what happened," I said. "But we can't tell you how we got our information."

Big looked over at Little and smiled. "I told you this was going to be good. Go ahead and lay your information on me."

"There were three vehicles missing from Hot Rod's shop," I said. "All black SUVs."

Big raised his eyebrows. "Interesting. So it's more likely they were looking for something stashed in a vehicle with that description. That would explain the way the job was handled. It didn't have any of the markings of a regular auto theft."

"That's what we thought," I said.

Big and Little both smiled.

"That's what you thought," Big said. "The three of you are dangerous enough as the good guys. You'd be hell as criminals."

"We'd be good at it," Gertie said.

"Really?" Big leaned forward a bit and looked at her. "You want to tell me how you know which cars are missing from Hot

Rod's shop? Because I know firsthand that place is being guarded by cops."

"Uh," Gertie said. "That's need-to-know information."

Now Big laughed, his whole body shaking. Even Little, who was usually the more composed of the two, let go with a chuckle or two. When Big finally stopped laughing, he wagged his finger at us.

"There was an explosion this morning near Hot Rod's shop. The police haven't determined the cause of the blast, but they found an open window on the back of the shop. When I heard about this, I figured someone clever created a distraction so that they could finish whatever job they started yesterday. But now the three of you sit here, with knowledge of what's missing from that shop, and I think about that explosion and I have to laugh. Because even though you won't tell me exactly what happened, I know how you work. And I've got a good imagination."

"We were gardening all morning," I said, and held up my arms. "Even got the scratches to prove it."

Big nodded. "Hey, I can roll with that story. When all this is over, I'd love to hear the real one, though. So did you come here just to ask if I knew anything?"

"Not exactly," I said, and pointed to Ida Belle. "She bought a vehicle from Hot Rod a week ago. A black SUV."

Big sobered and stiffened in his chair. He looked over at Little, whose smile had disappeared. "That's not good," Big said. "If whatever those men were looking for wasn't in the vehicles they took, they're going to go looking for the right one."

"That's where the favor comes in," I said. "We'd like to hide Ida Belle's SUV at your storage facility. It would give us a safe place to go through the vehicle ourselves and see if we can find anything. Plus, the thieves won't be able to find it and if they do, well, you have the security end of things covered."

Big looked over at Little, who nodded. "You can use the

storage facility," Big said. "On one condition. Mannie will help you search the vehicle."

"We would appreciate any assistance you can offer," I said, trying not to look excited.

Yes, Mannie was one of the "bad guys," but that just meant he knew way more than we did about hiding contraband in a vehicle. If anything was hidden in the SUV, Mannie would probably be able to spot it easier than we could. And the sooner the bad guys were rotting in a jail cell somewhere, the sooner Ida Belle could return to her regular programming.

Big looked over at Little. "There's an empty extra-large unit in the middle row, right in the center. That way, no one can get to it by blow-torching an outside wall. Set them up there. If anyone wants a look at what's in that unit, they'll have to pose for the cameras."

Little nodded and rose from his chair. "Increased security?"

"Yeah," Big said. "Get Deuce and Snake to cover it. They've been bored. Maybe they'll get to do something fun."

Fun. Like kill someone for breaking into a storage facility. I guess everyone needed a hobby, right? We rose from our chairs and I extended my hand across the desk to Big, who gave it a firm shake.

"Thank you," I said. "We really appreciate the help."

"Appreciate it when I get those animals that bashed in Hot Rod's skull," he said. "Oh, and ladies, no explosives at the storage unit."

He was still chuckling when we walked out the door.

———

WE WERE two miles down the highway from Big and Little's warehouse office before anyone spoke. I was processing everything we knew about the situation so far and trying to decide what could possibly be so valuable that it was worth going to all this trouble. I had no idea what everyone else was thinking.

"So?" I asked finally, breaking the silence. "What do you guys think?"

"Maybe it's diamonds," Ida Belle said. "Something small enough to escape detection from Hot Rod but worth enough to kill for."

"I think I need to buy a new handbag," Gertie said.

"I think we're going to start making you carry a coin purse," I said, "just so we can ensure our own safety."

"Don't underestimate a coin purse," Gertie said.

"We probably shouldn't allow her to wear clothes with pockets, either," Ida Belle said.

"You never know when you might need something," Gertie said. "The things in my purse have come in handy more than once."

That's when it dawned on me that Gertie wasn't carrying a purse at all. "I thought you had a backup. Why aren't you carrying it?"

"I forgot that I let my neighbor borrow it and there was an accident," Gertie said. "I didn't want it back afterward."

"You mean old Mrs. Cline?" Ida Belle said, and started laughing. "That was no accident. That's you in five years if you don't get better glasses."

"I'm almost afraid to ask," I said, "but I'm going to anyway. What happened?"

"Mrs. Cline borrowed Gertie's backup purse because she was going to one of those roving flea markets and needed something bigger to put her wares in," Ida Belle said. "Mrs. Cline's eyesight is even worse than Gertie's, but she refuses to wear her glasses unless she's reading, so she didn't find anything to buy at the flea market, probably because it all looked crappy blurred together. On the way home, she spotted her cat in the neighbors' bushes and figured he'd gotten out of the house. So she caught him and stuffed him in the purse."

"He's an inside cat with no claws," Gertie said. "That's a perfectly reasonable thing to do."

"It would have been reasonable if it had actually been her cat and not a skunk," Ida Belle said.

"No!" I said. "Did she figure it out before she brought it inside?"

Ida Belle started laughing. "Heck no. She trotted right to the kitchen and opened the purse, thinking the cat was going to hop out and wait for his dinner like he always did. Instead, the skunk strolls out of the bag and then Mrs. Cline sees her cat sitting on the kitchen counter. And he's not amused."

Gertie, who'd been trying to keep a straight face, couldn't hold back any longer, and she started laughing so hard her shoulders shook. "The cat, Horace," she said when she'd finally stopped guffawing, "bowed up and hissed and the skunk went crazy. He sprayed the cat, Mrs. Cline, the counter, the drapes...basically, the entire kitchen was a war zone of stench.

"So Mrs. Cline grabs a pair of glasses off the counter and puts them on and realizes she's got a skunk parading around her kitchen sending out a stink bomb like a lawn sprinkler. She runs to the back door and flings it open and the angry animal ran outside, giving her porch a final squirt before he hauled it into the bushes."

I couldn't help laughing. I'd seen Mrs. Cline at church holding the hymnal upside down and could imagine the entire thing going down just as Ida Belle and Gertie described.

"What did she do about the smell?" I asked. "Is there a hazmat team for random skunking?"

"The entire kitchen had to be repainted," Gertie said. "She washed the heck out of the drapes, but every time it got humid, they smelled like skunk all over again, so she finally tossed them. Mrs. Cline spent a significant amount of time bathing in tomato paste. Poor Horace had to be sedated and bathed, and for a good six months, he was on anxiety medicine."

"He never went back into the kitchen," Ida Belle said. "Mrs. Cline had to feed him in the living room."

"I didn't even bother trying to clean the purse," Gertie said. "When Mrs. Cline returned it, I wasn't home so she left it on the front porch. Carter got complaints from three of my neighbors before I got home. So I just threw it away, but then I forgot to replace it."

"I can see why you might want to let that one slip your mind," I said. "On the positive side, Ida Belle and I don't have to worry as much about what you're packing since you don't have a handbag."

"Oh, I just stuffed it all in my bra," Gertie said.

I looked at her in the rearview mirror, hoping she was joking, but she appeared to be completely serious. Ida Belle didn't even bother hiding her dismay.

"I am not frisking her bra," I said. "I'd rather risk an explosion."

"Agreed," Ida Belle said. "Nor am I interested in her going without one."

"You two are ridiculous," Gertie said. "Fortune usually has two guns strapped somewhere on her body. She probably takes one into the shower, and don't ever make the mistake of waking her from a dead sleep. You might get capped before she even opens her eyes." She looked at Ida Belle. "And you, with your Dale Earnhardt death machines. Who the heck needs an SUV that goes two hundred miles per hour?"

"I'm okay with fast things," I said. "Mostly. I mean, I've pretty much thought I would die several times with Ida Belle behind the wheel, but then I'm certain we would have all died several times if we hadn't been in something fast. So I'm still going with fast is worth the risk."

"Really?" Gertie said. "Even when the latest speed acquisition might have put a man in the ICU?"

It was a sucky point, but a point nonetheless.

We were all somber when I parked in front of the hospital and we entered the ICU. Ida Belle went directly to the nurse's desk and inquired about Hot Rod. The nurse stared at her for a moment with a "why do you want to know" look, then her expression shifted and she relaxed.

"You're Miss Ida Belle," she said. "You probably don't remember me—Shonda. Grandma Cline always spoke highly of your cough syrup."

"Good Lord," Ida Belle said. "Shonda. I haven't seen you since you were a little bitty thing. And now you're all grown up and working at the hospital. That's just great."

"Is that Mrs. Cline of the skunk-in-purse fame?" I asked. I couldn't help myself. I usually can't.

Shonda laughed. "That story never gets old. When Horace died, Grandma Cline refused to get another cat. I think Horace probably made her pay for what happened to him."

Gertie nodded. "Cats have a way of reminding all of us that they tolerate us only because of our opposable thumbs that open cans of goodness."

"So true," Shonda said. "I would love a puppy, but with the hours I work, it wouldn't be fair to either of us. I settled for a neglected cactus. I'm not doing so well with that, either."

She tapped on her computer screen, then shook her head. "I'm afraid I can't let you in to see Hot Rod, and even if you got through the doors, there's a cop sitting outside his room. He won't let anyone in except the medical staff."

Ida Belle nodded. "I figured that might be the case, but it didn't feel right sitting home and not checking."

"Of course not," Shonda said.

"Can you tell us anything about his condition?" I asked. "We don't want to get you in trouble, but we've been hoping for a bit of good news."

Shonda frowned. "He's in critical condition. It's really touch-and-go right now. I'm fairly new to this, but some of the older nurses said cases like his are fifty-fifty. I'm sorry I don't have anything better for you."

"Fifty-fifty is still better than the alternative," Gertie said.

Ida Belle pulled some bills out of her pocket and stuck her hand out, passing them to Shonda as they shook. Shonda uncurled her hand and looked at the bills, somewhat confused.

"For taking care of Hot Rod," Ida Belle said. "If there's anything I can do, please call. Hot Rod was a good man. He doesn't have any family here to look after him, so the least I can do is fill in."

Shonda's expression cleared in understanding and she nodded. "Of course, Miss Ida Belle. If I think of anything or if his condition changes, I'll let you know. Thank you ladies for stopping by. It's really nice to know that some things about Sinful haven't changed."

If she only knew.

CHAPTER SEVEN

It was late afternoon before Carter swung by my house. Even though it was still hot as heck, I'd gone into the backyard for some hammock sleeping and book reading. My cat, Merlin, who seemed to enjoy the heat, was sunning next to a rosebush. I was in between naps when Carter came around the side of the house and into the backyard, and I waved.

He gave the chopped hedges a hard look as he crossed the lawn, and I held in a smile. He might care for me, but he still didn't trust me. A normal woman might be offended, but I just thought it made him smart. Not that I couldn't be trusted at all. It was more like I couldn't be trusted about certain things—like not getting involved when a friend might be in danger.

"You might want to hire someone next time," he said, and pointed at the bushes.

"I know," I said. "Gertie offered to do it all, but I wanted to learn, and there's that whole other thing of letting Gertie loose with giant scissors."

"Smart," he said, and sat in the lawn chair that I keep near the hammock, mostly for Carter to sit in.

"So I hear that while I was doing a hatchet job on my bushes, someone set off a bomb at Hot Rod's shop." I figured if I got the facts wrong, he might make an attempt to correct me. "And for some reason you thought I might be involved?"

I had to give him credit. At least he appeared a bit apologetic.

"Sorry," he said. "It's sort of a trigger response given the company you keep, and then there's that whole history thing."

"So who blew up the shop?" I said, hoping that if he felt bad, I could take advantage of it.

"It wasn't the shop. It was in the woods surrounding the shop."

"Was it a still?" I figured given that a lot of Sinful residents made their own brew, it was the logical thing to ask.

"No. I'm not sure what it was, to be honest. Left a big hole in the ground and blew up some bushes."

"Kids?" It might not sound like a reasonable guess in other places, but Sinful was special.

"Could be," Carter said, proving my point. "There's a lot of highway construction going on. Someone could have snagged some dynamite for their own fun."

"Isn't it all supposed to be locked up and inventoried?"

"Of course. You say that like it changes reality."

I smiled. "Sorry. For a minute, I forgot I was in Sinful. So was anyone hurt?"

"Indirectly." Carter looked off at the bayou, and I could tell he was trying not to smile.

"Oh no!" I said, sitting up in the hammock. "You can't sit there with your lips quivering and not tell me what happened. It didn't have anything to do with the crime, so spill."

"Well, technically, the explosion is a crime of its own."

"Seriously. That's how you're going to play it?"

"Okay, fine. A deputy from a neighboring jurisdiction had called offering to help if I needed it. The sheriff's department likes to avoid involving the state police if we can help it, so I took him up on the offer and had him watching the shop. Sheriff Lee was there, but I figured he needed backup."

"Meaning someone to keep him awake."

"That and to make sure he didn't die on the job. I'm pretty sure that's what's going to happen. He's going to die on that horse, go into rigor, and no one is going to notice for days."

"I can see that."

"Well, anyway, it didn't happen today. What happened is that Sheriff Lee heard a noise in the woods and headed that direction to investigate. When he got close, the explosion happened. I don't know how much you know about horses, but even when they're a thousand years old and partially deaf, they don't mix with loud things."

"Oh no. Is Sheriff Lee all right? What about the horse?"

"The deputy got the worst of it, actually. The horse spun around and hightailed it away from the woods, and ran over the deputy, who couldn't dive out of the way in time. Sheriff Lee did a death cling and managed to stay on until the horse wore out and stopped running. Believe it or not, he managed five miles at full run."

"Wow. I can't believe he didn't keel over from a heart attack. Sheriff Lee, too."

"When the horse finally stopped running, he lay down in the middle of the highway. Sheriff Lee kinda rolled off of him. We had the eastbound lane blocked for a good half hour."

"But they're both okay?"

"The paramedics checked out Sheriff Lee and said he's fine, but he's going to be sore as heck. Both of them received oxygen."

"The horse received oxygen?"

"Apparently, he needed it. Anyway, a friend of Lee's brought a trailer and they managed to get the horse on his feet and in it. The horse and Lee are officially on medical leave."

"And the deputy?"

"Sprained wrist. Probably from trying to break his fall. I feel bad, though. Guy does me a favor and ends up injured."

I nodded; the deputy's situation was unfortunate, but I was relieved that there were no major injuries due to Gertie's "mistake." Given the players, it could have gone the other direction.

"Well, I'm glad everyone's all right. More or less. That poor horse."

Carter nodded. His smile had slipped away as he'd relayed the story, and I could see fatigue setting in.

"You look tired and frustrated," I said.

"That's probably because I'm tired and frustrated."

"Did you catch the guy who hurt Hot Rod?"

Carter shook his head. "No. And that's all I can say on the matter."

"That sucks. Not the 'all you can say' part, but the part where you haven't caught the guy. Ida Belle, Gertie, and I went to the hospital this afternoon." I figured it was better for me to offer up the information. That way, it would appear innocent, whereas if I didn't offer it up, he might think we were up to something.

"Why?" he asked. "They won't let anyone into ICU except immediate family, of which there's not any. Besides, I've got a guard on the door, and he's been instructed to turn away everyone but medical personnel on a very short list I supplied him with."

"I know, and I told Ida Belle and Gertie that would probably be the case, but apparently, there's some Southern requirement to grease the medical staff?"

"Ah. It's old-school, but given that Ida Belle just did business with him and he has no family, she would have felt obligated."

"That's what she said. I think it's nice...in a what-the-hell-happens-if-you're-not-bribing-people-to-do-their-job sort of way."

He laughed. "They'd all be offended if you called it a bribe. It's more of an appreciation thing. Kinda like tips for great service at a restaurant."

"Except it's prepaid," I pointed out. "The nurse couldn't tell us anything, but her expression said he's not doing well."

Carter sobered and shook his head. "No. He's still critical, and the doctor says it's too soon to tell. I hate this. Sometimes the vehicles he sells get people in hot water and more than a few have wound up in the ER, but he's a good guy. The only problem I've ever had with him is speeding."

"Makes sense. Are you hungry? I still have some roast beef."

"I grabbed a sandwich earlier. I don't think I'm going to get off in time for grilling, so our dinner is still on hold."

"No problem. I won't starve."

"But if you want to come over for dessert, I wouldn't complain."

"Yeah, about that. I'm going to have to go on a short-term diet."

He narrowed his eyes at me. "Why? What's up?"

"Why does something have to be up?"

"Because it's you."

"Well, nothing is up this time, except a problem with Ida Belle's plumbing. She has a leak and had to turn off the water to her house, so she's staying with me a couple days until some buddy of hers can take a look at it. He's giving her the friends-are-free deal."

"Why isn't she staying with Gertie?"

"Gertie sleepwalks."

"So?"

"She also sleeps in the nude."

Carter stared at me in dismay. "Please don't provide details as to how you know that. I don't want to live with those images in my head."

"Something we can both agree on."

"Okay, so you're putting up Ida Belle. So what? She's a big girl and can sleep alone. And even if you've not told her about our sleepovers, I'm sure she knows. Ida Belle knows about everything that happens in Sinful, sometimes before it even happens. If she had any interest in working and I thought I wouldn't want to shoot myself, I'd hire her as a deputy just for the intelligence gathering."

"Oh, I'm sure they both know. They've said as much although I refuse to provide details, much to Gertie's dismay. But I would feel bad leaving her here alone, and I'm sure it would be considered bad manners to abandon a guest in your home, even a capable one like Ida Belle."

He sighed, but I knew I had him with the manners argument. For all his practicality, Carter was still his mother's son, and Emmaline was a study in Southern manners. If she found out I was playing house with Carter while I had company, he'd never hear the end of it.

"It's only a couple of days," I said, hoping that was really the case. "Besides, you look like you could use some rest, and I'm not all that restful."

"Ha! That might just be the biggest understatement spoken in Sinful this year."

"Speaking of, have you had any more Celia problems?" I asked, Carter's words making me think about big mouths and lots of hot air.

He frowned and shook his head. "Nothing. Honestly, that concerns me more than if she were spouting her vitriol all over town."

"You think she's plotting her revenge."

"I'd bet on it. I'm sure I don't have to say this, but tell Ida Belle to watch her back. No matter how things go down, Celia always figures out a way to bring it back around to Ida Belle."

"Or me. You don't think she'll go poking into my background, do you?"

Carter's eyes widened, and I knew he'd instantly processed all the possibilities, none of them good. "If she digs too hard..."

"She'll find out that the real Sandy-Sue never came to Sinful."

"But she has no way of figuring out who you really are."

"No. But if she starts screaming loud enough to anyone who will listen, my picture and that bit of gossip could wind up all over social media. Do you really think Ahmad's cronies aren't monitoring that? They have better computer techs than Microsoft."

Carter jumped up from the chair and cursed, then starting pacing. "We have to figure out something to do about this."

"Like what? The only way to stop someone like Celia from talking is to kill her, and you keep telling me I'm not allowed to do that."

Carter stopped pacing and stared at me. "This is no time for assassin humor."

"There's nothing we can do. You know that. I know that. You just don't like it and neither do I, but I've had longer to process it."

"Why is it taking the CIA so long to catch that guy?"

I sighed, completely understanding his frustration, but I knew Harrison and my boss, Director Morrow, were doing everything possible to get me back to my real identity.

"Because he's really, really good," I said. "And unless they can figure out who the mole is, he's got someone inside the CIA helping him stay one step ahead."

I could have told him about Harrison's message that something was in the works, but I didn't want to give him false hope. It was bad enough that I was feeling hopeful. Disappointment sucked. No use in both of us feeling it when one would suffice.

"There's got to be something we can do," Carter said.

"The only thing we can do is sit tight and hope that the CIA gets Ahmad and that Celia doesn't make good on her threat. Trust me, I've rolled a million different ideas through my head, and there's nothing else."

"I swear to God that woman has turned this town into her own personal war zone. I wish she'd do everyone a favor and leave."

"She won't do that. She'll stay here until the day she dies, trying to get revenge on the people she believes ruined her life."

"Her life was ruined by a series of stupid choices. The only one who won't admit that is Celia."

I shrugged. We both knew the score. Beating a dead horse wasn't going to change who Celia was. I was fairly certain nothing would change Celia at this point.

"Anyway," I said. "I didn't bring it up to get you riled. I just wanted you to keep an ear open...just in case."

"Of course. And I will. If you think of anything I can do to help—anything legal, or close to it—let me know."

"I will."

Carter leaned over and kissed me, then sighed. "I best get back to it."

"Let me know if there's anything I can do."

He smiled. "You're already doing it."

I watched as he walked away, feeling a tiny bit guilty about the whole explosion thing. I hated lying to him, but until we knew for certain that something was going on, I couldn't see any reason to bring him into it. Not to mention he would never approve of my involvement with Big and Little. That one was something we'd have to discuss at some point. Because if I was ever free to try this whole PI thing, this probably wouldn't be the last time I used that connection to my own advantage.

For whatever reason, they liked me and were willing to help with our escapades. It might not be the smartest relationship to form in terms of the law, but it was useful in so many other ways that I thought it was worth the risk. The CIA worked with plenty of criminals to get the intel or access we needed to bigger fish. All law enforcement did, at some point.

All this thinking about the explosion and the PI thing brought me right back around to Celia. What I needed was a diversion. Something that drew her attention away from me and set her sights on something else. I just had no idea what that would be.

But I had friends who might be able to come up with something.

———

IDA BELLE, Gertie, and I decided against cooking or reheating that night and opted for Francine's instead. Ida Belle hoped that given what had happened with Hot Rod, more people might be out and about, which meant more gossip making its way around. The second-best place in town to get the local gossip was Francine's. The first place being Ida Belle's house.

But this time, Ida Belle's sources were coming up blank. Aside from periodic updates from Ida Belle's hospital contact about Hot Rod's condition, no one had anything to report. And that seemed strange. Usually there was speculation at the least, especially in a small town. There was always the guy who wore the funny hat or stared at people too long or never looked you in the eye. But not now. For the first time since I'd arrived in Sinful, lips weren't moving.

Ally was working the evening shift and hurried over when she saw us come in. "Your table in the back should be open in a couple of minutes if you want to wait."

Ida Belle scanned the café and shook her head. "The one in the middle will do fine."

Ally gave her a knowing look. "You want to see if there's any scuttlebutt."

"And?" Ida Belle said.

Ally frowned. "It's weird, but no. I figured by now, Celia would have gotten half her followers convinced that Fortune was to blame for the attack on Hot Rod."

"Why is it always my fault?" I asked. "Ida Belle's the one who bought a vehicle from him."

"Why would that give me a reason to crack him over the head?" Ida Belle asked.

"You didn't want to pay the note?" I asked.

"Huh," Ida Belle said. "I suppose it would be as good a theory as any, but I paid cash."

"Then I guess it wasn't you," I said.

Ally smiled and walked to the table with the menus. We took our seats and gave Ally our drink order. As soon as she headed into the kitchen, one of the women at the table next to us tapped Ida Belle on the shoulder. I recognized her as a member of the Baptist choir.

Midfifties. Five feet six. A hundred sixty pounds. Surprisingly decent muscle tone. With training, could probably produce a good left hook.

Her husband, a big beefy man, sat next to her, a sour expression on his face.

Late fifties. Five feet ten. Two hundred forty pounds. Muscle tone long gone. Personality gone with it. If it had ever been there to begin with.

"Have you heard anything about Hot Rod?" the woman asked.

Ida Belle told her what little we knew, and the woman shook her head. "It's so awful," she said.

Her husband cleared his throat. "What's awful are those death machines that man sells to unsuspecting citizens. He's going to get people killed with that tomfoolery."

The woman rolled her eyes. "Yes, Ralph, I'm sure those automobiles are so much more dangerous than the man who cracked Hot Rod over the head with a tire iron."

Ralph turned a bit red in the face and pushed himself away from the table. "I'm going to go outside and get some air."

The woman watched until he was a good ten feet away, then turned back to us. "If he goes outside still running his mouth with all that nonsense, he'll just make it hotter out there."

I smiled, somewhat surprised that she was willing to talk about her husband that way, but then maybe after decades with the same person, you stopped making excuses for their obvious personality flaws.

The woman looked at me and stuck out her hand. "I don't

think we've formally met. I'm Lucinda Fleming. That surly, pompous ass that just walked outside is my cousin Ralph."

"Cousin? Oh." I nodded.

"You thought he was my husband and that I was being indelicate with my comments, did you?" Lucinda asked.

I shook my head. "I thought he was your husband and you were being refreshingly honest with your comments."

Lucinda laughed, a giant booming laugh that had several patrons looking her direction. "I've heard a lot about you. I figured I'd like you, but then my requirements aren't all that high. As long as you're not a friend of Celia's, then you're pretty much a friend of mine."

"Then we're officially best friends," I said.

"Speaking of which," Lucinda said, "what is that old bat up to? No one I know has seen her since the announcement and that ridiculous display she made over the keys."

"We don't know," Gertie said. "None of the Sinful Ladies have seen her either."

Lucinda frowned. "Well, that's worrisome. I prefer for a boil to be out in the open where I can see it. When it's hiding down in a butt crack, it can be a real pain in the...you know."

"I guess it's too much to hope for to think she's depressed and drowning her sorrows in some homemade brew?" I asked.

Ida Belle snorted. "That woman doesn't know the meaning of depressed. She has two modes, mean and asleep. You can bet the only reason she's hiding in her house is because she hasn't figured out what she's going to pull next."

"Or she's busy working on it," Gertie said.

Lucinda nodded. "I don't know whether to be scared about that or look forward to the entertainment." She rose from the table and pulled her purse over her shoulder. "I better get going before Ralph leaves me to walk home."

She put some bills on the table for Ally, then leaned over and whispered something to Ida Belle. As she straightened back up, she patted me on the back. "Nice meeting you, dear," she said, and headed out of the café.

"What did she say?" Gertie asked.

Ida Belle stared out the café and frowned, then turned back to us, her voice low. "She said the Seal brothers were released from Angola last week."

Gertie's eyes widened. "That's not good."

"Who are the Seal brothers?" I asked, figuring all the whispering was an indication that I wasn't going to like the answer.

"Twins whose mother died in a car wreck when they were in high school," Gertie said. "They moved to Sinful and were raised by their uncle, as best as he could manage them anyway, until they turned eighteen and took off."

"So you knew them?" I asked.

Gertie nodded. "After I retired from teaching, I still did some subbing when needed. They were students in my class. Sullen, trouble, not interested in anything but getting out of Sinful, but they stayed put until they were legal adults. They were only in town six months or so."

"But that was plenty enough time to cause problems," Ida Belle said.

"What kind of trouble?" I asked.

"During that time," Ida Belle said, "there was a rash of stolen cars. It had never happened before and hasn't happened since."

"Until now," I said.

Ida Belle nodded. "The sheriff didn't have any proof, but everyone figured they knew the score. Still, with the brothers' connections, I think the sheriff was afraid to push the issue."

"What connections?" I asked.

"They claimed they're distant cousins to Barry Seal," Ida Belle said.

Okay. That was a name I knew. Barry Seal was a pilot who'd worked for the Medellín cartel. He'd ultimately turned informant and was assassinated while performing his public service work per his sentencing. The Feds had fallen under criticism for failing to provide adequate protection for Seal.

"You said they claim to be cousins," I said. "Does anyone know if that's true?"

Gertie shook her head. "I don't think so, but it doesn't really matter. They're bad news regardless of their family ties."

"I don't know," I said. "There's family ties and there's family ties."

"She's right," Ida Belle said. "If our theory about what happened at Hot Rod's is right, then the most likely candidate is organized crime. I saw the way Big and Little looked at each other when we talked with them. I guarantee you that's exactly what they think."

"But the Medellín cartel is long gone," Gertie said. "The Seal brothers are twenty-nine at the most. They could hardly have an association with an organization that was taken out of business when they were kids."

"They weren't all killed," I said. "And I seriously doubt those that got away became honest, hardworking citizens."

"Exactly," Ida Belle said. "Which means we need to find out more about the Seal brothers."

"This uncle that they lived with in Sinful," I said. "Is he still around?"

Ida Belle nodded. "You just met him."

CHAPTER EIGHT

We worked our way through dinner more quickly than usual and took our dessert to go, anxious to head back to my house where we could talk without being overheard. I grabbed my laptop off the kitchen counter and plopped down at the breakfast table as soon as we walked inside. Ida Belle retrieved three sodas from the refrigerator, and Gertie served up the dessert we'd brought from the café.

"Okay," I said. "First things first. Tell me everything you can about Ralph. You said he was the boys' uncle."

"Not much to tell," Ida Belle said. "He's an accountant, a bore, and a blowhole. You've seen the blowhole side. It probably comes as no shock that he's never been married."

"None whatsoever," I said. "Was he born here?"

Ida Belle nodded. "Born here, and aside from the four years he attended college in New Orleans, he's never left. His father was the local accountant and Ralph worked for him. When his father retired, Ralph took over his practice. He passed shortly after retiring."

"How is he related to the brothers?" I asked.

"His sister, Carol, was their mother," Gertie said. "I think her husband's name was Joshua."

"So they both grew up here, but Carol left and Ralph stayed?" I asked.

Ida Belle shook her head. "Actually no. The big scandal back then was Ralph's mother. She ran off with another man. She took Carol, who was just a toddler then, and left Ralph with his father. Ralph was maybe four or five. According to Ralph's father, he never heard from her again after the day she left, and she made no effort to contact Ralph. I think Carol reconnected with Ralph in college or maybe right after when she found out that she had a brother."

"Wow. That's unusual for these parts, right?" I asked.

"It happens," Gertie said, "but it's far more common for a woman to have her fun on the side and one of the kids belong to her fling. Usually the husbands never figure it out. But the wife usually doesn't take off with the other man, and it's also irregular for a woman to abandon all contact with a biological child."

"I'd bet that was her husband's requirement," Ida Belle said. "Given the rumors that were floating around at the time and the fact that Carol reconnected with Ralph but not his father, I figure Carol belonged to the guy her mother left with."

"Ah, that would make sense," I said. "In a daytime talk show kind of way. So Carol and Ralph reconnected as young adults. I assume Carol's husband died at some point prior to her car wreck, since the brothers went to live with Ralph after she passed?"

"Yes," Gertie said. "Some sort of accident. I think he worked in the oil field, but I'm not certain. Anyway, I want to think the brothers were much younger when that happened. I remember Ralph commenting one time about how Carol could have remarried a long time ago if the boys hadn't been such trouble, but instead she'd spent so many years stressing over them without any help."

"So the father doesn't sound like the connection between the brothers and crime," I said. "Especially if he passed when they were young. I don't suppose we have any reason to suspect Carol?"

"None that I'm aware of," Gertie said. "I believe she worked for the tax assessor's office or something to that affect."

"And the car wreck?" I asked. "Anything suspicious there?"

Gertie shook her head. "She ran off the highway and into a bayou one night. Blood alcohol content was sky high. She was probably unconscious before she went into the water."

"Her way of dealing with the brothers, I guess," I said. "What about Lucinda?"

"Born and raised in New Orleans. She and Ralph attended college at the same university, but Lucinda said they were never very close. She also worked for the government in some capacity, technical writer maybe. Did twenty-plus years for them, retired, and moved to Sinful."

"Why?" I asked. "It couldn't possibly be for Ralph's charming company."

"Her husband died and she wanted to get out of the city," Ida Belle said. "And Ralph is tiresome, but there's something to be said for having family around."

Something in the way Ida Belle delivered that first sentence made it sound as though she wasn't quite certain of what she'd said.

"You don't sound convinced," I said.

Ida Belle frowned. "There was some talk, that Lucinda's husband hadn't died but had run off with another woman. I never could trace it back to the source."

"If he died in New Orleans, wouldn't there be an obituary?" I asked.

"Not unless immediate family requested one, and in this case, that would mean Lucinda," Gertie said. "He was a native of Great Britain, so the gossip goes, and it was a late marriage for both of them. They were both in their forties. I believe Ralph said he was cremated and his ashes shipped back to the UK for burial in the family cemetery."

"But maybe he ran off and that was the story they told so that she could save face," I said. "Then she retired and moved away so no one would find out the truth. If that's the way it really went down, it sucks, but I can see why she wouldn't want that albatross of a past hanging over her head."

Gertie nodded. "Especially here. When a woman is widowed, she's treated completely differently by the local women than if her husband left her."

"Why?" I asked.

"Because a widowed woman is grieving," Ida Belle said, "and isn't as likely to go after someone else's husband."

"Good God," I said. "Like the men in this town are some big catch."

"Look at the wives," Gertie said. "It's all relative."

"Okay, so regardless of what really happened with Lucinda's husband," Ida Belle said, "she moved here shortly after Ralph got custody of the brothers. I guess she figured he could probably use some help."

Gertie nodded. "And now, she and Ralph have dinner together once a month at the café like clockwork. He probably sees it as doing his duty."

"Lucinda probably wishes he'd forget that part of his raising," Ida Belle said.

I nodded. What little I'd seen and heard of Ralph didn't give me any indication that spending time with him would be anything but miserable. But it also didn't give me any indication that he was involved in some big mob plot, even though he clearly had a problem with Hot Rod's creations.

"Okay," I said. "So what were the brothers up to after they left Sinful that landed them in prison?"

"Drugs," Ida Belle said. "The New Orleans police claimed they were moving twenty grand a night in heroin."

I stared. "That's a serious amount of product to move standing on the corner."

"They had an in with a club," Ida Belle said. "One of those trendy places that the kids with some disposable income frequent. The brothers went up for ten years. No time off for good behavior allowed, according to Ralph."

"Ten years?" I looked at Gertie. "You said the brothers were twenty-nine. They were busted a year after they left Sinful?"

Ida Belle nodded. "I remember seeing Ralph in the General Store shortly after the conviction. I told him I was sorry, and he looked so angry. Said they were an embarrassment to the family."

"Can't blame him on that one," I said. "What about the club owner? How much did he get? He might be out as well."

"I believe he disappeared," Ida Belle said.

"People don't just disappear," I said.

"No," Ida Belle said, "but Ralph said the police couldn't find him when the arrest order came down."

"Did they ever find him?" I asked.

Ida Belle shrugged. "I never followed up."

"Okay," I said, and opened my laptop. "What we can't find on the Internet, we can ask about tonight when we take the SUV to the storage facility. No way the brothers were moving heroin through the French Quarter without the Hebert family knowing about it."

"You don't think they'll be there tonight, do you?" Gertie asked.

I absolutely thought they'd be there. In fact, I was counting on it. If anyone could ferret out what might be hidden in that vehicle, it would be the Heberts. I was certain they were pushing their contacts for information. I didn't believe for a minute that they were sitting quietly in their office, waiting for information to fall into their lap. Men like Big and Little didn't wait for anything.

I nodded. "I don't think they'd miss it for the world."

It was just after midnight when we hit the highway to the storage unit. Ida Belle was driving her SUV, and Gertie and I were following her in my Jeep. I'd done a quick surveillance sweep on Carter's house before we'd headed out. His truck was in his driveway and all the lights were off. I had a moment of regret that I wasn't cuddled up inside with him, but I hoped he was getting some of that sleep he desperately needed. There would be plenty of time for cuddling once I was sure Ida Belle was safe.

The highway was a long, dark stretch in the middle of the night, with only lights in the windows of distant houses to pierce the black. A storm circling overhead had produced huge swirling clouds that were blocking any moonlight that might have illuminated our way. The upside was that it would be easy to spot anyone who attempted to follow us. The downside was if anything happened, there was no place to run.

"It's kinda creepy out here this late at night," Gertie said, her words echoing my thoughts.

"Yeah. The storm's not helping."

Gertie fidgeted a bit, then looked over at me. "Do you think Ida Belle's in danger?"

I knew the question wasn't the real question. Gertie had her moments, but her mind was sharp. She knew the score. She was just worried about her best friend and wanted me to tell her that the bad guys would go to jail and Ida Belle would be fine. And I really wanted to tell her just that.

But I couldn't.

Because I didn't know if everything would be fine. And I didn't want to lie to her.

"We're doing everything we can to protect her," I said.

"What if it's not enough?"

"You trust me, right?"

"Of course."

"Do you really think anyone is going to get to Ida Belle without going through me first? And then ask yourself how many people are capable of going through me."

She relaxed a bit. "You're a good friend, Fortune."

"You'd do the same for me," I said.

"Not nearly as well," Gertie said. "Maybe years ago I could have been trained like you were, but those days are long past. I don't like to admit that age is affecting me, but I'm not so foolish that I'm not aware."

"I don't think you're foolish. At least not about the age thing."

"So you think I'm foolish about other things?"

"You trapped an alligator with your pants and put him inside your house."

"Well, when you put it that way."

"We're going to figure this out," I said. "And Carter is going to catch the bad guys, and Ida Belle will be back in that age-reducing death trap before either one of us is ready."

"I like the sound of that."

"Me too," I said as I turned off the highway and onto the road that led to Big and Little's storage facility. Gertie and I were both silent the rest of the drive. I had so many thoughts running through my head, I was finding it difficult to settle on only one. God only knew what Gertie was thinking about, but since she wasn't carrying a purse, I figured I was on the safer side of things regardless of where her mind was roaming.

Mannie was up front at the gate when we arrived. He punched in a code and waved us through. "Second row," he said. "Unit 63. Right in the middle. It's open."

Ida Belle drove through and we followed her in my Jeep, figuring it was better for it to be hidden behind the gate with the SUV, just in case anyone got curious and came wandering up to the storage facility. The unit was large enough for two cars, but part of the space was already taken up by a lift, a tool chest, and Big and Little Hebert.

"You were right," Gertie said. "About them showing up."

I nodded. I just hoped it turned out to be a good thing and not a "fooled you, we're really the bad guys" thing. I hadn't gotten that impression when we'd met earlier, and my instincts were rarely wrong, but since I'd come to Sinful, my life had been full of first-time experiences. I just prayed this wasn't another one of them.

Big and Little nodded to us as we stepped out of our vehicles, and Big lumbered over to take a look at the SUV and motioned to Ida Belle to pop the hood. Mannie opened it and he leaned in to get a closer look.

"Hot Rod does excellent work," Big said. "I saw this before he went to work on it. I wouldn't have given ten dollars for it, but Hot Rod swore he could make it into something fantastic."

"He certainly did that," Ida Belle said. "Do you want me to pull it up over the lift?"

Little stepped forward. "Not yet. Given the extent of the work that's been done to the vehicle, it's unlikely that anything is hidden in any of the main mechanical areas."

"Because Hot Rod would have found it," I said.

"How do we know he didn't?" Gertie asked.

"We don't for sure," I said, "but I'm going to guess that the car thieves questioned Hot Rod before they popped him over the head. If he'd found something and given it up, there would have been no need to steal the other cars."

Big nodded. "You have a logical mind. Do you know much about cars?"

"Not enough," I said.

"Then it's a good thing I'm here. Because cars have always been my passion. And Mannie is an excellent mechanic."

It was as if saying his name made him appear because at that exact moment, Mannie walked into the storage unit.

"Deuce and Snake are up front," Mannie said. "I've checked all the cameras and repositioned those that shifted during the last storm. You have coverage of every square inch inside the gates. You just need to check the feed."

Little pulled out his phone and poked at the screen. "It looks excellent."

"Now that all the newfangled technical stuff is covered," Big said, "let me show you what us old-schoolers know about vehicles. Mannie, grab that toolbox and we'll get to work." He looked over at Ida Belle. "Please don't worry about the disassembly. I'll make sure everything is back to perfect."

Ida Belle nodded and I could see how relieved she was. The instant Big had said the word "toolbox," she'd stiffened like a parent who'd taken their child to the doctor.

Little and Mannie moved a park bench over next to the side of the SUV and Big took a seat. Mannie pulled the SUV forward into the storage unit and as he climbed out, Big told him to open all the doors.

And the show began.

CHAPTER NINE

I have to admit, I was impressed. Who knew there were so many places to hide something in a vehicle? Well, besides criminals. Every time Mannie removed a piece of the SUV and passed it off to Ida Belle, Gertie, or I, another cubby was revealed, which was both amazing and depressing at the same time. With this many options for hiding places and the possibility that what we were looking for was as small as a USB stick or a diamond, there was no telling how long it would take to find something. And that was all assuming there was something to find in this particular SUV to begin with.

Two hours later, all the seats, the carpet, and the entire dash had been removed and everything gone over with a fine-tooth comb. Unfortunately, we'd come up with nothing. Big, however, did not seem to be the slightest bit perturbed, and Mannie didn't show any signs of wear even though he'd been playing mechanic for two hours without pause. I briefly wondered when they slept and for how long, because I was starting to wane a bit and Gertie had finally given up her mechanic's assistant role and taken a seat on the edge of Big's bench.

Maybe they had really good vitamins.

"Don't give up yet," Big said, apparently cluing in to my thoughts. "There's plenty of vehicle left to search. If you need to get back to Sinful, I'm happy to continue and let you know if we find anything."

I didn't want to leave, and I knew Ida Belle wasn't about to abandon her SUV until she absolutely had to. Even as tired as Gertie was, I doubted she'd vote for going home. It wasn't as if we'd be able to sleep anyway. We'd be wondering what was going on here.

"We're good for a few more hours," I said. "We just have to get back before anyone notices we're gone."

Big nodded. "Then let's start on the doors. Mannie, remove the trim panel from the driver's door."

Mannie went to work on the door and a minute later, laid the black panel that contained everything you see on the inside of the door on the ground next to the SUV. Without the trim panel, the metal interior of the door was exposed and I was surprised to see a bunch more nooks and crannies. Slowly and deliberately, Mannie poked his fingers into every opening on the door, making sure nothing was occupying the space but air. When he slipped his fingers in the bottom of the door shell, he froze.

"I feel something here," he said. "It's hard and plastic."

Big shook his head. "There shouldn't be anything contained in that spot. Can you pull it out?"

Mannie jammed his entire hand inside the shell and pulled out a small black plastic box with magnets on one side.

"It's a key hider," Ida Belle said. "You stick a spare key in it and attach it under a wheel well in case you lock yourself out of your vehicle."

"Well, it certainly wouldn't do the driver any good to hide it inside the SUV behind a panel that has to be removed to gain access," Gertie said.

Big gestured to Mannie, and he handed over the box. Big shook it, but it didn't make any sound. I was about to grab the box from him and open it myself when he pushed the top off and pulled out a square of folded paper towel. We all crowded around as he unwrapped the paper towel and exposed a solid black key.

"He wrapped it to keep it from making noise," Big said.

"That's not a vehicle key," Gertie said, going straight for the obvious.

To be honest, it looked like something out of an old movie, where the interior doors on homes were all opened and closed by iron keys. This one wasn't as large as in the movies but it looked like a scaled-down version.

"What does it open?" Mannie asked.

Big stared down at the key, frowning. "I don't know," Big said. "It's definitely not something new."

"It looks like a skeleton key," Mannie said.

"Maybe someone put a curse on the owner of the SUV," Gertie said.

"I think he meant it was an antique," Big said. "A skeleton key, by definition, is a master key or passkey, regardless of its manufactured date, but around here, a key that looks like this is called many things."

"So I could be right," Gertie said.

Big smiled. "This is Louisiana, home of the mysterious, so anything is possible. But I doubt anyone would have gone to such trouble to hide a cursed key. It would have been simpler to slip it under the carpet in his floorboard."

"I can do some research," I said.

"Given the situation," Big said, "I doubt it would be safe to show this around."

"I meant on the Internet," I said.

"You aren't afraid of being monitored?" Little asked.

"I know how to reroute things. I can search all I want and it would never be tracked back to me."

Little nodded. "When this situation is resolved, I'd love to speak to you about that if you wouldn't mind taking the time."

Big sighed. "Damned computers are going to ruin the world. Always something new."

"Speaking of computers," I said, "I think we need to know who owned this SUV before Hot Rod acquired it. That might tell us everything we need."

Little nodded. "We know a guy...I'll get that information."

"Great," I said. That was the beauty about Big and Little. They always knew a guy.

Big handed me the key. "I'm entrusting this to you because you have a vested interest in finding answers. I also have an interest in those answers, just not as personal as yours. I'm allowing you to take the lead on this because of your personal interest and your skill set, but I want you to promise me four things."

"Okay," I said, a bit hesitantly. It was four chances that I wouldn't want to agree to something, but at this point, what option did I have?

"First," Big said, "you'll secure the key somewhere that it can't be found."

"I can do that," I said

"And two," Big continued, "if you figure out what it unlocks, you allow me to provide you protection when you go there."

"I would appreciate any backup you are willing to provide," I said. Why would I turn down hired guns? They might save me a whole lot of trouble.

"Three," Big said. "You leave the police out of this for now. I know that's difficult given your involvement with the deputy, but I won't help if I'm on law enforcement radar."

"I don't have any desire to tell Carter about any of this," I said. That definitely wasn't a lie. The last thing I wanted to cough up was my involvement with known Mafia. "What's the fourth thing?"

Big leaned forward and looked me straight in the eyes. "If you figure out who did this, you let me handle it."

It wasn't the right thing to do. If I figured out who the car thieves were, the right thing to do would be to turn that information over to Carter. But then, turning over information to Carter would mean explaining how I got the information in the first place, which got me right back around to things I didn't want to explain to Carter.

"I will tell you what I find out," I said, "but I can't control what the cops discover themselves. So if they get there first…"

"Then the problem is eliminated either way," Big said. He stuck out his hand and I shook it.

I'd just made my deal with the devil.

———

It was 3:30 a.m. by the time we pulled into my garage. We'd dropped Gertie off at her house just before, and I could practically hear a cold shower and crisp clean sheets calling to me as I walked into the kitchen through the garage door. When we made it to the living room, all dreams of shower and sleep disappeared in an instant.

Carter was sitting in my living room, staring directly at Ida Belle and me.

"Glad you could make it," he said. "Is there anything you'd like to tell me?"

I have to give Ida Belle credit. No matter the situation, she always manages to keep a straight face. I was good, but Ida Belle had me beat hands down. But then, she'd been at it for far longer and she wasn't in a relationship with Carter, so that might have a little bit to do with it.

"We were at Gertie's," Ida Belle said, without any hesitation.

I nodded. Technically, it wasn't a lie. We *had* just been at Gertie's.

"I'm sure that was true a couple minutes ago," Carter said, "but what about the rest of the night?"

Busted.

Ida Belle looked over at me, and I understood that she wanted me to take the lead. That way, I got to decide how much to tell Carter. She would go along with whatever I chose to offer. But this was a tricky one. I'd just made a deal with Big Hebert, and I wasn't about to tell Carter how deep we were in with him. I also didn't want to tell him about the key until I knew more about it. There was still the odd chance that it had nothing to do with what happened to Hot Rod. I didn't really believe that, but it was as good an argument as any. Besides, I was certain Carter had been over the records at Hot Rod's place by now, and he hadn't bothered to tell Ida Belle she might be in danger, which troubled me.

"I've never known Ida Belle to wait on a plumber to fix a leak," Carter said. "Besides, most leaks can be isolated by simply not using that area of plumbing. You usually don't have to shut off your water and abandon your home. So why don't you tell me what's really going on here."

I didn't like his tone, and that is never a good thing.

"Why don't you tell me what's going on here?" I asked. "Why are you hell-bent on assuming that we're up to something unless you're certain there is something for us to be up to? I'm not the only one keeping secrets."

He rose from the chair. "Refusing to talk about an open investigation is not keeping secrets."

"It is when the information you're withholding is about the safety of one of my friends," I said.

His eyes widened and I knew I'd hit a nerve.

"You knew, didn't you?" I said. "Of course you did. You knew that Hot Rod said he had to warn Ida Belle before falling unconscious. You knew she might be in danger and you never said a word. So I moved my friend in here to protect her and you have a problem with *me*? From where I stand only one of us is wrong, and it's the one who broke into my house and questioned me about the things I do to protect the people I care about."

He flushed a bit and I could tell that despite the fact that he was mad, he also felt guilty. "I planned on looking out for Ida Belle myself," he said.

"Yeah, because you're always around what with having no job or anything to do," I said. "And I'm sure Sinful residents wouldn't bat an eye if Ida Belle moved into your house. And hey, while we're talking about things that make no logical sense, let's talk about how Ida Belle would be safer alone in her house with your occasional patrol rather than bunking with someone whose entire life's work consisted of killing people."

Ida Belle looked from me to Carter, and I could see how badly she felt for the trouble between us, but I didn't blame her for any of it. This was totally between Carter and me, and if we couldn't figure out how to be ourselves when it came to things like this and not be at each other's throats, then it was going to be the shortest great relationship I'd ever had.

"This is exactly what I didn't want," Ida Belle said.

"This has nothing to do with you," I said. "It would have happened eventually, regardless." I looked at Carter. "Here's the bottom line. I'm never going to stop doing anything necessary to protect my friends. And when I leave the CIA, I guarantee you, it will not be to take up a profession that requires me to sit behind a desk. Given that, the likelihood of us running into this problem again is so high it's astronomical. So either you accept me for who I am or we don't have anywhere to go from here. Because I'm the last person who's going to back down when a friend is in trouble."

Carter sighed. "I don't expect you to back down. But that doesn't mean you have to get involved."

"I'm already involved. Do you really think I'm going to sit here in the kitchen, talking about knitting and eating Gertie's cookies while there's someone out there who tried to kill Hot Rod and might be targeting Ida Belle?"

He shook his head. "I guess not. I suppose that means you're not going to tell me where you were tonight."

"Are you going to tell me what is missing from Hot Rod's shop?"

"Black SUVs."

I blinked, a bit surprised that he'd spit it out just like that.

"That's what we were afraid of," I said, leaving out the part where we'd sorta checked for ourselves. "Did you really think we wouldn't put that together? The only interaction Ida Belle's had with Hot Rod was purchasing her SUV, and it was recent. Then someone breaks in his shop, tries to kill him, and the only thing he manages to say is about warning Ida Belle."

"It was still a bit of a leap," Carter argued. "Hot Rod might have been talking about something he realized was wrong with the car."

I nodded. "And we thought about that as well, but I've been trained to prepare for the worst possible situation and then be pleasantly surprised if things turn out better. Doing the opposite results in unnecessary casualties."

Carter looked over at Ida Belle. "I'm sorry I didn't tell you as soon as I knew about the SUVs. It was wrong, but I promise you, I wasn't going to leave you unprotected. I've asked the state police for backup, and I was going to keep watch myself until they were in place."

"I'm more qualified than the state police," I said. "And a whole lot more motivated."

Carter nodded. He couldn't really make an argument on either of those statements. "Is the SUV in your garage?" he asked Ida Belle.

She looked over at me, clearly not wanting to offer more than I was willing to.

"No," I said. "We secured the SUV in a safe place. That's where we were tonight."

"What safe place?" Carter asked.

"The storage units up the highway," I said.

Carter threw his hands up in the air. "You've got to be kidding me! You put the SUV in the Heberts' facility? For all you know, they could be behind all of this."

"I don't think so," I said.

"Oh, you don't think so," Carter said. "Because mobsters are such nice people who never hurt anyone."

"They liked Hot Rod," Ida Belle said. "He did the work on their Hummer."

"And that means they had no reason to get rid of him?" Carter asked.

"What do you think?" Ida Belle asked, and I could tell she was beyond exhausted and her patience was completely gone. "They dropped the Hummer off at his shop with a body in the back and then months later decided to make sure he never told anyone? Look, you can sit here and gripe at Fortune all you want, but it's not going to get you anywhere. All of this was my decision. Fortune is just a great friend who stuck her neck out for me. And now I'm exhausted and aggravated, so I'm going to bed. Anything else you have to say will have to wait until I've gotten some sleep."

She gave me a nod, shot Carter a dirty look, then headed upstairs.

"I'm not backing down from this," I said. "Don't even insult me by asking."

He shook his head. "Why couldn't I fall for a nice, boring accountant?"

"Because you'd never be happy with a nice, boring accountant. That's something you need to accept about yourself. I'm also exhausted and aggravated, so I'm going to bed too. Lock up when you leave."

I started up the stairs and Carter put his hand on my arm to stop me. "I'm going to need to see that SUV."

I nodded. "When I wake up, I'll call you."

I headed upstairs for the long-awaited shower and pulled out my cell phone to send Little Hebert a text. I didn't want anyone surprised when I showed up at the storage unit with the police.

I hid the key in the secret room in Marge's master bedroom closet that contained her personal armory, then headed for the shower. I felt a tiny twinge of guilt for not telling Carter about the key, but the twinge quickly disappeared. I'd promised Big and Little I wouldn't get them involved with the police, and I was already breaking that promise. Not that I had any choice, and I'm sure they would understand, but it didn't mean I was going to spill out everything else.

Carter had exposed his hand by keeping the missing SUVs a secret from Ida Belle and me. If he had the key, I was positive the withholding of information would continue in earnest. So I'd hold on to the key and move forward as planned. I'd do my own investigation, and when I figured out what the key opened, I'd call Big and Little for backup.

I just hoped I was doing the right thing.

CHAPTER TEN

My internal clock betrayed me and tried to force me awake at 6:00 a.m. I gave it the mental finger, rolled over, and went back to sleep. Finally, my overactive mind won and I rolled out of bed after a series of confusing dreams featuring alligators, exploding handbags, and cars that used odd-shaped keys to start them. Once I was upright and mostly awake, the dreams weren't as confusing as I'd originally thought. At least the elements made sense.

I checked the clock and saw it was 8:00 a.m. I'd officially slept late. It wasn't something I managed often, but then when you didn't fall asleep until after four, things like this were bound to happen. I pulled on yoga pants and a T-shirt and headed out of the bedroom. The smell of coffee hit me as soon as I stepped into the hallway, so I didn't bother to check the guest room on my way down.

Ida Belle was sitting at the kitchen table with a full mug of coffee. A quick glance at the coffeepot let me know it was either her first cup or she was on her second pot. Based on her lackluster greeting and her unusual slouch, I was going with option one. I poured a cup, sat down across from her, and took a big sip. Just a hundred or so more of those and I'd be good to go.

"I'm sorry I put you in this position," Ida Belle said.

I stared at her, somewhat surprised. "You didn't."

"It's my vehicle."

"So how does that make it your fault? Trust me, I put myself in this position by virtue of being who I am. I didn't know who that was for most of my life, but now that I'm starting to get a good idea, I have no intention of pretending something else. And if Carter decides he can't handle that, then it's unfortunate, but I'll get over it."

Ida Belle gave me a rueful smile. "I know exactly who you are. Probably could have saved you some time and filled in the blanks while you were working up your character bio, but I think it's something everyone needs to come to terms with themselves."

"I'll bite. Who am I?"

"You're me. The person I was many decades ago, anyway. I think that's one of the reasons that I took to you instantly. I look at you and I see myself at a time when I was younger, faster, stronger, and my whole life stretched in front of me like an endless sunset."

I frowned. "You say that like you have regrets."

"If you live to a certain age, you'll always have regrets. Most of them will be selfish."

I studied her for several seconds. I'd always known Ida Belle ran deep, unlike Gertie, who mostly showed you who she was up front. But Ida Belle rarely talked about personal things this seriously. In fact, I could probably count the times on one hand if you weren't including talking about the cases we'd gotten mixed up in.

"Is that 'certain age' not quite thirty?" I asked. "Because I already have plenty of regrets."

Ida Belle shook her head. "You shouldn't feel that way. You're a young woman who made decisions about your direction in life using what information you had. You're intelligent and very successful at what you do. Of all things, don't ever regret that. It helped make you the person you are today. And that person still has plenty of time to do all the things a young woman ever dreams of."

"Right now, I'm dreaming of a blueberry muffin."

Ida Belle sighed. "So much like me. I used to deflect just like that. Then I got tired and settled in my ways and just started saying exactly what I thought all the time. Neither is a good long-term plan, although they both have their usefulness."

I frowned. "I'm not sure what you want me to say."

"I don't want you to say anything. Maybe I'm just an old woman who didn't get enough sleep and now I'm rambling, but I think what I'm trying to say is I see you doing the same things I did. And I want to be certain you're thinking about all the ramifications."

Ah. The coffee was kicking in and it was starting to make more sense.

"You're talking about you and Walter."

The General Store owner had outright admitted to being in love with Ida Belle since the crib and still was. He'd never been married, preferring instead to carry a torch for the woman who wouldn't say yes to a relationship. I still didn't quite understand why, but every time I'd asked her about it, she gave me a piece of an answer, but never anything complete.

"You and Carter have something good started," Ida Belle said. "I just want you to consider all your options when you're making choices."

"Okay. You've danced around this since day one, but if you want to give me relationship advice, then you're going to have to explain to me why you never said yes to Walter. I mean, I'd totally get it if you don't have those kind of feelings for him, but I don't think that's it."

Ida Belle stared into her coffee cup, frowning, then finally looked back up at me. "I had a lot of reasons...good reasons, or so I thought. They made my choice easier. But I think the real reason is because I never trusted him enough."

"I don't understand. Walter would lie down and die for you."

Ida Belle nodded. "And that's the problem. Walter has never approved of the things I involve myself in because they put me at risk. He can't bear the thought of something happening to me. But putting myself at risk is who I am, and I'm not willing to pretend to be someone else, even for Walter. It might have worked for a little while, but in the end, I would have resented him for not accepting me the way I am and he would have resented me for putting him through hell."

"And you're afraid I'm in the same situation with Carter. But if you know we're so alike, then what makes you think I'd be any more likely than you were to give up who I am for a man?"

"I don't think that for a minute, but you're still discovering who you are. You're in a state of flux. Oh, there's things about you that aren't ever going to change, and if Carter is being honest with himself, those are the very things he loves most about you and that also scare the daylights out of him. My point is, you still have an opportunity to find balance. A way to be yourself but not outside the realm of what Carter can live with."

"You really think it's possible?" I asked, because the longer I thought about what my future might look like and what Carter would prefer it look like, the more I felt our differences were a giant chasm that would be almost impossible to bridge.

"I think you have a really good chance," Ida Belle said. "Based on who he is and the things he's done, Carter has a good understanding of you and what makes you tick. He could no more give up law enforcement than you would leave me to fend for myself with this car thing."

"Understanding is one thing, but can he accept it as part of his everyday life? That's a huge leap. Can we really make this work if we're constantly keeping secrets from each other?"

"That's where the trust part comes in. You have to trust each other that the only secrets you're keeping have to do with your work. You have to believe that it's not personal."

"I think *I* can do that. I know that Carter isn't legally allowed to give me information, although I still think he was out of line for not telling you that you might be in danger. The fact that we'd already figured it out doesn't matter. The problem is if I pursue this PI thing, will Carter respect my clients' privacy and let me do my job? If I continued to work for the federal government, he wouldn't have a choice, but confidentiality isn't a legal requirement for PIs. It's an ethical standard."

"I don't know if he can respect it. That's something the two of you will have to figure out. But I do think you've got a far greater chance of Carter accepting you as you really are than I ever had with Walter. I would have put that man into an early grave. And I love him too much to do that to either of us."

I stared at her, surprised that she'd admitted something so personal and so important. "It's not too late, you know. You're both still here and healthy."

Ida Belle shook her head. "And we're both still the same people we were all those years ago. I'm not made to sit in a rocker, knitting and exchanging casserole recipes. Odds are, I'll go out right smack in the middle of something that everyone else will say I had no business poking my nose into."

"Don't you think after all these years, he's used to it? Do you really think he cares less about you just because you aren't in a relationship?"

Ida Belle never answered. After about thirty long seconds of silence, I was about to say something else when my cell phone signaled that I'd received a text. I checked the display. It was from Little.

Everything is ready.

I had no idea what that meant exactly, but I trusted that when we showed up at the storage unit with Carter, he would see whatever he expected to see and nothing that Big and Little didn't want him to see.

"They're ready at the storage unit," I said, and explained my text to Little the night before.

"It's good you warned them," Ida Belle said. "I wouldn't have wanted to surprise them by showing up with Carter."

"Yeah, that fell directly under 'things that are a bad idea, especially when I promised no cops.'"

I heard the front door open and Gertie called out from the front of the house. Several seconds later, she shuffled into the kitchen, looking like an extra for *The Walking Dead*.

"What's wrong with you?" Ida Belle asked.

"I'm a little sore." She poured herself a cup of coffee, then hovered over the chair and dropped as if her knees had given out.

I got up and snagged a bottle of aspirin, then retrieved an ice pack from the refrigerator.

"Rotate this every couple of minutes on your knees," I said, and handed her the ice pack. "If you've eaten breakfast, then take some aspirin. If not, then I'll find you something to eat."

Gertie stuck the ice pack on her right knee and reached for the bottle. "I had leftover chicken casserole. Ate it cold right out of the pan. Didn't want to stand long enough to heat it or cook something else."

Ida Belle narrowed her eyes at Gertie. "You're that bad off from a little running?"

"It wasn't a little running," Gertie said. "It was a mad dash through the swamp, and then I got to bang around in the bottom of that boat because no one ever lets me sit in a seat."

"That's still not enough," Ida Belle said. "What are you up to?"

Gertie threw her hands in the air. "You always think I'm up to something."

"Only when you are," Ida Belle replied.

"Okay, fine," Gertie said. "Because I know you two nosy parkers won't leave it alone until you know everything, I've been doing some video exercising. You keep harping on me about getting in shape, well, I'm getting in shape."

"Getting in shape isn't supposed to injure you," I said.

"What kind of exercise video?" Ida Belle asked.

"Dancing," Gertie said, suddenly deciding that her coffee needed intense stirring while staring into it.

I looked over at Ida Belle, who shook her head.

"What kind of dancing?" Ida Belle asked.

"Break dancing," Gertie mumbled.

"Break dancing!" Ida Belle said. "Are you crazy?" She waved a hand in dismissal. "Never mind. That was rhetorical."

"Can't you just try one of those country-and-western line-dancing things?" I asked.

"It's boring," Gertie said.

"But not nearly as bad on the knees," I said. "Break dancing is for young people whose bodies haven't betrayed them yet."

"My body hasn't betrayed me," Gertie said. "It's just launched a mild protest."

"Your body went on strike thirty years ago," Ida Belle said.

"I'm getting decent at the head spins," Gertie said. "I can rotate almost halfway around."

"That's because you've got the hardest head in southern Louisiana," Ida Belle said. "And this proves it."

"You're one to talk. You and your fast cars and motorcycles."

"But I'm still in good enough shape to drive them," Ida Belle said. "And when I'm not, I'll get a nice big Bentley. It will be like riding around on my couch."

"I hope not," I said, "because your couch sucks."

"It's probably time for a new one," Ida Belle agreed.

"How old is that one?" I asked.

"When did *Happy Days* go off the air?" Gertie asked.

"Fine," Ida Belle said. "I'll buy a new couch if you agree to stop break dancing. Take up a nice waltz."

"I don't have a partner," Gertie said. "What about hip-hop?"

"Take the deal," I said to Ida Belle. "It's as good as it's going to get. And besides, we have far more important things to deal with."

Gertie nodded. "Like the key."

"Like the fact that Carter was sitting in my living room when Ida Belle and I got home this morning."

Gertie's eyes widened. "Not good. What happened?"

I filled her in on our fight, Ida Belle's declaration, and Carter's insistence that he see the SUV today.

"I sent Little a text last night," I said. "I just got word back that they're ready."

"Have you heard from Carter yet?" Gertie asked.

"No, but I told him I'd call when I got up."

As if on cue, my phone rang. So much for waiting on me to call.

"Speak of the devil," I said, and answered.

"I'd like to see the SUV this morning," Carter said. "Is Ida Belle available to go to the storage unit with me?"

I frowned. So this is how it was going to be.

"No," I said. "Ida Belle isn't available to go to the storage unit with you. But Ida Belle, Gertie, and I will be happy to meet you there in an hour."

"This is an official police investigation," Carter said. "You have no business there."

"Given that I'm the one who acquired the storage unit," I said, "I'm going to go ahead and disagree with you. I can stay home, of course, but I seriously doubt the Heberts are going to let you into my unit without a search warrant."

I heard him huff and knew he was mad. He'd thought he had an ace in the hole, but he didn't. And while I had no doubt he could acquire a warrant, the waste of time was something I knew he wasn't interested in.

"Fine. One hour."

He disconnected and I put my phone on the table.

"That went well," Gertie said.

I sighed. "I have a feeling this day is not going to get any better."

CHAPTER ELEVEN

Carter was already at the storage facility when we pulled up. So was Mannie, standing in front of the security gate, arms crossed, and looking scary as only Mannie could do. Carter appeared more annoyed than impressed with Mannie's display, but he was smart enough not to push the issue. Mannie might be hired muscle, but he was well-trained hired muscle. He knew to ask for a warrant if Carter started insisting.

I said good morning to Mannie, who nodded and opened the gate for me. We pulled around to the unit, Carter trailing behind. Mannie showed up a minute later and handed me a key to the padlock.

"Forgot to give this to you last night," he said. "I'll give you a card with the pass code for the security gate as well so you can come and go as you need to."

He turned around and left without so much as a glance at Carter, but I knew somewhere in an air-conditioned office, Big and Little were watching the show from the security camera feed. I removed the padlock and rolled the door up. I was glad Carter was behind me and couldn't see my face, because the scene in front of me didn't look anything like it had the night before.

The completely intact SUV sat in the middle of the otherwise empty unit. No toolbox. No bench. No lift. Absolutely nothing to indicate that we'd disassembled a huge part of the vehicle the night before. Carter walked into the unit and around the SUV.

"Do you have the keys?" he asked Ida Belle.

"Left them in it," she said. "What are you looking for?"

"I don't know," he said. "Something that's not supposed to be there, I guess."

"The vehicle has been heavily modified," Ida Belle said. "Everything engine-wise isn't supposed to be there. At least according to the manufacturer."

I stood there watching as Carter started up the vehicle, then killed it and started peering under the seats. He still hadn't said a word to me and I was growing more and more agitated by the minute. Finally, I walked over to him.

"If you don't need us for anything else," I said, "we've got some errands to run. I'll leave the unit key with Mannie and let him know to lock up after you leave."

"What kind of errand?" Carter asked.

"Ida Belle needs a new couch, and all three of us need to get our minds off this," I said, "so we're going to New Orleans to go furniture shopping. Unless, of course, couch shopping on Wednesday is against the law."

"Only in 1973," Gertie said, "but it was every day of the week, not just Wednesday. Horton Myer fell asleep smoking and caught his couch on fire. The whole thing went up as though it was covered in rocket fuel. The mayor thought it would be better if no one had couches, but residents argued that the existing ones had to be grandfathered in. So he just banned buying new ones. It was only in effect for a month though. The mayor's couch broke right off its legs and he hated his wife's sewing chair."

"That is the most ridiculous story I've ever heard," I said, "and in Sinful, that's saying a lot."

"The mayor was an idiot," Ida Belle said. "We get to say that a lot. About all the mayors."

"Not anymore," Gertie said. "Now we have Marie."

"Yes, that's all lovely," I said, "but I'd like to leave." I looked at Carter. "Do you need anything else from us?"

He stared at me a couple seconds, but I couldn't tell what he was thinking. His expression was a mixture of frustration and that look like when you want to say something but can't. Or won't. Whatever. It didn't matter. What mattered was that I got out of there before I said something I might regret. Even if it was the truth.

"I don't need anything," he said finally. "I'll drop the SUV keys off later at your house."

"Great," I said, and whirled around. "Then let's go find something comfortable. I think one of those electric recliner couches is the best option. I saw a nice one on television last week."

Gertie and Ida Belle hustled after me, Gertie glancing back at Carter.

"Well, that was uncomfortable," Gertie said as we climbed into my Jeep.

"It's not going to get any better unless he checks his ego at the door," I said. "If anyone but Ida Belle had owned that SUV, Carter would have told them they might be in danger. He deliberately avoided telling Ida Belle because he didn't want us sticking our noses into what he thinks is his business. Well, it stopped being only his business when Ida Belle became a potential target."

Gertie frowned and shot Ida Belle a worried look. "Aren't you going to say something?"

"What would you like me to say?" Ida Belle asked. "She's right. He wouldn't have withheld information from anyone else. How she wants to feel about that is up to Fortune. I have my own feelings on the matter and will have a talk with Carter about said feelings when all this is over."

I glanced over at Ida Belle and from the way her jaw was set, I didn't envy Carter that conversation. He'd made a big mistake not warning her and an even bigger one pulling the cop card with me. Ida Belle was seriously pissed.

Mannie nodded as we pulled up to the security gate and handed me a business card. "The code for the gate is on the back of the card. It will let you in any time."

"Thanks," I said, and stuck the card in my pocket. "And thanks for cleaning all that up. It looked like the truck had never been apart."

"We figured things would go better for everyone if the situation looked as, uh, clean as possible," Mannie said.

"Well, we appreciate the forethought," I said. "Carter is going over the vehicle. I gave him the key to lock up and told him to give it to you on his way out. He can have all the time he wants or as much as you want to give him. Whatever."

Mannie's eyebrows went up. "Problems in paradise?"

I stared at him. "Men are never a problem for me."

Mannie grinned. "I kinda had a feeling about that. Go ahead and get going. I'll keep an eye on things here and make sure the SUV is secure when Carter's done. If you run into anything I can help with, give me a call."

I gave him a nod and we headed back to the highway. I knew exactly the sort of help Mannie provided. He was the illegal version of me—a hired gun. And while I appreciated the backup, I was really hoping we didn't need it.

Not this time.

———

AN HOUR LATER, I parked the Jeep in front of an antiques shop in the French Quarter and hopped out. Gertie and Ida Belle followed me into the store, both of them looking slightly confused.

"You don't want Ida Belle to buy an antique couch, do you?" Gertie asked. "Because that's just icky."

"Are you afraid it might be haunted?" Ida Belle asked drily.

"No," Gertie said. "I'm afraid of the germs from all the people who sat naked on it before you."

"Okay," I said, "that's an image I just didn't need. And no, I'm not suggesting Ida Belle buy an antique couch. They're all straight-backed and have no padding, and I'm pretty sure nothing in here has an electric recliner."

"Then why are we here?" Gertie asked.

"We're working," I said, and waved at a salesperson back in a storeroom.

He put down the packing tape he was holding and headed our way.

Seventy if he was a day. Five feet eleven. A hundred seventy pounds. White hair. Nearsighted. Intellectual. Only a danger as a college professor.

"I'm Errol Jones," he said, and stuck out his hand.

"Sarah Wilson," I said, and shook his hand. "I'm wondering if you can help me with something. I inherited my great-aunt's house and I've been going through her things. I found a key that looks like something that would open antique furniture, but it doesn't fit anything in her house. I thought maybe you could tell me if I'm off base."

"I can surely try," he said.

"Great," I said, and pulled the key out of my pocket.

Errol took the key and studied it, turning it around to see it from all angles. "I can see where you thought it might fit furniture. It does have the general look of a key that might unlock a wardrobe or a desk, but I think it's bigger than any furniture key I've seen."

He frowned and drew the key closer to his face, then lowered it and headed for a desk toward the back of the store. "Come with me, please."

He pulled a magnifying glass from behind the counter and used it to take a closer look at the top of the key. "Ah," he said. "I couldn't be sure because it's been eroded over time, but if you look through the magnifier, you can see the remnants of letters on the top of the key."

I looked through the magnifying glass and saw what he was referring to. "I see it. Does that mean anything to you?"

"It might," he said. "I thought I'd seen a key similar to this before but couldn't place it at first. It belonged to an old client whose family went back over two hundred years in the city. It was a key to a door."

"Like a door to a house?" I asked.

He shook his head. "A door to a crypt."

"Oh," I said. "Wow. I didn't see that one coming."

"I'm sorry if I upset you," he said.

"No," I said. "It was just unexpected. My family doesn't have a crypt, so I can't imagine where my aunt would have gotten a key to one. Or why she had it."

"Perhaps it belonged to a friend who had no one else to oversee things," Errol said. "So many families move away or simply die out, and the crypts crumble because there's no one left to tend to them."

"Maybe so," I said. "Still, if there's someone left in the family this belongs to, I'd like for them to have it. Is there any way to figure out whose crypt the key opens?"

"Not by the key alone," Errol said. "Perhaps if the lettering were still legible...maybe you'll find something in your aunt's paperwork."

"I hope so," I said, and stuck the key back in my pocket. "I appreciate your time."

"Of course," Errol said, and smiled. "It was a pleasure meeting you, and good luck with your search."

We headed back outside and Gertie was practically bouncing.

"That's awesome," Gertie said. "You figured out what the key opens. I would have never thought to bring it to an antiques shop."

"It was a great idea," Ida Belle said, "but we *still* don't know what it opens. It's not like there's a shortage on crypts in this area, and for all we know, it might not even fit a crypt around here."

I nodded. "We need to know who owned that SUV before you. That might help with the crypt identification, because there's a lot of things I'll do, but traipsing through every cemetery in New Orleans and trying to unlock a room full of dead people is not one of them."

"Big said he was going to get that information," Gertie said. "Maybe you could follow up?"

I pulled out my cell phone and sent Little a text.

Working on the key. Did you find out anything about SUV owner?

I sent the text and pointed to a café across the street. "While we're here, might as well have beignets."

"Now you're talking!" Gertie hurried across the street, her desire for beignets apparently overriding her bad knees.

"Sooner or later," Ida Belle said, "you're going to have to address things with Carter."

"I will, but not until I'm certain you're safe."

Ida Belle nodded, and we headed across the street and into the café. Gertie had already acquired a table underneath a ceiling fan. I shot her a grateful look as I sat. It was so hot, and the old building in the French Quarter didn't hold air very well. Added to that, no one wanted AC eating up all their profits, so owners were probably using only enough air to keep customers from melting. If you wanted to actually be cool, you'd have to do it at home and on your own dime.

I would have loved a latte, but no way was I adding to the heat factor, so we placed orders for iced tea and beignets. As soon as the waitress headed off, my phone signaled an incoming call from Little. I jumped up from my chair.

"It's Little," I said, and hustled outside where I couldn't be overheard by any of the restaurant patrons.

"Miss Morrow," Little said, "I have some information for you. The previous owner of the SUV was First Rate Auto Sales in New Orleans. They acquired the car from the widow of a Preston Wilks, who passed at age eighty-two."

"So probably not involved in anything nefarious."

"Oh, I've met quite a few old boys who were still in the business, but I couldn't find anything on Wilks that would indicate he had criminal ties."

"So who put the key in the SUV?"

"There were no owners listed between the car lot and Hot Rod, but sometimes people buy cars from these small lots and the paperwork never gets processed."

"Why not?"

"Many reasons. The car lot forgot. The buyer didn't want the vehicle in his name. Some are trying to avoid taxes."

I sighed. "So we still don't know anything."

"I'm afraid not in this regard. I did get another name for you to run down. Willie LeDoux. According to my source, he was a friend of the Seal brothers, but my source knew nothing about Mr. LeDoux beyond that. I've found no connection other than the club owner where they were dealing, and as far as my sources know, he's still MIA."

"Well, at least that's one more name than we had before. I'll see what we can find on this Willie LeDoux."

"I am also still trying to locate the Seal brothers but haven't had any luck. I will keep looking and let you know if I find anything else. Please let me know if I can help in any other way."

I thanked him and headed back inside and filled Ida Belle and Gertie in on the conversation.

"So we should find this Willie LeDoux, right?" Gertie asked.

I had already entered his name into the Internet browser. "Doing it now," I said, then groaned.

Over three hundred hits.

Gertie looked at the screen and shook her head. "Why can't the bad guys ever be named something like Thadius Thistlebone? Where there's only one of them in the country?"

"It would definitely make things easier," I agreed. "Maybe I can narrow it down if I search by name and Louisiana."

That got me down to forty hits, which was definitely better.

I scanned the hits for an obituary but didn't come up with anything in the right century. Could be Willie was still kicking. Or could be that he died somewhere else or didn't have friends or family who felt they needed to publicize his death. Too many variables.

Then a thought occurred to me—somewhat out of left field. I tried again, this time searching for Willie and the name Seal.

I got one hit.

An article about three men arrested for car theft—the Seal brothers and Willie LeDoux.

"Here we go," I said.

THREE MEN WERE ARRESTED *early Saturday morning during a theft in progress at a used car dealership in Belle Chasse. The three men were identified as brothers John and Bart Seal of New Orleans, Louisiana, and Willie LeDoux of Lafitte, Louisiana. Two black Escalades had already been removed from the lot by the time law enforcement arrived on the scene, and the whereabouts of the vehicles are still unknown.*

The three men were wanted for questioning in connection with a heroin ring bust that involved several local nightclubs. The men were booked on charges of grand theft auto.

"WILLIE MUST HAVE BEEN WORKING with the Seal brothers," I said.

Ida Belle nodded. "And this is how they all got caught."

"And ultimately sent to prison," I said.

"Then Willie must have gone as well, right?" Gertie asked.

"Not necessarily," Ida Belle said. "He might have flipped on the Seal brothers for a reduced sentence or even walked. Or he might not have been as deeply involved in the heroin dealing or perhaps not at all. He might just be a car thief."

I frowned. "Which makes you wonder why the Seal brothers didn't offer up information to get a reduced sentence. I mean, ten years for a first offense is pretty harsh."

Ida Belle shook her head. "The brothers were bad news, but they weren't smart. They might not have known anything."

"They had to have a supplier," I said. "Unless the guy wore a clown suit to exchange money for product, they should have known who he was."

Ida Belle shrugged. "Maybe they were too scared to give up a name. Maybe the guy they dealt with was some middleman whose name wasn't worth a deal."

"True," I said. "I wish we had a way to find out more about this case. The Internet is woefully underwhelming when it comes to details."

"It wasn't a big enough story to keep reporters on it," Gertie said. "They're looking for the big splash. Dirty politicians...that sort of thing."

I shook my head. Things still didn't fit. Why were three guys who were about to go down for dealing heroin taking the time to steal cars when they should have been hightailing it out of Louisiana?

Then something occurred to me.

"Black SUVs," I said. "They were stealing black SUVs."

Gertie's eyes widened. "They were looking for the key then?"

"Maybe," I said.

Ida Belle blew out a breath. "What the heck is hidden in that crypt?"

"Something big," I said, "otherwise, they'd have been lying low or getting out of town."

"It has to be money, right?" Gertie asked. "Enough money to skip the country."

"That's as good a guess as any," Ida Belle said.

"But who did the money belong to?" I said. "If they were looking for the vehicle back then, who hid the key inside? Who hid something in a crypt? It couldn't have been any of these three or they'd know what vehicle they were looking for. And if they'd known which crypt the key unlocked, they would have just taken a sledgehammer to it."

"You're right," Ida Belle said. "This whole thing is a question without an answer."

"It's a mess," I agreed. "So, we don't know how, but someone knew Hot Rod had the SUV with the key."

"But they didn't know which vehicle it was," Ida Belle said.

I nodded. "And all of this happens when the Seal brothers get out of prison. It's not a coincidence."

"I agree," Ida Belle said. "Whatever they were looking for before, it's valuable enough to look for it again. But if they didn't know what SUV the key was in then, they'd have an even harder time now."

"Except that if you hadn't bought the Blazer, they would have had the key this time," I said. "Which means they figured out some way to narrow down the search to Hot Rod."

I blew out a breath. There were entirely too many tentacles on this octopus.

"We need to find Willie LeDoux," I said. "Little hasn't come up with a line on the Seal brothers, so he's our only lead. If he was helping them steal vehicles before, then he has to know something."

"But how do we find him?" Gertie asked. "The name's too common. We can't run down every Willie LeDoux mentioned online. We'd be at this forever. If we were cops we'd have access to arrest records and driver's licenses and all kinds of other cool things, but we don't know anything else about him."

"Except that he used to live in Lafitte," I said. "What's that town like? Maybe we start there."

Ida Belle nodded. "It's Sinful with a different name. About thirty miles south of here."

"So, small and packed with a bunch of nosy people who probably know all the latest dirt on any local criminals," I said.

"Exactly," Ida Belle said.

"But can we get them to talk to us?" I asked.

"Leave that to Gertie and me," Ida Belle said. "We know their language."

"Okay. Then I guess when we're done here, we're taking a drive to Lafitte."

CHAPTER TWELVE

I pulled into Lafitte a little over an hour later and studied the row of buildings that constituted both businesses and homes. It was more or less what I'd expected based on Ida Belle's description, but it lacked the charm and quaintness of Sinful. I hoped it wasn't lacking in the nosy citizens who liked to gossip.

Ida Belle pointed to a convenience store, and I pulled up in front.

"Wait here," she said, and she hopped out and walked into the store. She exited a couple seconds later and gestured to Gertie. "You're up. There's an old woman sitting behind the food counter knitting."

Ida Belle looked at me. "Wait a bit, then come in after us. She's more likely to talk if she thinks we're two dithering busybodies from another bayou town."

I grinned. "What you're saying is you don't want my youthful appearance and Yankee accent ruining your ploy."

"I look youthful," Gertie said.

"Sure you do," Ida Belle said. "Especially with all that hobbling around. You could easily pass for a hundred and eighty-two."

Gertie gave her a dirty look and climbed out of the back of

the Jeep. Then she started up the sidewalk, and I could tell she was trying not to wobble. Ida Belle shook her head and trailed into the store behind her. I waited a bit, then finally decided enough time had passed and my desire for a cold drink was high, so I headed inside.

Gertie and Ida Belle were standing at a food counter at the back of the store, pointing to stacks of odd-looking fried things and murmuring between themselves. The woman Ida Belle had spotted sat in a rocking chair behind the counter, studying her knitting and not even glancing up at Ida Belle and Gertie.

Five foot four. One hundred ten pounds with the knitting bag. Blind or deaf or dislikes people as much as I do.

I headed over to the soft drink cooler that was about ten feet away and proceeded to study my options while sideways glancing at the food counter, waiting to see Ida Belle and Gertie in action.

"Excuse me, ma'am," Gertie said. "Can you tell me how these gizzards were seasoned?"

I looked again at the stack of fried stuff. Gizzards? Yuck.

The woman kept rocking and knitting and never so much as blinked.

"She's deaf as a doornail," Ida Belle said. "This ought to be fun."

Gertie waved her hands in the air and yelled. "Excuse me, ma'am!"

The old woman looked up from her knitting, then put it down and pushed herself out of the chair, struggling a bit to rise.

"Sorry about that," she said, and fiddled with something on her ear. "I'm getting a bit hard of hearing, but when this darn thing is turned up, I can hear rats pooping on a leaf in the bayou. I keep it off unless I have customers. What can I do for you?"

"I wondered about the seasoning on the gizzards," Gertie said.

The woman launched into a discussion of the many sauces and flavors she'd used on the gross gizzards and her preparation techniques. Gertie nodded the entire time, looking more interested than I felt the conversation required, but it was Louisiana. Last week, I'd heard two women at Francine's Café discuss the best way to clean socks for well over an hour. I figured if socks needed that much cleaning, it might be time to just buy new ones.

"I'll take two orders," Gertie said. "You're old-school in your preparation. So many people go for the fast methods these days, but the taste isn't the same."

The old woman gave her an approving nod and started putting the icky gizzards into a foam container. "Whereabouts you from?" the woman asked.

"Sinful," Gertie said.

"You're a ways from home," the woman said. "You come to fish?"

"No," Gertie said. "Wasting time is more like it. I have an old Cadillac with some rusted-out spots, and one of the old fishermen said he knew a guy from here a while back that could fix anything car-related. I couldn't find a phone number for him, but my friend and I had nothing better to do so we figured we'd take a drive this way and see what we could come up with."

The woman nodded and handed Gertie the container. "Lots of hidden talent out in these swamps. What's this feller's name?"

"Willie LeDoux."

The woman scowled.

"Is there a problem?" Gertie asked.

"Willie LeDoux's been nothing but a problem his entire life. Hell, he was even a problem in the womb. Got sideways there too, and had to be taken out. Darn near killed his mama."

"His father couldn't get him in line?" Gertie asked.

"Ha," the woman said. "That no-account ran off when Willie was still a baby. His mama sent Willie to live with his daddy in New Orleans when he was a teenager. I think she was hoping he could get Willie straight, but his daddy wasn't exactly an upstanding citizen so I don't know where she got that idea. He got himself killed trying to rob a convenience store a couple years back."

The woman shook her head and sighed. "Oh well, at least his mama passed before Willie went to prison."

Gertie gave her a sympathetic shake of the head. "I've known a few like that myself. Such a hard task to parent a child who's determined to go the wrong route. So I guess he's not around anymore?"

"Oh, he's around. That no-account came back here last month after he got released from prison. Dealing drugs. Stealing automobiles." She shook her head. "Then he waltzes back into town like he's been on vacation all that time. I ran him right out of the store. Once a thief, always a thief, I say, and I don't want his kind hanging around."

"Well, that's disappointing," Gertie said. "I was really hoping he could fix my car. I've talked to several other repairmen, but none of them would touch it."

"He'd probably do the work," the woman said. "I'm sure he needs the money, and much as I hate to admit it, the boy did know his automobiles."

Gertie bit her lower lip and glanced over at Ida Belle. "I don't know, of course. I mean, if it's not safe then I'll just figure out a way to put together money for a new car even though Social Security being what it is makes it kinda hard."

The woman nodded. "I don't think he'd hurt you, if that's what you mean. He never was violent. And as much as I don't want to send him business, I don't want you trying to manage buying a car on the pittance we draw."

She reached for a pad of paper and started writing. A minute later, she handed the sheet of paper to Gertie. "That's a map to his place. Was his mother's place before she passed, God rest her soul. There's no road names, so I drew some landmarks."

"Thank you," Gertie said. "I really appreciate the information. And the gizzards."

The woman nodded. "You ladies have a nice day and good luck with your car repair."

I hurried to the counter and paid for my soda, then headed outside and hopped into the Jeep. A couple minutes later, Ida Belle and Gertie climbed in, and I gave Gertie a high five.

"Great work," I said.

Ida Belle smiled. "Gertie always knows just the thing to say to get the old gals talking. I never was good at it."

"That's because you don't know how to make all the sympathetic faces," Gertie said. "When you're talking nonsense, you mostly just look like you smelled something bad. People don't get chatty with someone who looks like they just sniffed a horse's butt."

"This butt-sniffing discussion is incredibly interesting and probably useful, but it needs to wait," I said. "Pass me that map."

I took the sheet of paper from Gertie, looked at the squiggles, then read the cryptic phrases, identifying the turns.

"Right at the lightning tree. Left at the beehive. Left at the Millers' old barn...what the heck is this?"

"Typical local directions," Ida Belle said, and took the paper from me. "Just head south kinda slow and I'll let you know where to turn."

I pulled out of the parking lot and drove out of town, all fifty yards of it, scanning the trees even though I had zero idea what I was looking for. We were about a mile past the downtown area when Gertie grabbed my shoulder and pointed.

"There!" she said, clearly excited. "That's the lightning tree."

I looked at the giant cypress tree that looked as if it had been torn down the middle. What the heck. It made as much sense as anything else in Louisiana.

"Great," I said, and I made a right turn onto a dirt road. "Find me a beehive, preferably one we can drive quickly by. They can come in through air vents."

The dirt road led into a forest, so I slowed down some, partly because of the crappy road but mostly because I figured it might be hard to spot a beehive in all the foliage. I wasted my time worrying.

The hive was huge. Like the size of guest bathroom.

"What the heck kind of bees made that?" I asked as I made a left turn onto an even smaller dirt road. "It's like something out of *Jurassic Park*."

"They've been at work there for a long time," Ida Belle said. "I bet there's some stellar honey in it."

The noise of the Jeep must have alerted the bees to an invader present. A group flocked out of their McMansion and flew straight for us. I swear, they were the size of small birds.

Gertie leaned forward, watching them fly back and forth across the front of the Jeep. "Well, at least we don't have to worry about them getting in an air vent."

Ida Belle nodded. "You'd need a heavy-duty flyswatter to take out one of those babies."

I stared at her. "You'd need a nine-millimeter to take out one of those things, which is precisely why that hive is so big and undisturbed. It's guarded by prehistoric creatures."

"I hope they don't follow us all the way to Willie's house," Gertie said. "Without my purse, I've got nothing to take them out with."

Thank God for small favors. If Gertie's purse of death were still with us, she'd probably have been shooting at the bees through the windshield.

"I'm sure they'll leave before we get to the house," Ida Belle said. "After all, someone's been living there for decades. If those monsters were hanging around outside, they would have moved years ago."

"Maybe that's what happened to the Millers," I said, and pointed to a dilapidated barn with an overgrown path leading up to it. "And their livestock. They were probably carried away under the cloak of night and used for parts to build that hive."

I made the last turn after the barn and we inched along on a narrow slit of dirt, trees branches rubbing both sides of the Jeep.

"How do people keep paint on their cars out here?" I asked. At the rate I was going, I was going to owe the real Sandy-Sue a paint job, at the least, when I turned over her inheritance. Possibly even a new vehicle.

"When you're driving a road regularly," Ida Belle said, "it stays cleared better, and most people cut the worst of the branches out of the way."

"And some just don't care," Gertie said. "That's why you see so many trucks with rusted-out spots on the sides."

The Jeep dipped into a huge hole that had been hidden by marsh grass and we all flew up and back down onto our seats.

"I'm more worried about a back injury," Gertie said. "I hope Willie's house isn't that far."

"I hope we don't need to leave in a hurry," I said.

"Why would we need to do that?" Gertie asked.

"Because Willie is a convicted felon and he might have tried to kill Hot Rod for a key that unlocks a crypt that even Willie hasn't identified?" I said. "And if he didn't try to kill Hot Rod, he probably knows who did, which means he's still tied to murderers, potentially the Seal brothers. And then there's the part where it's the three of us and things just seem to turn out that way."

"I see your point," Gertie said. "But I'm going to be optimistic. This time, everything will be fine."

"Sure," Ida Belle said. "Willie will probably be on his front porch whittling. He'll offer us tea and tell us why everyone is after the key and we'll be on our way. Or maybe he'll just leave a note pinned to the front porch and we won't even have to bother with pleasantries."

"I'll just settle for no shooting," I said. "If we could get through one investigation with no shooting, I'd throw a party."

"I don't mind the shooting," Gertie said, "because you and Ida Belle are always the best at it."

I glanced over at Ida Belle, started to say something, then shook my head.

"I think I see it," Ida Belle said.

I leaned forward a bit and caught sight of a gray structure just off to the right. The path made a right turn, and I stopped about twenty yards from the house.

"Looks a bit rough," Gertie said.

That was an understatement. At one time, the place had been painted, probably a bright yellow, but now, tiny remnants of its previous sunshine splendor were dull and clung to splintered, rotting wood. The roof sagged on one side, and we watched as a raccoon crawled through a hole in the roof and strolled up a branch that had settled on the corner of the house. The one window appeared intact. The rest that I could see were covered with plywood.

There was no vehicle out front, which was a good sign, but that didn't mean Willie wasn't inside. He could have caught a ride with someone. Or for all we knew, he might have a motorcycle in the living room. It would probably dress the place up.

"I guess the house fell into disrepair while he was in prison," I said.

"My guess is it would still look the same even if he'd never gone to prison." Ida Belle looked at the house and frowned. "How do you want to do this?"

I stared at the dilapidated structure for a moment, considering our options, which were severely limited by terrain for both approach and escape. We hadn't driven all this way to turn around and go back to Sinful, but I wasn't interested in putting any of us in more danger than was necessary.

"Here's the plan," I said finally. "I'm going to turn the Jeep around so that it's ready to roll. I'm going to go up to the house. Ida Belle, I want you to take the driver's position in case things go south and we need to make a getaway."

"What about me?" Gertie asked.

I pulled my backup pistol from my ankle strap. "As much as it pains me to do this, if I have to make a run for it, I need you to cover me."

Gertie took the pistol with a little more glee than I found comfortable.

"Remember," I said. "No shooting unless someone is shooting at us."

Ida Belle nodded. "And for God's sake, don't shoot Fortune."

Gertie gave us a dirty look. "Just take care of your end of things and I'll take care of mine. He's probably not in there anyway given that the raccoon was in residence."

I raised my eyebrows. "Really? Says the woman who let an alligator live in her house?"

I backed the Jeep up and got it turned around and ready to roll, then hopped out and let Ida Belle take over the driver's seat. "Keep it running," I said. "If everything's clear, I'll call you in."

Ida Belle nodded and I pulled my nine-millimeter out of my waistband and headed for the house, scouting every inch of the surrounding forest as I went and checking the one window that wasn't boarded up for any sign of shadow movement inside. The regular sounds of birds chirping and wind blowing through the trees were the only things I could pick out, but that didn't mean Willie wasn't inside. He could just be sitting there waiting to see what we were doing. That's what I would do if I were him.

I crept onto the porch, trying to pick my way around the worst of the rotted spots. The boards creaked with every step, and I winced and moved as quickly as possible for the door. I lifted my left hand and knocked, my back against the wall to the side of the door. If Willie was inside and decided I was the enemy, he'd likely open fire through the front door. Standing to the side gave me an opportunity to avoid being shot and get the heck out of there.

If he opened the door and didn't appear as if he was going to shoot me, I'd hide the nine and launch into our car repair story. It wouldn't get us what we came for, but it would probably get us out of there without incident. I didn't hear anything inside, so I knocked again, but the house was silent. I decided to change tactics.

"Mr. LeDoux. My name is Sandy. I got your address from the lady at the convenience store. She said you did repair on old automobiles."

I waited a bit, but nothing stirred inside. I inched toward the doorframe and slipped my elbow around the edge, then pressed it against the door. The door creaked open a bit and I frowned. Granted, you couldn't exactly sneak up on the place with a vehicle, but someone could easily hike through the woods and come up on the cabin without Willie knowing. Leaving the front door unlocked was an odd thing for a con to do, especially if he was back in his old line of work.

I moved over and pressed my elbow harder against the door and opened it enough to see inside. The front room was kitchen and living room. It looked more abandoned than occupied, but a stack of beer cans and a new pack of smokes on the end table indicated that Willie had been around at some point, raccoon or no. There was an opening on the back wall of the living room that I assumed led to the bedrooms.

I slipped across the living room, thankful for the hideous worn rug that masked the worst of my passage, and peered into the opening that led to a hallway that ran the width of the cabin. I counted three doors and decided it was probably two bedrooms and a bathroom. I crept down the hallway and poked my head into the first bedroom. It was tiny and had probably been Willie's when he was a child. It had since been turned into a sewing room. The only furniture was a sewing desk along the back wall and a table along the front wall, piled high with old fabric.

The next room was the bathroom, with crumbling tile and rusted fixtures. I lifted my pistol into ready position as I inched toward the last door. When I reached the doorway, I paused and listened, but the only thing I heard was the steady buzz of insects. I had a good idea what I was about to discover, but I went through the motions anyway. I whirled around the opening, gun leveled, and cursed when I got a good look at the inside of the room. The smell had been a dead giveaway, so to speak.

CHAPTER THIRTEEN

Willie LeDoux, or at least I assumed it was him, wasn't going to threaten anybody. A single bullet hole through the center of his forehead had cemented that fact. He was sitting partially upright in the bed, leaned back against the headboard and slumped to the side. His eyes were wide open, and I figured he knew the bullet was coming before it was fired. I turned around and headed back outside to the Jeep.

"It's clear," I said, and motioned to Gertie. "Give me the pistol."

She grumbled a bit but passed the weapon back to me and I secured it on my ankle. I opened the glove compartment and grabbed latex gloves.

"Put these on. We can't afford to leave fingerprints."

Ida Belle and Gertie climbed out of the Jeep and pulled on the gloves as we walked.

"You think Willie is going to lift fingerprints and come after us?" Gertie joked.

"Willie's not going after anyone," I said. "He's dead."

"What?"

"No!"

They both spoke at once.

"Single bullet through the forehead," I said. "In bed. He was probably asleep when the shooter sneaked up on him. Looks like he woke up in time to die."

"We should do something," Gertie said.

"Like what?" I asked. "It's a little too late for CPR and since Willie can't talk, we need to go through his stuff and see if we can figure out what that key unlocks. He's not going to get any deader. An anonymous phone call to the police once we're long gone from here is the best idea. It's bad enough that we were at the convenience store asking for directions to his house."

"She's right," Ida Belle said. "Once the police know, it won't take a minute for the news to sweep through the entire town. The woman at the convenience store will tell them about us and they'll be knocking on your door in Sinful."

Gertie's eyes widened. "They'll think I killed him. Oh my God! I can't go to prison. They won't even allow me knitting needles."

"Oh, for Christ's sake," Ida Belle said. "You're not going to prison. When the cops come, you tell them we knocked on the door, no one answered, and you left. There's not a shred of evidence to indicate you did anything unless you go leaving some in that relic. Just be glad Fortune didn't talk to the woman at the store along with us."

"She's right," I said. "Besides, he's been dead for at least a day, probably more. It would hardly make sense for you to kill him, then come back later and ask for directions to his house."

"Okay," Gertie said, somewhat mollified. "I suppose that's true."

"Then let's get in there and try to find something and get out before we do get caught," I said. "And be careful. It's a minefield of broken crap that can gouge skin. The last thing we need is someone bleeding."

I walked in the front door and waved my hands. "Gertie, take the kitchen. Ida Belle, you get the living room. I'll cover the bedroom with the dead guy."

Gertie looked relieved and headed off to the kitchen. I went into the bedroom and started tossing the room while reminding myself to breathe with my mouth. There was a single nightstand but it didn't have a drawer, and the top contained only a lamp and an ashtray. The dresser drawers had women's underwear in them, which I assumed had belonged to his mother. Or maybe Willie had been into the freaky stuff. If so, that secret could be between him and the coroner.

The closet contained mostly women's clothes shoved to the side. A couple pairs of men's blue jeans and some ragged T-shirts hung in the center. A pair of worn-out boots was in the bottom. The top shelf contained only bed linens and a worn pair of women's slippers. I felt the back of the closet wall for a secret hiding place, and checked the floorboards as well, but the room appeared clean. The last thing I had to do was a sweep in between the mattress and the box springs. I held my breath and passed my arm between the two layers, then hurried to the other side and did it again.

Nothing.

The room was clean. Aside from a couple items of clothes and the ashtray, there was no sign that Willie even lived here. I went into the bathroom and found a half-used package of antacids and a bar of soap. A shelf above the toilet contained two rolls of toilet paper and a stack of car magazines. I shook the magazines, to make sure nothing was hidden between the pages, then headed into the sewing room and gave it a once-over, but it yielded nothing but dusty old fabric.

Disappointed that I had nothing to show for my effort, I headed back into the front room.

"Anything?" I asked.

Gertie shook her head. "A bunch of chipped dishes, some

holey dish rags, and two cans of beans. All that's in the refrigerator is beer."

Ida Belle looked up from the coffee table, where she was flipping through more car magazines. "No television," she said. "He must have spent all his time reading."

I nodded. "There's a stack in the bathroom too."

"You didn't find anything?" Gertie asked.

"Nothing," I said. "You can barely tell he lived here."

"It is rather sparse," Ida Belle said, and lifted another magazine. She flipped through the pages and a sheet of paper fell out. I picked it up and opened it.

"It's a flyer for an auto auction," I said. "And look! There's your SUV."

Ida Belle stepped closer to me and eyed the flyer. "Yep, that's mine all right. I'd recognize that custom grille anywhere."

"The car lot must have put it up for auction. That's probably how Hot Rod acquired it."

"There are four other black SUVs on the flyer," Ida Belle said. "Hot Rod might have picked up more than one at the auction."

I nodded. "Willie didn't have this stuffed in a magazine for no reason. All he had to do was find out who bought the vehicles and he'd know where to find them. He might have even been at the auction when they were bought."

Ida Belle frowned. "But if Willie is the one who attacked Hot Rod, then who killed Willie? The Seal brothers? It had to be more than just Willie stealing the SUVs from Hot Rod's place. Why kill Willie when they didn't find the key?"

I shook my head. There were a couple of things I was pretty sure about, but a whole lot I needed to dwell on for a while and not while standing in the middle of a crime scene. There were a ton of moving parts and right now, some of them appeared to be floating around with no pieces fitting together. Those that did fit, didn't get me any closer to the answers I needed.

"Let's finish up and get out of here," I said. "I'm getting a really bad feeling about all of this. I don't want whoever shot Willie to come back to search the place like we did."

Gertie's eyes widened. "Why would they come back? Surely they searched the place before."

"I don't think so," I said. "This place would look completely different if it had been searched, especially by amateurs who weren't concerned about covering their tracks."

"And the Seal brothers would fit that bill," Ida Belle said, "but it wouldn't explain why they killed Willie."

"Could be a bunch of things," I said. "Maybe they had a falling-out over something. They got the information on the location of the SUV out of him and they didn't need him for anything else. Or maybe it was someone else entirely. Willie's not exactly a corporate banker. There's no telling who else might have it in for him."

Gertie took the auction flyer from me, folded it, and stuffed it in her bra.

"That's evidence," Ida Belle said.

"And?" Gertie asked. "What are the local cops going to do with it? They won't be able to connect it to anything, and that's if they bother to spend much time investigating the murder of a career criminal at all."

"She's right," I said. "Whatever Willie knew or didn't know might have been worth killing him over, but the police wouldn't know the significance of the flyer. Honestly, it doesn't tell us anything either except how Willie located the SUVs."

I looked over at Gertie, then back at Ida Belle. "Besides, she's not going to give it up voluntarily, and I refuse to take it from her given the current positioning."

Ida Belle shook her head. "Let's flip through the rest of those magazines just to make sure there's nothing else that Gertie can use to stuff her bra, then we'll trek back to Sinful."

"I'm going to check outside," Gertie said. "Take a lap around the house in case there's an outbuilding or somewhere else he might have hidden something."

"Good idea," I said.

Gertie headed outside, and Ida Belle and I flipped through the remainder of the magazines one at a time, but there were no more hidden papers inside.

"I guess that's it," Ida Belle said. "It seems rather underwhelming considering a man was killed."

I nodded. "I'm afraid that what we need to know might have only been in Willie's head."

"Which means figuring it out the hard way," Ida Belle said.

She sounded so defeated that it made me sad. "Don't worry," I said. "I have some ideas."

"Really?"

I opened my mouth to reassure her that I wasn't going to stop until we had answers when I heard Gertie scream. I pulled out my gun and bolted for the porch. Ida Belle was right behind me. I practically jumped from the front door to the ground and as I landed, Gertie came running around the side of the house, screaming bloody murder and waving her hands in the air.

"What the hell?" Ida Belle slid to a stop beside me as I tried to figure out what the heck was going on.

"Bees," Gertie yelled as she sped by about twenty feet in front of us. "The bees are after me."

It was hard to see anything with Gertie flailing about, but I finally caught sight of tiny black flecks zooming around her and said a silent prayer of thanks that I'd taken my backup pistol from her earlier.

Ida Belle ran for the corner of the house and shouted, "There's a water hose."

"Run this way!" I yelled at Gertie, who was off in the other direction.

She made a spinning turn, which her injured knees were probably going to complain about later on, then came running back toward me. I sprinted for the end of the house, where Ida Belle was standing in position with the hose.

"The hose!" I yelled, and stopped next to Ida Belle, figuring standing behind the wall of water was the safest place to hide when those bees got doused.

Gertie ran our way and when she was about ten feet away, Ida Belle opened the hose on her. Gertie fell onto the ground and flopped around like a fish for a bit while Ida Belle drenched her with the hose.

"I don't see the bees," I said, and Ida Belle cut the hose off.

Gertie rolled onto her back and blew a stream of water out of her mouth. She was soaking wet and covered with mud, given that Willie's property didn't have grass to speak of. Just weeds and dirt.

"Are you all right?" I asked, scanning her face and arms for stings. For the most part, bee stings were only an annoyance, but some bees were highly poisonous and too much of any bee sting could be a problem. Unfortunately, I couldn't see anything given the layer of mud that covered most of her exposed skin.

"I think I'm okay," Gertie said. "How badly am I stung?"

"I can't tell," I said. "You're too muddy. Can you stand?"

I extended my hand and helped her up, then Ida Belle turned the hose on her again, this time with a little less force, and rinsed off the worst of the mud. I looked closely as each bit of skin was exposed, and was relieved when I didn't see any welts. Only a couple of small red dots.

"I don't see much," I said. "Did you feel them sting you?"

"Heck yes," Gertie said. "Right on my arm. I was bending down to look under the back of the house when they flew out and attacked me."

I frowned and bent over, staring in the dirt. Finally I spotted what I was looking for and started to laugh. "That wasn't bees. It was flies. Look."

Ida Belle and Gertie bent over to see the trio of huge flies I was pointing at.

"Deerflies," Ida Belle said. "They bite hard. They were probably clustered when you bent over."

Gertie stared at the ground, clearly disgusted. "I darn near ran myself into a heart attack over deerflies?"

"If you—" Ida Belle started to speak, and Gertie put a hand up to interrupt her.

"If you tell me this wouldn't have happened if I had decent glasses," Gertie said, "I'm going to take Fortune's gun from her and shoot you."

"Now that you've said it," Ida Belle said, "I guess I don't have to. Can we please get out of here now? Someone might be close enough to have heard Gertie screaming like a banshee."

Gertie's eyes widened. "The auction flyer!"

She reached into her blouse and dug around far too long for my comfort, then produced the folded paper, which was surprisingly dry given the drenching Gertie had gotten with the hose.

Gertie grinned. "It was tucked underneath—"

"Stop!" Ida Belle said. She grabbed the flyer from Gertie's hands and pointed to the Jeep.

We hurried back to the Jeep and took off down the trail as quickly as the bumpy path allowed. I kept to the speed limit through town, but as soon as we were out of sight of the main drag, I punched the accelerator and headed up the highway. I needed to get home, sit down at the kitchen table, and sort all of this out.

In some way I couldn't see, all of this had to make sense.

CHAPTER FOURTEEN

We stopped at what was probably one of the last pay phones left on earth. I scanned the area for cameras and people, but it was an old industrial area and mostly empty. I called and reported Willie, wearing latex gloves of course, then we headed back to Sinful.

We were all quiet on the drive home. My mind jumped between the key and the car thieves and my problems with Carter. I couldn't seem to focus on one thing, and I knew that had to change. I needed to get home, take a cold shower, and get myself focused. There was no way I would come up with a solution with everything roaming around in my head all at once. I needed to pick one thing and concentrate on it until I had a solution.

As I pulled into Gertie's drive, Ida Belle's cell phone rang.

"It's Myrtle," she said, and answered.

I watched Ida Belle's face shift from pensive to worried, but all she did was mumble "uh-huh" so I had no idea what was going on. Given Myrtle's position with the sheriff's department, it could be anything.

"Thanks," Ida Belle said. "I really appreciate it."

She hung up the phone. "Myrtle got a call at the sheriff's department from one of my neighbors. It seems there was a black sedan parked on my street most of the morning. Two men inside and they were just sitting there."

"Did she dispatch someone?" I asked, surprised that they had risked watching Ida Belle's house in broad daylight. That was either ballsy or desperate.

Ida Belle nodded. "With the Hot Rod investigation going on, the only person available was Sheriff Lee. That darned horse of his is still refusing to come out of the barn, so he walked over, but by the time he got there, the car was gone. Ralph verified what the other neighbor said, though."

"Ralph?" I asked.

"He lives on my street," Ida Belle said. "He said he didn't recognize the car and didn't get a look at the people inside."

"Did the neighbor get a license plate?" I asked.

"Yeah," Ida Belle said, "and they ran it but it doesn't exist."

"That's not good," Gertie said.

"No, it's not," I agreed.

"Stolen and fake plates?" Ida Belle asked.

"Possibly," I said. "Gertie, take your shower or whatever and pack a bag. Our cover is blown with Carter, so you might as well stay with me. If someone goes looking for Ida Belle, they'd probably check your place, too. I don't want you here alone."

"If Carter hadn't made me get rid of Godzilla," Gertie said, "that wouldn't be a problem."

I couldn't think of a single argument because in a ridiculous sort of way, she had a point.

"All interest in attack alligators aside," I said, "I'd rather have you at my house. Besides, we have a lot of things to go over, and I'm going to need to talk it through. I think this is the most confused I've ever been. Nothing makes sense."

Ida Belle nodded. "I agree. I have yet to come up with a single theory that checks all the boxes. We need to brainstorm this until we figure it out. Fortune's house is the easiest to defend given the location of all the upstairs windows, and besides, she's got Marge's secret artillery if we need it."

"Not to mention that Carter will probably be lurking somewhere nearby, waiting for us to do something he can arrest us for," I said. "So we've got backup, whether we want it or not."

"I have a casserole we can heat up," Gertie said.

"Only if it's not fish," I said, the memory of Gertie's horrible creation for Godzilla still lingering in my nostrils.

"It's chicken," Gertie said as she climbed out of the Jeep. "I'll put together some things and be there in about an hour."

Ida Belle looked over at me as Gertie walked away. "The casserole is already made and she needs an hour to put things together? We need to search anything she brings into your house."

"Definitely." I pulled out of Gertie's driveway and headed around the block toward Ida Belle's street, looking up and down the roads as I went. I figured the guys in the black sedan were long gone, at least for now, but I knew I had to check or it would be nagging at me the rest of the day. Ida Belle didn't even ask what I was doing. She silently scanned the streets along with me until we reached the end of the neighborhood.

"They're not visible," Ida Belle said, "but I don't think for a moment that they're gone."

"No. They probably saw your neighbors peeking at them through the blinds and decided it would be wise to vacate until dark. They're sitting still somewhere, and I'd bet they'll be back tonight, probably once they think everyone is asleep."

"And when they don't find me here..."

"We'll be ready for them," I said.

"Maybe we should stay at my house instead," Ida Belle said. "It would be a shorter wait."

"No. You were right about the advantages my house has, and there's that whole police backup thing. I'm not overly happy with my situation with Carter right now, but relocating to your house would just be out of spite for me and would reduce our safety. I'm not irritated enough to decrease our chances of catching these guys."

Ida Belle sighed. Not an exasperated sigh but the kind of sigh you let out when you're resigned to something crappy that you can't change. I knew her frustration wasn't over just her own situation but the problems it had caused my relationship.

"What would you do?" I asked quietly.

"It doesn't matter what I would do. It's your life and you have to live with the consequences."

"I'm not putting you on the hook for the outcome. But as someone I respect and trust, I'm asking you what you would do if you were me."

Ida Belle stared out the windshield for a while.

"I'd be true to myself," she said finally.

It was an answer and yet at the same time, it wasn't, because it didn't tell me exactly what choice to make. But I understood her point. I had to figure out what constituted the "me" that I couldn't live without.

One more thing I had zero answer for.

———

AN HOUR LATER, we were all parked at my kitchen table. Gertie had put together sandwiches as she'd miscalculated her casserole supply, and Ida Belle had dumped some chips and salsa in bowls and retrieved us all a much-needed beer. I was making notes on my laptop about everything we'd found.

"Are you sure that's a good idea?" Gertie asked. "Putting it all in writing like that? I mean, what if someone else sees it?"

"By someone, I assume you mean Carter?" I asked.

Gertie nodded. "He is the first one that comes to mind when I consider access to your home and the person who would be the most upset about us finding a dead man and taking evidence from his house before calling in an anonymous tip."

"It's a risk I have to take," I said. "There's too much going on, and we have to figure out which parts of this mess tie together and how. I can't do that with it all roaming around in my mind. I thought seeing everything typed out might help."

"I'm good with whatever you want to do," Gertie said. "But I felt I had to say something because you're the one with the most to lose."

I looked over at her and smiled. "You're a good friend."

"The best," Ida Belle agreed.

"Oh sure," Gertie said. "You say that now, but you searched me like you thought I was ISIS when I walked in with that box."

"We were worried you might have more in it than just food," I said.

Gertie shook her head. "Then you're going to have a heart attack when you search my overnight bag. I've got it locked in the trunk for safekeeping."

I made a mental note to go light on the beer lest I forget to frisk Gertie's bag later on. I scanned all my notes and then looked up.

"There is a whole lot going on here," I said. "I think we need to tackle one thing at a time and flesh it out rather than running all directions and not making enough progress on anything to figure this out."

Ida Belle nodded. "That sounds reasonable, but where do we start?"

"The key," I said. "Everything centers on the key. Everything we've found so far points toward Willie and the Seal brothers looking for it before they went to prison. So they get out of prison and are looking for it again. Maybe with each other. Maybe not."

"Which means it could have been any of them who attacked Hot Rod," Gertie said.

"Yeah, but someone killed Willie," Ida Belle said. "And if the Seal brothers are still walking around, my money's on them."

"That's the logical answer," I said. But somehow it felt as if there were more to it.

Ida Belle studied me for a couple seconds. "You think we're missing something."

I shook my head. "I just don't know."

"What about Willie's time of death?" Gertie asked. "Couldn't that tell us whether he was at Hot Rod's shop or not?"

"Not really," I said. "Stiffness in the body was dissipated, which normally takes a day or more but in this heat could have happened faster."

"So he could have been killed three days ago or last night?" Gertie asked. "That sucks."

"What about flies?" Ida Belle asked. "Don't they tell you something about time of death?"

"Sure," I said, "but I'm not a forensics expert. I don't know how to estimate time of death by the amount of or stages of larvae, and temperature and exposure affect everything."

Ida Belle sighed. "So we still can't narrow it down."

"I can't," I said. "The coroner probably can but I don't think they'll be calling us with that information."

"So for now," Ida Belle said, "we work the theory that either the Seal brothers got the information on the location of the SUV from Willie then killed him, or the three of them boosted the SUVs from Hot Rod's shop and had a falling-out later. Maybe because they didn't find what they were looking for. Maybe for another reason."

I nodded. "I think that's as good as we can do for now."

"I think we need to find out more about the Seal brothers," Ida Belle said.

"I agree," I said. "Any ideas on that?"

"We should speak to Lucinda," Ida Belle said. "Ralph won't talk, but if anyone knows the dirt about those boys it will be her."

"Then let's pay Lucinda a visit," I said.

As I was about to stand, my cell phone rang, and I frowned when I looked at the display. "It's Little," I said, and answered it.

"Miss Morrow," Little said, "I hope I didn't catch you at a bad time."

"No," I said. "Your timing is great. Is anything wrong?"

"I'm afraid so. We picked up a notice on police channels that a Willie LeDoux has been found dead in his home. I know you were trying to track him down, but it appears someone has beaten you to it."

I started to talk but then couldn't decide what I would say. Did I tell Little we had already searched the cabin or did I protect our cover? Turns out I didn't have to decide, because Little spoke for me.

"I assume your hesitation in reacting is because you were the anonymous tipster that called in Willie's unfortunate circumstances," he said.

"I, uh, might know something about that."

"Big and I suspected as much," he said, and I could practically see him smiling when he said it. "Did you discover anything that identifies the men who attacked Hot Rod?"

"I'm afraid not. We found an auction flyer that had Ida Belle's SUV on it, though. We think that was how Hot Rod acquired the vehicle. Willie had the flyer stuffed between the pages of a magazine."

"That's interesting," Little said. "So Mr. LeDoux had knowledge of where the SUV was located, which means he could have been the person who attacked Hot Rod."

"Yes, but then there's a question of who killed Willie."

"And given his colorful pursuits," Little said, "his death might have been because of the key or something else entirely."

"Exactly."

"I'll do some more asking around about our friend Mr.

LeDoux and see if someone else had a reason to prefer him out of commission. I assume you had no luck with the key?"

"I'm afraid not," I said. "Aside from Willie, who couldn't talk, and the auction flyer, there wasn't much to find. Definitely nothing the key would fit. We know Willie worked with the Seal brothers in the past, and they're our best suspects now, but like you said, Willie probably had dealings with plenty of shady types."

"And that complicates things," Little said. "Unfortunately, inquiries as to the Seal brothers' whereabouts have also turned up nothing. It's as if they walked out of prison and vanished."

Which was interesting in and of itself, because most people who were released from prison went looking for money, either from people who owed them before or an easy crime to pick up some walking money. Which brought me right back around to the key. Maybe it was that simple.

"Thanks for trying to run them down," I said. "If you come up with anyone else Willie might have been involved with, let me know. Maybe the next guy will still be breathing."

"I can't make any promises there," Little said. "I doubt Mr. LeDoux spent a lot of time in the company of suburban dads or your average office worker."

"Probably not."

"It goes without saying that you need to watch your back," Little said. "If you want assistance in that regard, all you have to do is call. I can provide Mannie at your disposal as long as you need him and in whatever capacity."

"I appreciate it, but we're good for now."

"Very well then. I'll be in touch when I have more information."

I disconnected and filled Ida Belle and Gertie in on the conversation, then we headed out for a chat with Lucinda.

DESPITE THE HEAT, Lucinda was out front doing something to flowers in her beds. Gertie called it deadheading, but that didn't sound right. I suppose I could have asked for clarification, but then I was afraid someone might ask me to help do it. Lucinda looked up from her flowers as we climbed out of my Jeep and waved at us.

"You're just in time to save me from heat exhaustion," she said. "I made a fresh batch of sweet tea this morning. Let's go inside and have some."

She didn't have to ask me twice. I still thought Louisiana heat combined with the ridiculous humidity the state managed should be illegal. The only other time I'd experienced something like it was on one mission in the Brazilian rain forest. The dry heat of the desert was much kinder to equipment and my lungs.

We headed inside through a pleasant living room painted a muted shade of green and down the hallway to a kitchen off the back of the house. The kitchen was not muted at all. It was bright yellow with blue and yellow decorations. Lucinda motioned to the kitchen table, and we took a seat on white farmhouse chairs with blue plaid seat cushions.

"I like your kitchen," I said.

Ida Belle and Gertie stared at me, both looking somewhat confused.

"What?" I asked. "It's cheerful. I didn't say it made me want to cook or anything."

Lucinda laughed and set a pitcher of tea on the table. "It was this way when I bought the house. The whole thing was rather bright. The living room used to be this very odd shade of orange and the master bedroom was a vivid purple. I changed everything but the kitchen. I don't like rooms shouting at you as soon as you walk in, but for whatever reason, I couldn't bring myself to change the kitchen. It just looks right somehow, even though it's not my taste at all."

She placed glasses with ice on the table and poured us all

glasses of tea, then took a seat across from me. "So what are you ladies out doing this fine hot day?"

I looked at Ida Belle, indicating I wanted her to take the lead. I didn't know Lucinda and still hadn't quite gotten the hang of that Southern chat thing they were so good at.

"Actually," Ida Belle said, "we wanted to talk with you about the Seal brothers."

Lucinda nodded. "The café wasn't really a good place to get into such talk and God knows, Ralph has a conniption fit every time I mention them."

"Has he heard from them since they got out?" Ida Belle asked.

"Yes," Lucinda said. "They called the day they got out, asking for money. I thought Ralph was going to have apoplexy just trying to tell me about it."

"Did they really think Ralph would give them money?" Gertie asked.

"Who knows what they think," Lucinda said. "Those boys were never bright and always trouble. Their mother bailed them out until she drank herself into that car wreck and then they wound up with Ralph. I think they thought he'd be a pushover like their mother. I'll give him credit for trying, but those boys were more than Ralph was equipped to handle."

Gertie nodded. "Hard enough taking on kids that aren't your own, but when you've never raised any yourself and the kids you're taking in have been running wild all their life, well, he didn't have much of a chance."

"No, he didn't," Lucinda agreed. "I tried to help what little I could, but I had never raised children either and quite frankly, had no idea what could be done. I think he finally just gave up and prayed nothing horrible happened until they turned eighteen."

I shook my head. "They must have been really desperate to hit Ralph up for money. Surely they knew the answer before they called."

"Oh, they tried to assure him it was just a loan," Lucinda said.

"That they had a line on work and would pay him back in no time, but he didn't buy it." She frowned.

"What's wrong?" Ida Belle asked.

Lucinda sighed. "I'd never say this to Ralph, of course, because it would just cause him to stress over something he can't control, but I can't help but wonder if it was them that broke into Hot Rod's place."

"But New Orleans is their home turf," I said. "Wouldn't it make more sense for them to boost cars there? Why come all the way out here? Hot Rod had a couple of nice things, but nothing like the cars you can get off a lot in the city."

Lucinda shook her head. "That's something I don't have an answer for, and I could be completely wrong besides." She paused. "But the timing just seemed odd, you know? All these years and no car thieving around these parts—I mean no more than drunk teens joyriding—and then this."

Ida Belle nodded. "I see why that might have occurred to you, especially given that you had close proximity to their past exploits."

"I pray I'm wrong," Lucinda said. "For Ralph's sake. He's a bore and a grump but he doesn't deserve any more grief from those boys. He did what he could, but they were too far gone by the time they got here."

I leaned forward in my chair. "Gertie told me the brothers claimed they were related to Barry Seal. Is that true?"

Lucinda rolled her eyes. "That old story again. I never met the boys' father. That loser died before I met Carol. Always unemployed. Always running some kind of scam. Do you know he was killed while trying to steal equipment from the drilling company he worked for?" She shook her head. "I doubt the boys even remember him very well. Carol sure knew how to pick 'em."

"So the boys made it up?" I asked. "I just wondered since they *did* go to prison for drug dealing..."

"Of course." Lucinda nodded. "Makes sense to wonder from

an outsider's perspective and it is a good yarn, but I'm guessing the boys made it up to make themselves more important. I know it sounds odd."

"Not really," Ida Belle said. "Given that the boys ran with a rough crowd, having a famous criminal as a relative might have gotten them street cred."

"Even though he was a snitch?" I asked.

Lucinda shrugged. "The people who made Barry Seal into a folk legend like to believe he was playing the federal government and was supposed to be recovered from that work crew and whisked off to live the rest of his life on an island, rather than killed, like he was."

"I guess when you don't have anything," Gertie said, "that's as good a lie to believe as any."

"They were a pitiful case," Lucinda said. "And not very bright. I heard the police clued in to their gig in New Orleans because of their spending habits. Flash and show are not good traits to have if you're doing something illegal."

"A low profile is definitely the more common route for that type of career," Ida Belle agreed.

Lucinda sighed. "I really hoped they'd get out of prison and try to do things a different way."

"But you don't think they're going to?" I asked.

She shook her head, her expression sad. "No. I'm afraid I don't."

CHAPTER FIFTEEN

When I pulled away from Lucinda's house, I looked over at Ida Belle and Gertie. "I've burned off my sandwich," I said. "Let's grab some dinner at the café. That way, no one has to cook anything and we get something better than sandwiches."

"You don't have to convince me," Gertie said. "I always end up doing the cooking, which normally, I don't mind. But I'm not feeling it today."

Ida Belle nodded. "Too much other stuff cluttering things up there. I could do with a good hot meal and no dishes afterward."

I headed for Main Street and parked in front of the café. Ally was working the dinner shift and waved us to our favorite table in the back when we walked inside.

"Any news on Hot Rod?" she asked as we sat down.

"No change in his condition," Ida Belle said.

Ally looked disappointed. "I didn't figure, but I still had to ask. There's always the chance something good could have happened between now and ten minutes ago when I asked someone else."

Ida Belle nodded. "We're still hoping for positive news but right now, I'm afraid it looks pretty grim."

"Speaking of grim," Gertie said, "where's your aunt? She's been suspiciously quiet and it's making us all a little nervous."

"That's a good question," Ally said. "I went by her house Monday evening to check on her...you know, the whole niece thing, and I saw a suitcase in her living room. She tried to shove it behind the coffee table, but it was sticking out enough that I saw it."

"Did you ask her about it?" I asked.

Ally shook her head. "She would have just lied. Clearly, she didn't want me to know she was going somewhere. I stopped by her house this morning and rang the doorbell and knocked for a while, but no one answered. I went around back and peeked in the windows, but other than a light on in her kitchen, there was no sign of life."

Ida Belle frowned. "I wonder what she's up to now."

"If she had any kind of sense," Ally said, "she'd get out of town long enough to give people time to forget her latest stunt."

"She doesn't have enough sense to be embarrassed," Ida Belle said.

"True," Ally said. "Besides, she's back already. I saw her driving down Main Street toward the highway about an hour ago. So whatever she's up to only required a day."

"You're just assuming she was gone somewhere overnight," Gertie said. "For all you know, she could have been hauling body parts out with that suitcase."

Ida Belle shook her head. "If she'd been hauling body parts, one of us would have been in there."

"I guess we'll have to wait and see if someone doesn't turn up for church on Sunday," Ally said. "Let me go grab your drinks."

"Any ideas?" I asked as soon as Ally walked away.

"Plenty," Gertie said, "and none of them good."

"I'm afraid she's right," Ida Belle said. "Celia doesn't leave Sinful for just any old reason, and if she was gone overnight, it must have been something important."

"Do you realize," Gertie said, "that if it were anyone but Celia, we'd think she had a booty call."

"There's an image I didn't need in my mind," I said.

"Just replace it with one of Willie and the bullet hole through his head," Ida Belle said. "We've got bigger fish to fry than whatever nonsense Celia's up to. And whatever it is will come out soon enough."

I nodded and looked out the window at the street. The sun was setting and the light from it had disappeared over the back side of the building. The streetlights were just starting to flicker on, but it wasn't so dark that I didn't see the black sedan parked at the edge of town with two shadowy figures inside.

Immediately, my senses went on high alert. I didn't recognize the car. Not that I knew what everyone in Sinful drove, but I'd probably seen most every vehicle in town at some point or another. It was a black sedan, and there were plenty of those around, but what made this one different was the limousine tint on the windows. I wasn't sure about the laws in Louisiana, but in most places limo tint was illegal for regular vehicles. I'd never seen it on a car in Sinful.

And even if the car hadn't stood out, I could feel them inside, watching the café storefront. With the streetlamp reflecting off the glass, they probably didn't have a good view of us, if they could see us at all, but if they saw us pull up, then they knew we were inside.

"Fortune?" Ally's voice broke into my thoughts.

She smiled when I looked up at her. "You must be thinking about Carter," she said. "You were a million miles away. What can I get you to eat?"

I gave her my order and watched as she walked away. I glanced back out the window but the car was gone.

"What's wrong?" Ida Belle asked.

"There was a black sedan parked at the edge of town," I said. "Two people inside. Limo tint on the windows."

Ida Belle and Gertie glanced at each other.

"Where did it go?" Gertie asked.

"I don't know," I said. "It was gone after I finished giving Ally my order."

"Do you think it's the same people who were watching Ida Belle's house?" Gertie asked.

"Yeah. I do," I said.

"Is it one of those feelings you have?" Gertie asked.

I nodded.

"Then that's as good as having a signed confession," Gertie said.

"It's probably the disappearing Seal brothers," Ida Belle said.

"So what do we do about it?" Gertie asked.

"Nothing," I said. "I mean, nothing that we didn't already have planned. We all bunk at my house and be ready if needed."

Gertie frowned. "They've seen us all together. When they find Ida Belle's place empty, they'll know to check yours and mine."

"Let's hope so," Ida Belle said, her jaw set. "I've moved past worried and right to pissed off. They hurt Hot Rod, one of the nicest people in Sinful, and he might die from it. They killed Willie, and even though we don't know what the key is hiding, I'm guessing it's not something he should have died over. I'm ready for them."

I knew exactly how Ida Belle felt. I'd been there several times on mission when things crossed the business-only line and I developed personal feelings about a victim. It was best not to, of course, but sometimes it was impossible to avoid. In this case, it was personal to Ida Belle. It was her truck they were after, and that vehicle was the reason Hot Rod was in critical condition.

And while I didn't doubt for a minute Ida Belle's capability with a weapon, I also knew firsthand what being emotional could do to judgment. As much as I hated to do it, I was skipping dessert tonight and going with a cup of coffee instead. I needed to stay awake. Whatever happened, I had to be the first responder.

The door to the café swung open and Carter walked in. He spotted us and headed our direction, his expression grim. I stiffened and watched his approach, afraid that this was it. Something had gone wrong at Willie's and he was coming to arrest me. He stopped at our table and motioned to the empty chair.

"Do you mind if I sit for a minute?" he asked.

"Of course not," Gertie said. "Let me flag Ally down so you can order. We just put ours in."

"That's okay," he said. "I don't have long and I ate a sandwich earlier."

He glanced around the café, then leaned across the table closer to us and looked directly at Ida Belle.

"There was a report this afternoon of a suspicious car parked on your street," he said. "It was a black sedan with two people inside."

"Limo tint?" I asked.

"Yes. How did you know?" he asked. "Is Myrtle telling police business again?"

"No," I said before he could get worked up. "The neighbor who reported the strange car is telling police business, and it made it around to us. Not the part about the limo tint, though. That part I know because the same car was just parked at the end of the street."

"What?" Carter's eyes widened. "How long ago? Did you see which direction they went?"

"About ten minutes ago," I said. "I looked away to place my order and when I turned around they were gone. I would assume they went the opposite direction rather than pull right in front of the café, but that's just a guess."

"Probably a good one," he said.

"Did you find out who the car was registered to?" I asked, figuring it was good to pretend we didn't have that information he'd just accused Myrtle of handing out.

"No," he said. "The plate doesn't exist."

"Does that mean the car was stolen?" Gertie asked.

"They're car thieves," Ida Belle said. "What do you think?"

Carter ran one hand through his hair. "Maybe the three of you should get out of town...take one of those girls' trips you're always talking about."

"That's your solution?" Ida Belle asked. "That we flee our homes for an indefinite period of time? Our lives are here. Our obligations and responsibilities are here."

"Maybe it would only be for a day or two," he said, but he knew he'd already lost the argument.

Ida Belle shook her head. "Those men aren't going away until they can access my SUV and either retrieve what they're looking for or ascertain that mine is not the vehicle they want."

"Unless they find what they're looking for somewhere else," Carter said. "And that's entirely possible. I went through that SUV with a fine-tooth comb. It's possible something is still hidden inside, but not likely. I even brought in a dog. No drugs. No explosives."

"There's a bit of good news," I said. "When you get your vehicle back, you won't go up in a mushroom cloud of blow."

"That's an interesting visual," Gertie said, sounding entirely too perky.

I kicked her under the table. The last thing we needed was Carter associating Gertie with explosives again. I still wasn't sure we were out of the weeds over the fiasco at Hot Rod's shop.

"Look," I said, "we both know Ida Belle's not going to leave town, but we're all bunking at my house. We're on alert and so are you, and there's not exactly a lack of capability among the four of us."

I knew he understood exactly what I was saying. Other than me, Carter was the only person in Sinful who knew the truth about Gertie's and Ida Belle's military service in Vietnam. And he certainly knew my skill set. He'd seen it firsthand.

His shoulders slumped a bit and he sighed. "I'll be on patrol all night, watching for the car. I'll likely do a lot of it on foot so I'm not seen. But I will have my phone on me. If you see or hear anything, call me immediately. I don't care if it turns out to be raccoons or loud frogs. You hear anything at all, you call."

We all nodded.

"I do have a bit of good news," he said. "I talked to the doctor before coming over here and he said Hot Rod's condition has stabilized. He's still unconscious, but his heart is working fine."

I felt a bit of relief sweep through me. It was a small thing given the severity of Hot Rod's injuries, but at least it was something.

"That's great news," Gertie said. "One step at a time. I'm telling you, he's going to come out of this just fine."

"Your mouth to God's ears," Ida Belle said.

Carter rose from his chair. "I've got to get back to work. Remember, call."

He turned around and headed out.

"This tension between the two of you is horrible," Gertie said. "I could practically cut it with my knife."

"I know," I said. My back was still tight and showed no signs of loosening any time soon. "But there's nothing I can do about it right now. Might not be anything I can do later, either."

"Surely the two of you care about each other enough to meet in the middle," Gertie said.

"The middle of what?" Ida Belle asked. "Fortune skirting or downright breaking the law? Either she stops completely or he accepts that she does it. If that's not a rock and a hard place, I don't know what is."

"Maybe you could have one of those relationships where you never talked about your work," Gertie said.

"I'd be all for that," I said. "And if we lived in a city the size of DC our work would probably never cross paths. But here in Sinful, what are the odds?" I shrugged. "Discussing it now is pointless because I don't know when I'll be free to make a decision about my future anyway."

"But you can't keep going like this," Gertie said, "or it's just going to be worse if you end it later."

I knew she was right, but I didn't have to like it. The last time Carter had written me off, I'd fallen into a pit of depression and sorrow unlike anything I'd felt since my mother died. I hadn't even known I was capable of feeling that bad. The thought of doing it all over again was awful, but then so was the idea of trying to change who I was. The feelings of sadness over a failed relationship with Carter probably wouldn't last. The feelings of regret over letting someone else dictate what I did with my life again would probably never fade.

CHAPTER SIXTEEN

It was long after midnight when I made the rounds upstairs, peering through every bedroom window and scouting for any sign of movement around the house. Ida Belle made patrol with me, going one direction while I went another, both of us making the full loop then meeting back in the hallway at the top of the stairs. Gertie had crashed on the living room couch about thirty minutes before and we could hear her snoring carrying all the way up to the second floor.

"If they get close enough to the house, they'll definitely know we're in here," Ida Belle said. "I bet they can hear Gertie snoring in the next parish."

"Maybe they'll think we're in here juggling chain saws, and it will scare them away."

Ida Belle laughed, but I could tell it was strained.

"Why don't you get some rest?" I asked. "I'm wired enough and I can wake you if I need a break."

"I couldn't sleep even if I tried."

I nodded. "Then let's head to the kitchen for another cup of coffee. This night isn't getting any shorter."

We headed downstairs and into the kitchen, and Ida Belle poured us both a cup as I retrieved the sweetener.

"I didn't see Carter this time," Ida Belle said as we took seats at the kitchen table.

"No. But I'm sure he's somewhere close. He probably ditched his truck and is lurking in the bushes across the street."

"You could have invited him to stay, you know."

I shook my head. "They were watching us in town. If Carter was here and they figured it out, they'd never make a move."

Ida Belle stared. "You want them to make a move, don't you?"

"I want to get this over with, so yeah. Why not? If it was only about being safe, we'd be sitting in a hotel in Florida about now, having room service and looking at the ocean."

"I think I got ripped off," Ida Belle said. "Next time, I'm going with that 'get out of town' option, especially if you're doing the planning."

"Maybe that's something we should do...take a trip. There's nothing stopping me really. I doubt Ahmad has people combing the beaches for me."

"No, but there's far less of a chance of him having people in Sinful."

"True, but a big floppy hat and huge sunglasses go a long way to disguising a person."

"Traveling with two old ladies would probably pass scrutiny as well." Ida Belle plopped her mug on the table, sloshing the coffee up the sides. "Hell, let's do it then. As soon as this crap is over, we head for sand and surf. We can sit under an umbrella and drink fancy drinks. Gertie can knit, I can sleep, and you can figure out what you're going to do with the rest of your life."

"I think a beach and drink service would be the perfect setup for deciding what I'm going to be when I grow up."

"No one said you had to grow up. That's just mean."

I started to laugh, but Ida Belle grabbed my arm and pointed to the door. I could hear scratching and went over to let my cat,

Merlin, inside. He walked in with the stroll that only cats can manage—the one that says I'm king and I'm irritated all at the same time. He let out a loud squall, then sat in the middle of the kitchen, his tail twitching back and forth.

I looked down at him and frowned. "He's mad."

"Did you forget him outside?"

"No. He doesn't always come in at night. I figure sometimes he's tomcatting around. I called for him earlier and he just stared at me from the lawn chair. That usually means he won't show up until first thing in the morning, demanding his breakfast. But this is different."

I walked over to the kitchen window and peered between the blinds. "Something has him riled."

Ida Belle stood up. "Something's not right outside."

I nodded. "The problem is it could be nothing more than a rival cat or another animal he feels is encroaching on his territory."

"But it might be something else."

"Go upstairs and check the street...see if there's a car that wasn't visible before. And remember, it might not be the same one we saw today. No telling how many vehicles these guys have lifted."

Ida Belle hurried out, and I waited until I heard her going up the stairs before slipping through the living room and into the office located off the living room at the back of the house. I rarely went in there but right now, it had something I needed—a window that led into the backyard and was hidden by the bushes. Ida Belle would be angry when she realized I'd sent her upstairs mostly to get her out of the way, but I'd deal with that later. The bottom line was suitability. Ida Belle was a crack shot, but I was lethal in hand-to-hand combat. Besides, if someone was lurking around my house, they had to get here somehow. As long as she had eyes on the street, I had coverage from above.

I shoved up the window and peered outside. The hack job

we'd done on the bushes had thinned them a good bit, but I'd had the forethought to wear black pants and tee, so they probably wouldn't see me exiting the house. I just had to make sure they didn't hear me. If they were in the backyard, then they'd seen me let the cat in and knew I was awake.

I slipped my legs over the window and lowered myself to the ground. So far, so good. I hadn't rustled so much as a single leaf with my exit. A faint rustling sound echoed somewhere off to my right, and I crouched down and crept to the end of the hedges, peering out as I went. The light from the back porch illuminated a small piece of the backyard and provided enough light to get me halfway down the hedges, but after that, progress was by feel and memory only. I prayed we weren't all in the bushes, headed on a collision course. I hated the thought of having a fight among all the jagged branches.

When I got to the end of the house, I stopped and peered around the corner. The streetlight lit up a good piece between my house and my nosy neighbor Ronald's, and it was clear. I heard the rustling noise again and this time it was behind me, somewhere in the backyard. I scanned the backyard through the bushes, squinting as I tried to make out movement, but the clouds overhead blocked the moon, leaving most of the yard in complete darkness.

I was just about to head back the other direction when the clouds parted a bit and the moon cast a faint glow over the yard. I scanned from one end to the other and then I saw it. A shadow slipping behind the storage shed. The shed held lawn and fishing equipment and some power tools, but it wasn't big enough to hold an economy car, much less an SUV. Why would someone be lurking around there? The only thing I could figure is that they must be using the structure to conceal themselves while they watched the house, because there was no good reason to break into the shed.

I waited for the moon to disappear behind the clouds again,

then dashed across the open space into Ronald's yard. He had a thick row of azalea bushes on the property line and I hurried down them toward the shed, planning to ambush the intruder as soon as I had enough light to spot him. When I reached the stretch of bushes across from the shed, I stopped and stared into the darkness. My eyes had started to adjust and probably would have been able to pick out someone standing in the middle of the yard, but with the trees and bushes, the area around the shed was pitch black.

Come on, moon.

The seconds ticked by like hours, and I grew more antsy. The more time went by, the more chance there was that Ida Belle would find the open window and come out to help. I could hear rustling near the shed and was just about to move on the sound when the clouds cleared and I spotted two shadowy figures at the small window on the back side of the building. One of them took out a flashlight and shone it inside.

I had everything I needed.

CHAPTER SEVENTEEN

I launched through the bushes and threw a flying kick at the guy holding the flashlight. The flashlight flew across the yard, and he flew backward into the second man, sending them both to the ground, which was exactly what I'd been hoping for. Before they could scramble to get up, I pulled out my pistol and chambered a round. There's no mistaking that sound.

"Move and I'll shoot," I said. "Put your hands up in the air and don't make an attempt to leave a sitting position."

The dim glow from the moon didn't allow for me to see anything more than the silhouettes of their bodies on the ground, but I could see their arms go up over their heads.

"There's been a misunderstanding," one of them said.

Were they kidding me? A misunderstanding? As though they'd accidentally strolled through my flower beds or delivered a package to the wrong address? Not the kind of misunderstanding where they were here to steal an SUV and potentially bash us over the head when they didn't find it. Were these two the Seal brothers? Ida Belle and Gertie had said they weren't very bright, but did they really think I would buy that line of bull?

"You're darned right there's been a misunderstanding," I said.

"You're trespassing on private property. Threatening women. Who sent you? And what are you after?"

"We're not at liberty to say," one replied.

"You're going to be at liberty to wear some hot lead in your butts if you don't."

I was just about to fire off a warning shot, both to get them talking and to call for backup, when a spotlight hit us all and lit up the area surrounding the shed as if we were on stage. I put my left hand over my eyes and turned my head slightly to block the worst of the light, but made sure I kept my pistol trained on the two men on the ground, who, now that I had a good look at them, didn't appear to be the Seal brothers at all.

Unless the Seal brothers had aged and liked to wear black suits.

Uh-oh.

There was only one kind of person who drove an unregistered black sedan and who crept around at night wearing a black suit.

"I'm Deputy Carter LeBlanc," I heard Carter's voice sounding from behind the spotlight. "Everyone stay exactly where they are. Miss Morrow, could you please lower your weapon?"

"Not a chance," I said. "Not until I know who these men are and why they're sneaking around my property."

Carter stepped up next to the men, spotlight in one hand and pistol in the other. "I've got them covered."

I stuck my pistol in my waistband and stared down at the two suits. The back door flew open and Ida Belle and Gertie came running outside and hurried over to me.

"What's going on?" Gertie asked.

"I'm still waiting for them to answer that question," I said.

"You heard the lady," Carter said. "Who are you and what are you doing lurking around her property?"

"I need to reach for my ID," one of them said.

"Two fingers," Carter said.

The guy reached into the inside pocket of his jacket and

pulled out a wallet, then opened it, showing the federal identification that I'd been expecting to see.

Carter peered down at it. "ATF? Would you like to tell me what you're doing in Miss Morrow's backyard?"

"We're not at liberty to talk about an investigation in progress," the ATF agent said.

"Really?" Carter said. "Well, I'm not at liberty to allow the harassment of citizens in their own homes, so you can come down to the sheriff's department and wait there until you acquire that liberty you need to loosen your tongues."

"You can't be serious," the ATF agent said.

"Hey," Carter said. "I'm doing you a favor. This is not the sort of town where you go sneaking around private property at night. You're lucky she didn't shoot you, and I might add, she would have been well within her rights to claim a threat. You can spill it now or later, but rest assured, I have enough federal connections of my own to find out why you're here. So you can save all three of us a long night of stale coffee by just spitting it out."

"Fine," the agent said. "We got a report that these three women were involved in the manufacturing and distribution of illegal alcohol products."

I stared. It was all starting to make sense now. Celia's trip and her smug threats. This was her next play.

"I'm going to sue Celia Arceneaux for harassment," I said.

The agent flinched, and I knew I'd hit the nail on the head. I leaned forward and stared down at him. "Did you really think I had a still in my shed? Do I look like someone who's that stupid?"

"All right," Carter said, his jaw twitching. "Get up and get out of here. I don't know what you've been told and frankly, given the source, I don't care. That woman is nothing but trouble, and if you'd bothered to do a little research before you started sneaking around, you could have found that out rather easily."

"So you're saying these women do not sell illegal alcoholic

products?" the agent asked. "Because Mrs. Arceneaux brought a sample."

"It's cough syrup," Gertie said. "Herbal remedy, and we've been selling it for decades."

Ida Belle shook her head. "You've been played. There's nothing here to see but a bitter, angry woman who can't get the better of three women she hates. You're welcome, of course, to search our houses and sheds and anything else we own, but you're not going to find what you're looking for. She's wasting your time."

The two agents got up and the first one shoved his ID back in his suit coat. They brushed the grass off their jackets and glared at all of us.

"This matter is not concluded," the agent said.

"Sneaking around my town at night is concluded," Carter said. "You want information, you better be knocking on front doors in broad daylight and holding a warrant. Get out of here. People have lost enough sleep over you."

The two agents stomped off across the yard toward the front of the house.

"I can't believe her," Gertie said. "The ATF? What did she think that would accomplish?"

"Making trouble," Ida Belle said. "That's all she's really after. She probably thought if she fed them a big line of bull, they'd poke their nose around and find a smoking gun she wasn't aware of."

"If they'd been smarter about it," I said, "her plan might have succeeded. At least in my case."

"Oh my God," Gertie said. "I hadn't thought... That bitch. She could have blown your cover."

I nodded. "This war with Celia is becoming a real problem."

"I'll deal with the ATF," Carter said, but I could tell he was worried about how bad this could have been.

"That only solves this particular problem," Ida Belle said.

"Celia's not going to stop, and until Fortune's situation is resolved, she will continue to be at risk."

"If that woman's stupid crap forces the CIA to relocate Fortune," Gertie said, "I swear to God, I'm going to shoot her myself." She looked at Carter. "And you can put that on record. If Celia gets shot, just go ahead and prepare my cell. I'll even make it easy and turn myself in."

I smiled. While I didn't want to see my friend on trial for murder, I appreciated the sentiment.

Carter held his hands up in the air. "I don't think it will come to that. Let me see what I can do, and please, let's all keep our weapons to ourselves."

"Well," I said, "since the odds are against two sets of intruders in one night, I vote we go to bed. For real this time. No more patrol." I looked over at Carter. "Thanks for the backup. I was about to fire a warning shot. That probably would have been a lot more trouble."

"I suppose just calling, like I asked you to, was out of the question?" he asked.

"Oops," I said. "Sorry, I kinda went into mission mode and forgot."

This time, it was the absolute truth. When I'd thought there was someone outside, I automatically shifted into action. My only external concern had been keeping Ida Belle out of the fray.

He sighed. "I figured. Hey, just wondering—how did you get them both on the ground?"

"Oh, I did a flying kick and knocked one into the other," I said.

Gertie shook her head in admiration. "You must kick like a mule."

"I would have paid to see that," Ida Belle said.

Carter smiled. The first time I'd seen him smile in forever. "I would have, too. You ladies get inside and lock up. I'll be watching things a little longer but I think Fortune is right. I think all the excitement for tonight is over. If anyone else was intending to make a move, all this commotion would have scared them off."

Ida Belle, Gertie, and I headed for the back door. I could feel Carter's eyes on me as I walked. What did that smile mean? Was he coming to terms with my outlaw personality that had me consorting with known criminals and generally doing things most girlfriends never even thought about doing?

Or was he simply amused that two Feds got their butts kicked by a girl?

————

WE WERE a tired bunch at the breakfast table the next morning. Even though we'd all gone straight to bed after the throw-down with the Feds, I was betting no one had slept well. Based on the dark circles under everyone's eyes, I was also betting no one would take that bet. We all shuffled into the kitchen around 8:00 a.m., poured coffee, and plopped into chairs.

"Who's up for running a marathon today?" I asked.

"Ha," Gertie said. "I took a good five minutes to think about whether I was up for getting out of bed. You don't want to know how long it took me to put on pants. Or take them off, for that matter."

Ida Belle nodded. "I don't think I've slept this poorly in a long time. Between Hot Rod, the SUV, and Celia, I can't get my mind to stop worrying, and I'm usually not a big worrier."

"I'm better at it than you," Gertie said, "and I freely admit to being near heart attack stage. Something has to give. Either we catch the guys who hurt Hot Rod or we kill Celia. At this point, I'm not sure which one presents more difficulty."

"I have a feeling that if I shot her," Ida Belle said, "she'd just pop right back up for round two."

"She does have a rather inhuman quality about her," I said. "Especially when it comes to living with embarrassment. She seems to have no limits to what she'll endure to try to get one up on you."

Gertie shook her head. "I don't think she owns a pair of underwear the entire town hasn't seen."

"The town's seen a few pairs of yours as well," Ida Belle pointed out.

"Yes, but mine aren't as big," Gertie said, "and they're always trendy."

"Can we skip any more talk about underwear?" Ida Belle asked. "Especially the big kind on Celia's butt? This is only my first cup of coffee and it doesn't even have alcohol in it."

I nodded. "It does seem rather cruel to continue down that train of thought this early."

"Fine by me," Gertie said. "So what are we going to do?"

"About which problem?" I asked.

"All of them," Gertie said. "It's not like we can ignore any of them. None are going away. I know Carter said he'd handle the ATF, so I guess we can push that one to the end of the list for now, but Celia and the car thieves are both major problems. So, what are we going to do?"

I tapped the side of my coffee mug and stared out the kitchen window at the shed. I wasn't worried about the ATF agents. Not because they couldn't cause problems but because there was nothing I could do about it if they did. I had to hope that threats from Carter and the embarrassment of being outwitted by a woman would be enough to get them to leave town and forget they had ever talked to Celia Arceneaux, but sometimes when men felt played, they doubled down instead of doing the smart thing and walking away.

So one of the things I needed to do when I could be assured of the free time for a conversation was to send Harrison an email and ask him to call me. There was no way I could explain the situation in our email code. Not in a way he'd understand. We had burner phones to use only for emergency contact, and the threat of a federal agency investigating me definitely constituted an emergency. Plus, a call would give me a chance to talk to Harrison firsthand about the lead they were working to locate Ahmad.

Celia was definitely a problem, but without a way to predict the things crazy, obsessed people did, I wasn't sure what could be done about her. At least not at this moment. The car thieves, on the other hand, were something I could work with. Ever since I'd done that flying kick into the ATF agent the night before, the wheels had been spinning. In fact, I'd thought of little else the entire night. And now, staring at the shed in the light of day, I knew what we had to do.

"I have an idea," I said.

"I like the sound of that," Ida Belle said.

"You might not when you hear the idea," I said. "That whole thing with the ATF last night got me to thinking. We need to find the Seal brothers, but nobody seems to know how to locate them. So I was thinking maybe we get them to come to us."

Ida Belle straightened in her chair. "Set a trap with the SUV?"

"Yeah," I said. "We'd have to bring it back to Sinful, though. I don't care how foolish the Seal brothers are, they can't possibly be dumb enough to break into a storage facility owned by the Heberts."

"We broke into a storage facility owned by the Heberts," Gertie pointed out.

"That was different," I said. "We were breaking in to look at evidence the Feds stored there, and there's no love lost between Big and Little and the Feds. Besides, they like us."

"They find us amusing," Gertie said. "I'm still not sure they like us."

I shrugged. "Works out for us either way."

"Fortune's right," Ida Belle said. "It's the quickest way to get this over with. Use the SUV to draw them out and trap them."

"But how will bringing the SUV here make a difference?" Gertie asked. "We've been waiting on them to show up and they haven't. They don't know the SUV is at the storage facility, so if they were coming, wouldn't they have done so already?"

"I've thought about that," I said, "and the reality is, we don't know what they know. They could have already checked Ida Belle's garage. She doesn't have an alarm on it, and her back door is easy enough to jimmy. I'm always pulling the Jeep in and out of my garage so anyone watching would know it's the only vehicle that even fits inside with all that other crap Marge has out there."

"But if they've already checked and know it's not here," Gertie said, "then why would they come back?"

"We'd need to draw them out," I said. "I'm betting that the Seal brothers are keeping watch on Sinful for the SUV. Maybe they think Ida Belle has it in the shop somewhere and it will be back soon. They don't know that we're onto them."

Gertie nodded. "So we drive the SUV down the highway and through Sinful and hope they're watching. Does that mean we're letting Carter in on it?"

"No," I said. "Even if Carter agreed to using the SUV as bait, he'd never let us be in on it. We'll have to get it back into Sinful without Carter knowing."

"So you want *us* to catch them?" Gertie asked.

"Yes, but with a little help," I said. "Just not the law enforcement kind. In fact, I was thinking just the opposite."

Gertie's eyes widened. "You want the Heberts to help?"

"Why not?" I said. "If Carter catches the Seal brothers, they won't talk because admitting they're looking for the key means admitting they bashed Hot Rod over the head and then they go right back to prison. But if the Heberts are doing the questioning..."

"They'd go somewhere far worse than prison for not answering," Gertie said. "Are you sure you want to go that route?"

The CIA assassin in me had gone that route enough times to be able to handle it. After all, it was part of the mission and for the greater good. But the new civilized me found several ethical problems with the setup.

"I think I can convince them to scare the information out of the brothers and then we can turn them over to Carter," I said.

Gertie glanced over at Ida Belle, and I could tell neither of them was convinced that I could get the Heberts to deal, but I was willing to give it a try, especially if it meant Ida Belle could go back to sleeping at night and in her own bed.

Before I could change my mind, I picked up my cell phone and sent a text to Little.

Have a plan and need to talk. When can you and Big meet?

"There," I said. "We'll talk to them and see if they'll agree to do things my way."

"And if they won't?" Ida Belle asked.

I shook my head. "The reality is, they could set up a trap themselves if they wanted to, and if it hasn't already crossed their minds, it will. They have the SUV in their possession and the ability to put out the word that it's being repaired at some shop in New Orleans, or whatever. How many people do you think owe them favors? They wouldn't have any trouble setting up a garage to borrow."

Ida Belle frowned. "I hadn't thought about that."

"So basically," Gertie said, "you're going to pitch the idea before they move on it themselves. Otherwise, we'll be just as left out as we would be if Carter did it."

"Exactly," I said. "I don't like it, but it's a better than being sitting ducks. I was lucky with those Feds last night. They weren't expecting anyone to be outside and they certainly weren't expecting someone with my capabilities. But people like the Seal brothers spend every waking moment looking over their shoulder and anticipating a possible attack."

Ida Belle nodded. "You're right. I hated pacing the house last night, checking the windows every twenty minutes and feeling like a caged animal. I need this to be over with."

My phone signaled an incoming text and I checked it.

Meet us at the storage unit at 10 a.m.

"Ten o'clock," I said. "We have less than two hours to figure out how to convince two mobsters to do things our way."

"We're going to need another pot of coffee," Gertie said.

CHAPTER EIGHTEEN

I pulled up to the storage unit and punched in the code for the security gate. We'd talked about our pitch over and over again until we'd worn out every possible angle—asking politely, insisting gently, pleading just a little, and even crying. I'd finally decided that the truth was the easiest way to go. It might not get us what we wanted, but I was fairly sure none of the other options would, either.

The door to the storage unit was already open, and Mannie was standing outside. I pulled up in front of it and saw Big sitting inside on the bench and four other chairs surrounding him. We greeted Mannie and headed inside. Little rose from one of the chairs and waved his hand at them.

"Please, take a seat," Little said. "It's not the most comfortable of furniture, but we have other business being handled at our offices today and couldn't meet there."

We all said our hellos to Big, who nodded, and we took a seat. Mannie stood off to the side, as usual. I wasn't sure I'd ever seen him sit except when driving.

"You've been busy," Big said. "It's unfortunate that Mr.

LeDoux turned out to be a dead end, quite literally. Have you discovered anything else about the key?"

"Nothing that is a big help, I'm afraid," I said. "We talked to an antiques dealer and he thinks it opens a crypt, but we have no idea which one and there's not exactly a shortage of them around these parts."

Big nodded. "A crypt. Interesting. But yes, I see where that's a problem, especially with Mr. LeDoux no longer able to answer questions. I've heard Hot Rod's condition has improved. That was a bit of good news."

Ida Belle nodded. "We were really happy to hear that."

"Well," Big said, "I'm sure you didn't come here to chat, so what can we help you with?"

"I want to set a trap," I said. "We're tired of looking over our shoulders and patrolling the house at night, waiting for the car thieves to come looking. I want to bring the SUV back to Sinful and take them down."

"Nice," Mannie said.

I explained my plan, as well as I'd fleshed it out so far.

Big glanced at Mannie, then looked back at me. "While I appreciate your desire for a speedy resolution, I'm not certain your plan is the best option. At least, not in the way you've presented it."

"Why not?" I asked.

"Well," Big said, "while I have no doubt at all about your ability to secure the thieves should they take the bait, I'm afraid the events at your home last night have provided information that you're under surveillance."

I threw my hands in the air. "How do you know that? Do you have hidden cameras on my lawn?"

"No," Big said. "We haven't surveilled you ourselves since we bugged your house that one time, and all of that equipment has been removed. Now that we know each other better, I wouldn't do such a thing without inquiring first, but I will admit there are times I would enjoy the footage."

"We have some friends in high places," Little said. "We were aware that the ATF was in Sinful, but had no information as to why. After they flubbed their mission last night, word of it made rounds. But our friends have not heard that the investigation has been canceled. Until such time, we have to assume that the ATF could still be watching."

I sighed, unable to control my disappointment. But Big and Little were right. I could hardly go apprehending car thieves in Ida Belle's driveway with a federal agency watching us. That might look a little suspicious, not to mention I needed to question the thieves myself, and Feds rushing in to aid the helpless female would mess up everything. The thieves would go straight to jail and I'd never get a chance to question them.

"If I may," Little said. "I think I might have a solution."

"I'm listening," I said.

Little nodded. "I'm sure we can all agree that attempting to draw the thieves to the storage unit would also be folly, which I'm sure is why you want to take the SUV back to Sinful. Because of this situation, I understand you're all staying at Ms. Morrow's home at night, correct?"

"Yes," I said, "but you're right, if the ATF is still hanging around, my plan won't work. They'd come out of the bushes and honk everything up."

Little nodded. "It could definitely get a little crowded, especially as I'm sure your deputy friend is also lurking about. What I'm going to suggest is that we give the thieves exactly what they want but in a different way than you suggested."

I frowned. "But they want to find the SUV in Ida Belle's garage...oh, I get it. Since everyone's watching my house they won't be watching Ida Belle's."

Little nodded. "Classic misdirection. While all interested

parties are watching your house, Big and I can arrange to have the SUV placed back in the garage."

"The staging part makes sense," I said, "but I want to be the one doing the takedown. I can't do that if I'm playing David Copperfield with the Feds and local law enforcement."

"I know you want to be involved," Little said, "and I'm not saying you can't be. Just that you can't be at Ida Belle's."

"You're suggesting *you* take down the thieves?" I asked. "And then what, call us up and we stroll over? How is that any better?"

"I'm suggesting that we acquire the thieves and transport them to a place where they could be questioned without the worry of federal agents or local law enforcement getting in the way," Little said. "I have every confidence in your ability to get out of your home without being seen."

"We could get out of the house, sure," I said. "But we can't exactly drive my Jeep out of the garage and I'm not interested in jogging to the storage unit or your warehouse, or wherever else you have in mind."

"Of course not," Little said. "We will be happy to provide you with a vehicle—not stolen—that you can use to meet us at a specified location. All you have to do is get out of your house and to the vehicle without being seen."

"That sounds good and all," Ida Belle said, "but I think you're forgetting the nosy neighbor side of things. Those ATF agents parked on my street yesterday and stirred up my neighbors. They're going to be watching. If you grab people in my driveway and toss them into a van, my neighbors are going to notice."

"I wasn't planning on grabbing them in your driveway," Little said. "I was planning on letting them leave town in the SUV and acquiring them when they were well out of view of Sinful residents and law enforcement."

"You're going to let them steal my SUV?" Ida Belle looked less than enthused. "I know the key's not in it for them to find anymore, but I love that vehicle. What if they wreck it when you go chasing them down the highway?"

"I'm afraid this is where you're going to have to trust me," Little said. "I assure you I can create a situation where the thieves leave Sinful with your SUV but do not engage in a dangerous driving situation. Your SUV will not be damaged."

Ida Belle narrowed her eyes at Little. "And just how the hell are you going to do that?"

"Oh!" Gertie clapped her hands. "You have one of those radio beam things, don't you?"

Ida Belle glared at her. "You've been watching that sci-fi stuff again."

"Have not," Gertie said. "Okay, well, maybe I have, but the radio beam thing is for real."

Ida Belle opened her mouth to argue and I held up a hand. "Gertie's right. The radio beam thing does exist, but I'm guessing it would be easier to simply stick the gas indicator on Full and remove all but a tiny bit of gas from the tank."

Mannie grinned. "Smart. Practical. You sure you aren't military?"

"Pretty sure," I said. "But thanks for the compliment."

Little smiled. "Ms. Morrow is correct with her assessment. The easiest route to follow is to allow the thieves to drive the SUV out of town and to acquire them when they come to a stop on the highway. I assure you I can provide many reasons for them to abstain from attempting a run in your vehicle."

I figured the many reasons were mostly made up of big scary guys and even bigger, scarier guns. It was a good plan. Most people wouldn't move if a small army told them to stay put.

Ida Belle looked at me, and I knew she would defer to my opinion because she trusted my instincts. I didn't think it was an airtight plan, but it was a pretty darn solid one. The trickiest part would be getting the SUV to Ida Belle's without Carter seeing it, because if he did, the gig was up.

I looked at Little. "You have to get the SUV into Ida Belle's garage without Carter seeing it, or he'll know right away what we're doing."

"We'll bring it in after dark," Little said, "and we'll avoid downtown, although I think a little driving up and down the highway is in order. It would help if you could arrange for the deputy to be otherwise involved when we arrive."

"That's easy enough," Gertie said. "You're talking to his main distraction."

Big laughed. "Let's try to keep things PG. You wouldn't want to scare the ATF."

"I can provide a distraction," I said, and gave Gertie a pointed look. "*Not* that kind of distraction. Just give me a time frame."

"Let's say ten p.m.," Little said. "It's too late for sunlight and a tad too early for car thieving, but gives us time to drive around a bit and get noticed."

"You know," Ida Belle said, "all of this makes a big assumption —that the thieves will show up at my house tonight for the car. What if they've looked already and moved on?"

"It's a possibility," I said. "It's also possible that they don't come tonight because they're busy somewhere else. I still say we put the SUV in there and leave it until they show up. It's bound to happen sooner or later. Regardless, this way we get to stay involved. If Carter gets them..."

"I agree with Ms. Morrow," Big said. "If not tonight, then another. We are available until this situation has been handled to everyone's satisfaction."

I looked at Big. "You have to make me a promise."

"I'm intrigued," Big said. "What do you require?"

"When we get what we need out of the thieves, we turn them over to Carter."

Big smiled. "Of course. I never considered anything else."

I stared at him for a moment, trying to decide what I believed. He'd said in the beginning that he wanted me to tell him who had attacked Hot Rod. Now he was backtracking and saying he'd gladly turn the bad guys over to Carter. I wondered briefly what kind of condition they'd be in when that turnover finally happened. Not that I cared overly much. As long as the car thieves ultimately ended up in a jail cell wearing handcuffs rather than in the bottom of the bayou wearing cement boots.

Part of me worried that Big was just humoring me and things were going to go very badly for the thieves once he got a hold of them, but at this point, it was wasted energy. My idea was out in the open. Either we got to be involved and maybe I could talk the Heberts out of killing the thieves if it came down to that, or they'd execute the plan without us and I wouldn't have any say at all.

I looked at Little and nodded. "Then I believe we have a plan."

———

AT 9:45 P.M., Ida Belle, Gertie, and I were up to our wrists in crap. Literally.

"Are you sure this is going to work?" I asked for the hundredth time. I couldn't help it. This entire Operation Distract Carter plan had Gertie's name written all over it.

"It will work," Ida Belle said. "Do you think I'd be doing it otherwise?"

She had a point. Gertie was willing to throw caution and sanitation to the wind, but Ida Belle was a little pickier. If it didn't work out well, then I had only myself to blame for going along with it. And I was perfectly willing to admit that the hope that it did work was why I'd agreed to it in the first place. The very idea of success had me more gleeful than I'd felt in days.

So we'd commandeered Marie's house, because it was located next door to Celia's, and set to work with our diabolical plan. First, we'd hauled buckets of cow poop over the fence. Then a fertilizer sprayer filled with regular water. It was a three-stage process. First, we sprayed an area of grass with water to wet it down, then we put a layer of fresh cow poop onto the wet grass. Finally, we added dried cow poop to the top of the fresh cow poop. We created five of these piles about two feet apart from one another and ten feet away from Celia's back porch.

"That's the last one," Ida Belle said.

"We have some leftover," I said, pointing to a half-full bucket of the fresh stuff.

"I'll use it on my flowers," Gertie said.

I grimaced at the thought of how her flower beds would smell, but then the upside is it probably kept people from trampling anything. They wouldn't even get near enough to pick a flower. We all pulled off our latex gloves and dropped them into one of the empty buckets. I stacked the buckets, the one with the fresh poop on top, then headed to the fence Marie and Celia shared with the buckets and the sprayer.

We'd positioned a ladder in Celia's yard to help with a quick escape, so I scaled it and leaned across the fence and to the side, placing the buckets and sprayer on the ground in Marie's yard. I hurried back to the poo piles, ready to get the show on the road.

"The buckets and sprayer are on the right of the ladder," I said, "so when you go over the fence, go straight or to the left."

Ida Belle and Gertie nodded.

"Are we ready?" Gertie asked, practically bouncing up and down.

"Definitely ready," Ida Belle said, looking happier than I'd seen her in a while.

"I want to do the lighting," Gertie said. "You promised."

"You can do the first one," I said, "then I want you to haul it for that ladder. With your crappy knees, you can't move as fast as us, and I need you out of Ida Belle's way when she runs for the ladder."

"What about you?" Ida Belle said.

"I don't need the ladder," I said.

"Of course you don't," Gertie said. "If I were twenty years younger…"

"You'd still need the ladder," Ida Belle said. "Break out the matches."

Gertie pulled books of matches out of her pocket and passed one to each of us. She struck a match and lit the first pile of poop on fire. She paused long enough to make sure it was burning, then took off with a sorta jogging limp for the ladder. Ida Belle and I lit the remaining piles, then ran for the fence.

Gertie was on top of the fence hanging across the middle of it when we reached her.

"Hurry up," I said.

"I'm stuck," Gertie said. "My shirt is caught on a nail."

"Let it tear," I said. "Just get out of Ida Belle's way."

Ida Belle hurried up the ladder and assessed the situation. "It's not a nail. You've managed to wedge a hunk of your blouse in between the fence slats. Just roll over the edge and buy a new blouse."

I glanced back at Celia's, worried that we were running out of time. A second later, a light clicked on upstairs.

"Celia's awake," I said. "Get the hell out of here!"

CHAPTER NINETEEN

The backyard was wide, and the rear had no lighting outside of the weak bulb on the back porch. With no moon to speak of, I knew Celia wouldn't be able to see us from the window, but any second now, she'd be outside.

I hadn't even finished my sentence when Ida Belle vaulted over the fence to the side of Gertie. I grabbed the ladder and flipped the whole thing over then leaped up, grabbed the fence, and followed suit. I did a somersault, then bounced back up and whirled around, expecting to see Gertie on the ground, but she was still dangling from the middle of the fence, Ida Belle frantically motioning at her.

Marie hurried over to us and I pointed at the ladder. "Get that back where it goes."

As she grabbed the ladder, I looked up at Gertie.

"Drop," I said. "Now!"

If she'd just rolled over the side the way a sane person would have, things probably would have been okay. But Gertie had to do things her way.

Her way called for using her right hand to try to pull her blouse out of the fence. One good tug and she lost her balance and pitched over the fence, landing feet first in the bucket. Before she could even attempt to move, I scooped up one arm and Ida Belle grabbed the other and we lifted her off the ground. I grabbed the sprayer with my free hand and we started running for Marie's house, the bucket of poo stuck to Gertie's feet as we hauled her to the house.

Marie had placed the ladder next to the porch and was gesturing at us from the back door.

"The bucket," Ida Belle said.

"Later," Marie said. "I can hear her yelling."

Now that Marie mentioned it, Celia's loud mouth was beginning to carry across the yard. We hauled Gertie and the bucket up the porch steps and went sideways into the laundry room, where Marie had wisely covered the floor with a tarp. She grabbed the bucket, and Ida Belle and I pulled Gertie out of the stinky poo.

"Hurry," Marie said. "We have to get upstairs and see the show."

"Not you," Ida Belle said to Gertie.

Ida Belle and I ran upstairs behind Marie and hurried to the window in the back bedroom that had a clear view of Celia's yard. I yanked open the curtains and we perched in front of the window. The lights were off in the room so Celia wouldn't be able to see us watching her. A couple seconds later, Gertie elbowed me in the side.

"Stop hogging the view," she said.

I glanced over and realized more of Gertie was currently exposed than covered. Her blouse was torn and dangling from one shoulder, and the bottom half of her clothes were missing entirely except for a pair of traffic-stopping orange underwear.

"Celia's coming out!" Ida Belle said.

All our noses instantly pressed against the window as Celia ran out her back door and onto her porch, her hideous green bathrobe flapping as she went. She paused a second, then took off again down the steps and into the yard, running straight for the steaming piles of poo.

"Wait for it," Gertie said as Celia slid to a stop in front of the first pile, then lifted her foot and stomped right in the middle of the flames.

Ida Belle, Gertie, and Marie all let out a whoop at the same time, and I watched in amazement as Celia yanked off her slipper and tossed it across the yard.

"I can't believe she actually stomped on it," I said.

"Works every time," Gertie said.

"It's a natural reaction," Ida Belle said, "when the fire is small."

"Now she's going for the hose," Marie said. "Party's over."

"Maybe not," Ida Belle said. "This is Celia we're talking about."

Celia ran for the corner of the porch and yanked a water hose off a reel and then hurried back to the poo and blasted the stacks to her right with the hose. As she turned to the right to aim, the bottom of her robe flew out and grazed one of the stacks to her left. Flames shot up the back of the robe and Celia whirled around like a magician with a cape, trying to get it off of her. A second later, a woman ran into the yard, grabbed the hose, and turned it full blast on Celia, who was still trying to get the robe off.

Completely drenched, Celia turned around and started yelling at the woman, waving her hands in the air.

"Wow," I said. "You'd think if you were on fire and someone put you out, there would be a little gratitude."

"It's Celia," Ida Belle said.

The woman dropped the hose and gave Celia the finger before stomping back across the yard and out the gate.

"No good deeds living next to Celia," I said.

Ida Belle's phone beeped and she checked it. "Myrtle says Carter is on his way to investigate a fire at Celia's."

"Awesome," I said, and pulled out my phone to send a text to Little.

Your window is open.

"Okay," I said, "let's wrap this up and get out of here before Carter shows up."

We figured given the proximity of the houses and the mayoral race, Marie would be first up on Celia's blame list. We didn't want any evidence around when he showed up for his obligatory check.

We hurried back downstairs and headed to the laundry room. I put on gloves and grabbed the buckets. The sprayer was Marie's and would go back into the garage. Gertie's poopy clothes got folded up in the tarp to take with us, and all evidence was ready to ride.

"Make sure you spray some deodorizer in here," Ida Belle said as we hurried out. "And thanks again for letting us use your place."

Marie grinned. "Are you kidding me? I wouldn't have missed being a part of this for anything."

"What about Gertie?" I asked. "She can't go traipsing around half naked."

"Gertie won't fit in anything Marie's skinny butt goes into," Ida Belle said.

"Well, I'm not letting her get into my Jeep wearing half a blouse and neon orange underwear that say 'Bad Ass' on the rear."

"Pretty sharp, huh?" Gertie grinned.

Ida Belle rolled her eyes. "Just grab the tablecloth and wrap up in it. You can launder it and bring it back tomorrow."

Marie, whose nose was twitching from the smell, glanced at Gertie's orange-clad butt and said, "You can keep it. I need a new one anyway."

Ida Belle snagged the tablecloth and Gertie wrapped it around her body like a toga, then we headed into the garage, where we'd hidden my Jeep. Since Gertie was wound up like a burrito, Ida Belle climbed into the backseat and secured the bucket of poo on the floorboard next to her. I went over to the passenger side and half lifted, half shoved Gertie into the seat, then hopped into the driver's seat and hauled it out of the garage and onto the street.

Our plan was to head the opposite direction of Celia's house with no headlights so that she couldn't see my vehicle. Plus, Carter would be approaching Celia's from the shortest route, which was from the opposite direction. I floored it to the end of the street, checked for cars, then rounded the corner without stopping. A second later, red lights flashed behind me.

"You've got to be kidding me!" I yelled. "Now they decide to have traffic patrol?"

"Is it Deputy Breaux?" Gertie asked.

"Can't tell," Ida Belle said. "The headlights are shining right at us."

"Just play it cool," I said.

"I'm wearing a tablecloth," Gertie said. "If you've got any ideas on how to make this cool, then lay them on me quickly."

I saw a flashlight bobbing in the side mirror and put my hands on the steering wheel, the way you're supposed to when you're stopped. I rolled down the window and said a silent prayer as the figure stepped up to the window. Automatic relief coursed through me when Deputy Breaux peered in the vehicle at us.

"Ladies," he said. "Are you aware that you're operating this vehicle without headlights and you ran a stop sign?"

"Yes," I said, "but no one was coming and I'm in a hurry to get home."

"Why are you in a hurry?" Deputy Breaux asked.

"Because I have a bathroom emergency," I said.

Deputy Breaux looked confused and Gertie leaned over the console.

"She has to pee," Gertie said. "And you're not helping matters any holding us up."

"I'm just doing my job," Deputy Breaux said, looking slightly pained.

"This Jeep has cloth seats," Gertie said. "That's all I'm saying."

Deputy Breaux leaned forward more and took a harder look at Gertie. "Why are you wearing a sheet?"

Gertie froze and I still hadn't come up with anything reasonable. Thank God Ida Belle was thinking for all of us.

"Toga party," Ida Belle said.

He frowned. "Why aren't the rest of you wearing sheets?"

"Mine were in the laundry," I said.

"And I don't take part in such nonsense," Ida Belle said. "I was just there for the free beer."

He wrinkled his nose. "What's that smell?"

"I stepped in dog crap," Ida Belle said. "Happens every time I walk across the lawn. I should know better."

Still confused, he looked back at me, and that's when he noticed my hands on the steering wheel.

Crap! I was wearing the latex gloves.

"Ms. Morrow," he said, "why are you wearing plastic gloves?"

"Wax treatment," Gertie said. "Makes your skin really soft but it's messy. She has to wear the gloves until the wax is hard, then we'll peel it off."

"You dipped your hands in wax?" He stared at me as if I'd lost my mind.

"It's special wax," Gertie said. "It doesn't burn. I'll be happy to come by the sheriff's department and do your hands for you next week."

The thought of having girlie treatment on his hands at the sheriff's department must have scared Deputy Breaux more than whatever we were up to, because his eyes widened and he shook his head.

"That won't be necessary," he said. "My hands are just fine. You go ahead and get going and take care of that bathroom thing...and your hands."

He was still standing there shaking his head when I pulled away.

"Nice thinking with the toga explanation," Gertie said to Ida Belle.

"It worked on Deputy Breaux," Ida Belle said, "but the gig's up as soon as he tells all this to Carter."

"So what," I said. "He won't have any proof and even if he did, do you really think Carter's going to arrest us for lighting poo on fire in Celia's yard after the trouble she caused with the ATF? As long as he thinks this was a juvenile prank and nothing more, we're in the clear."

"Who are you calling juvenile?" Gertie asked.

I looked over at her, wrapped in a yellow tablecloth, hair askew, and orange underwear lurking below, and grinned.

"Who indeed?"

———

AT 10:30 p.m. came the knock on my front door that I'd been expecting. I jumped up from the couch and looked at Ida Belle and Gertie.

"Time for game face," I said.

It was going to be hard. We'd been grinning ever since we'd walked into my house a half hour ago, and I wasn't completely certain we could stop anytime soon. As I turned the dead bolt, I put on the best bored and sleepy look I could manage and swung the door open. Carter stared at me, eyebrows up.

"Miss Morrow," he said, cluing me in that it was official sheriff's department business. "There's been a disturbance at Celia Arceneaux's house tonight and she's suggested I ask you some questions."

"Of course she has," I said, and waved him in.

He stepped into the living room and nodded at Ida Belle and Gertie. "Ladies."

"So what kind of disturbance did Celia manage this time?" I asked.

"This time," Carter said, "she managed to step in flaming cow poop and set her robe on fire."

"What in the world would she do that for?" I asked. "Can't she find something to watch on television like the rest of us?"

His lips quivered and I could tell he was trying not to smile. "Someone—not Celia—put the cow poop in her backyard and lit it on fire."

"And she's blaming us," Ida Belle said. "Guess that means she didn't burn her lips off. What a shame."

"She doesn't burn," Gertie said. "You know, hell and demons and all."

"Well," I said, "I don't know what to tell you, except that I don't play with poop...cow or otherwise. And it sounds like Celia shouldn't either. I can't imagine her neighbors were happy seeing her out in her yard without a robe on. God only knows what she sleeps in."

"So you've been here the entire night?" Carter asked.

I knew right away he'd already talked to Deputy Breaux, but if he wanted to continue this ridiculous dance of lies, I was game.

"We were at a toga party earlier."

"And where was this toga party held?" Carter asked. "I'd like to check your alibi."

"You're looking at my alibi," I said. "It was a large party of three at Gertie's house."

"I see," he said, "and when you left Gertie's house, you drove the long way around to get home, with your headlights off, and ran a stop sign because you had a bathroom emergency. Even though you'd just left a house with two perfectly good bathrooms."

"Some people just can't hold their sweet tea," Gertie said.

"So if I checked around," Carter said, "I wouldn't find a container with poop remnants, would I?"

"Nope." Because I'd tossed the entire bucket, poo and all, into the bayou, much to Gertie's dismay.

"Do we have to keep this up much longer?" Ida Belle asked. "Because I'm a little tired. We didn't get much sleep last night what with Fortune out taking on the ATF and all."

The smile that had been hovering on Carter's lips finally broke through. "I just wanted to see how far you would take it," he said.

"As far as required," Gertie said. "And for a lot longer than you can hold out for. What do you think we are, amateurs?"

"I thought nothing of the kind," he said. "Well, since you all have an alibi, I guess my work here is done."

"We always happy to help," I said, and followed him to the door.

He walked onto the porch, then turned around and looked at me, his expression now serious. "I'll be making periodic passes by throughout the night. If anything even feels off, call me."

I nodded.

"I mean it," he said. "No more taking down strange men lurking around your lawn. You might run up against someone more capable than the ATF."

I shrugged. "They'd have to be more capable than me before it would matter."

"Humor me."

"Just this once?"

He sighed. "Please?"

"Fine, I'll call if I hear or see anything nefarious. I'm not going to say out of the ordinary because that would be pretty much everything in this town."

"That's good enough for me."

He turned around and headed for his truck. I watched him for a couple seconds, then closed the door. When I turned around, Gertie and Ida Belle were both grinning at me.

"Let's talk about the poop stomping one more time," Gertie said.

I smiled. "Maybe just once more."

———

AN HOUR AND A HALF LATER, I'd paced the living room so many times that I worried I would wear out the soles on my tennis shoes. It was ten minutes past midnight and my phone had remained agonizingly quiet the entire night. Was this how it was going to be? I spent every night pacing until someone showed up to steal the SUV? I might make it a couple days, but if they hadn't shown up by the third night, I was going to consider advertising the vehicle in every auto sales paper I could find.

"If you don't sit down," Ida Belle said, "you're going to start a fire on those hardwood floors through friction alone."

"You're one to talk," I said. "You only stopped an hour ago."

"I didn't even start," Gertie said. "I got tired just watching the two of you."

I flopped into the recliner and sighed, something else I'd done more times than I could count in the past hour and a half.

"This waiting is killing me," I said.

Gertie nodded. "If we have to do this every night for a week, you're going to have to refinish the floor."

"If we have to do this every night for a week," Ida Belle said, "I'm hitting the hard stuff."

Gertie shook her head. "You two just need to look at the positive side of things. We have a plan to catch the car thieves and people to help with it—*qualified* people. The SUV is tucked safely in Ida Belle's garage and Carter doesn't suspect a thing. And if that's not enough for you, Celia stomped right into flaming cow crap and set her robe on fire."

I smiled. "The foot in flaming cow crap thing was really funny."

"So was the look on Deputy Breaux's face when he pulled us over," Ida Belle said.

"Okay, so the night wasn't entirely bad," I said, "but the cow crap was a onetime gig, so if we're sitting here tomorrow, we won't have a recent memory to laugh over."

"I'll still be laughing about the cow crap tomorrow night," Gertie said.

"Okay," I agreed. "I can probably get another night out of it, especially since everyone in town will be talking about it tomorrow, but if we move on to night three, something's going to have to give."

"Oh, oh!" Gertie said, and bounced in her chair. "We should pull a drive-by and use water guns to spray her porch with fox urine."

I looked over at Ida Belle. "Should I even ask?"

"Ten times worse than cat pee," Ida Belle said. "She'd have to burn the house down."

"Okay," I said. "We'll keep that one in reserve."

I was just about to suggest another round of chocolate chip cookies when my phone signaled a text coming in.

SUV is on the move. Head out.

My pulse began to race just as it did every time I was closing in on a target. I looked over at Ida Belle's and Gertie's expectant faces and smiled.

"It's on," I said.

CHAPTER TWENTY

I da Belle and Gertie jumped up from their seats, and I could tell they were as excited as I was. Everything about our escape route was already planned and we'd gone through the steps a million times. I grabbed the getaway car keys that I'd found that afternoon, somewhat disturbingly, on my kitchen table, along with a description of the car. It was parked in the location I'd specified to Little when we'd talked earlier, which was four houses down from mine and in front of a panel van that was always parked at the curb.

Ida Belle ran upstairs and a couple seconds later yelled down. "Street's clear."

We'd been watching all night as Carter made sweeps around the neighborhood. He must have been making regular stops at his house because we only saw him every thirty minutes, but it was like clockwork. Which was a really good thing given what we needed to do.

"Last pass was ten minutes ago," I said. "Let's go."

We headed into the study and I opened the window. I'd already placed a stepladder underneath it to help all of us exit without incident. And by all of us, I meant Gertie and her bad knees. Ida Belle went first, then made sure Gertie got out without incident, then I climbed out last, and we set off down the side of the house, keeping our position behind the bushes. I stopped at the end of the house and peered out, making sure there were no random ATF agents lurking about. I didn't think they would be foolish enough to pull the same thing twice, but if my job had taught me anything it was that humans weren't often rational.

The space between the houses was clear, so I ran across to Ronald's yard, Ida Belle and Gertie close behind. We moved across his backyard and two more houses before turning and heading for the street. I stopped at the edge of the house and scanned up and down the road, looking for any sign of movement or oncoming headlights in the distance, but everything was quiet.

The place I'd chosen for the pickup car, a completely nondescript Honda Accord, was directly between two streetlamps, so almost no light reached the vehicle. The owners of the house it was parked in front of were the cheapest people on the block and had something against burning outside lights. It provided the least visibility for our passage.

I set off across the yard at a fast walk. If anyone drove by and caught sight of me, they would probably take running or even jogging as my attempt to escape a pursuer. That meant a call to the sheriff's department, so I settled for fast walking. Ida Belle followed at almost the same pace, while Gertie lagged behind. Ida Belle and I were already in the car and ready to go while Gertie negotiated the last quarter of the yard.

"Close the door," Ida Belle said when Gertie climbed in the car. "If I'd known you were going to make this a midnight stroll, I would have gotten you a wheelchair."

I started the car and drove one block back from Main Street, then headed for the highway.

"Why didn't you just make me wait in the car like a good retriever?" Gertie asked.

"That whole bathroom thing would have been a problem," Ida Belle said.

I clutched the wheel as I turned the car onto the highway. Usually, I'd be joining in or at the very least laughing at their banter, but right now, I was too wired. Too ready to get answers and get everything back to normal. My issues with Carter were bothering me more than I was willing to let on, and with Ida Belle's safety and Hot Rod's health hanging in the balance, I couldn't clear my mind enough to make the tough decisions I needed to make.

I peered out the windshield, scanning the highway in front of me, looking for the SUV, but the road was clear. Ida Belle noticed my unusual level of concentration on the road and frowned.

"Do you think they screwed up?" she asked. "Miscalculated the fuel and they had enough to get away?"

"I doubt it," I said. "But maybe he never left town."

"Or maybe they have him already," Gertie said. "This is the Heberts we're talking about. I'm going to bet on efficiency where things like this are concerned."

She had a point. The Heberts were on the wrong side of the law when it came to most things, and speed and stealth were two of the things that kept them out of jail.

Still...I handed Ida Belle my phone. "Send a text to Little and ask if they have the thieves."

Even though we were 99 percent sure the Seal brothers were the guilty party, I was still using the generic description because if life in Sinful had taught me anything, it was that things were rarely as they appeared.

Ida Belle sent the text and watched the screen. A couple seconds later, my phone signaled an income text.

"He says they are en route to the storage facility," Ida Belle said.

I could hear the excitement in her voice and felt it as well. This was turning out to be surprisingly easy. All we had to do now was get information out of the thieves and prevent the Heberts from killing them when it was over.

Piece of cake.

It was the second item on that agenda that occupied most of my thoughts on the rest of the drive. By the time we arrived at the storage facility, I had decided on either a logical argument or begging if it came down to it. Prayer might be thrown in there as well.

A couple of cars were parked in front, including Big and Little's Hummer, but Ida Belle's SUV was nowhere in sight. I saw one of the Heberts' employees waving me toward the gate and drove through as he opened it.

"They must have put the SUV back in the storage unit," Ida Belle said.

I nodded. "Probably the best thing until we get all of this sorted out. For all we know, there might be more people than these guys looking for it."

"There's a cheerful thought," Ida Belle said. "When we figure out what that darn key is hiding, I'm taking out a full-page ad in every newspaper in the parish, letting everyone know that the treasure hunt is over."

"It's not the worst idea," I said. "Unless, of course, there's something else hidden in there and we didn't find it."

Ida Belle stared at me in dismay. "Don't even go there."

"Maybe you should paint it bright pink and put daisies on it or something," Gertie said. "Dudes would never steal a bright pink vehicle, even if it had a million dollars and ten naked supermodels hidden inside."

"That would defeat the purpose, since then I wouldn't drive it either," Ida Belle said.

"The unit door is partially open," I said, feeling my pulse tick up a notch.

Mannie was standing outside the unit and waved to us as I

pulled up and parked. I jumped out of the car and practically ran the couple of steps over to him.

"Everything went okay?" I asked.

Mannie grinned. "Like clockwork. They're waiting for you inside."

He leaned down and lifted the door the rest of the way, and we got our first look at the result of our successful plan.

Big and Little stood in the middle of the storage unit, two men duct-taped to chairs in front of them. I greeted the Heberts as I walked over and got my first personal look at the Seal brothers.

Identical twins. Five feet eleven. A hundred seventy-five pounds. Decent muscle content but lean. Smart enough to be scared. Even if they weren't duct-taped to chairs, I could take both of them with little effort.

Ida Belle and Gertie stepped up next to me and looked at the brothers. Gertie shook her head. "I can't believe after all these years, you still haven't learned a thing."

The brothers looked at the three of us and glanced back at Big and Little, clearly confused by the mix of people in front of them.

"Have they said anything?" I asked.

"Oh, they've said plenty," Big said. "But most of it was begging, so it doesn't count. We were waiting on you for the questioning. We are merely hosting your party."

"Look," one of the brothers said. "I think there's been a big mistake. We were supposed to be picking up an SUV for a friend of ours. I don't know what you think we've done, but you've got the wrong people."

Ida Belle narrowed her eyes. "So someone gave you keys to my house and my SUV? Who might that be, that you think had permission to give away my personal property and allow you to trespass into my home?"

"Willie LeDoux," the brother said.

"Oh," I said, "you mean that dead guy. Funny how dead people can talk and produce keys these days." I looked over at Mannie. "You find any keys in the SUV?"

"Hot-wired," Mannie said.

"Shocking," I said, and leaned forward to look at them. "Here's how it's going to go. We're going to ask you some questions and you're going to tell us everything we want to know. And if I'm satisfied with your answers, I'll ask the Heberts to go easy on you. Do you understand?"

They glanced at each other and I'm sure they were wondering who the hell I was, but since Big and Little were letting me run the show, they weren't about to do anything but nod.

"And don't bother lying," I said. "I can spot a liar a mile away. Are you ready to talk?"

They nodded again.

"Good," I said. "We know you're the Seal brothers, so let's start with first names."

The one who'd spoken earlier said, "I'm John. He's Bart."

I smiled. "See how easy that was? Now, tell me why you stole the SUV."

"We're looking for something hidden in it," John said. "A key."

Ida Belle, who'd been standing quietly by, apparently reached her breaking point. She stepped forward and pointed her finger in their faces. "I always thought the two of you were useless, but a good man is in the ER because of you, and if he doesn't make it, I'm going to personally see that you pay for it. *Without* benefit of a judge or jury."

Their eyes widened, and they both started shaking their heads.

"No!" John said. "We didn't do that to Hot Rod. I swear."

"Then who did?" Ida Belle asked. "Your friend Willie? I guess you killed him once you found out where the SUV was."

"We didn't kill Willie," John said. "He was our friend. Jesus. This is all wrong. You have it all wrong."

"Then you better get to straightening us out," I said. "Before we decide we've waited long enough."

"Okay, okay," John said, "but I have to go back some for it all to make sense."

"Go back to Genesis for all I care," I said. "Just spill it."

"We were running drugs through a club in New Orleans," John said. "And we were doing good. Everyone was making some money. But then this kid died. A cop's kid. And people said it was our drugs that did it, but I swear we ain't never seen that kid in the club before. Neither had Gary."

"Gary Thibodeaux?" I asked. "The club owner?"

John nodded. "Next thing you know, the cops are looking to bust us for drug trafficking and for killing this kid, but Gary said we was set up. That we was going down for murder. But we ain't killed nobody. We don't even know the kid. I swear it."

The ten-year sentence suddenly made sense. The DA might not have been able to directly tie the brothers to the death of the cop's kid, but with that theory floating around, the judge handed out the longest sentence he could manage.

"This cop have a name?" I asked.

"Patrick Marion," John said.

"Okay. So who set you up?" I asked.

John shrugged. "We don't know. But Gary found out somehow. He couldn't find us because we was laying low, but he found Willie at his job at a mechanic's shop. Gary told Willie he had proof but he wasn't taking his chances with the law getting things right. He had a way out of the country and he was taking it. He said he'd hid the proof and some money in a family crypt and he gave Willie the key to give to us."

"Then why didn't Willie do that?" I asked, still confused.

"Willie was freaking, you know?" John said. "Gary told him to hide the key until he could give it to us, so he hid it in one of the SUVs that was in for repair, figuring we'd boost it later and get the key."

"That is the dumbest thing I've ever heard," Ida Belle said. "You expect us to believe that Willie hid the key in a stranger's SUV instead of just putting it under a rock somewhere at his house?"

John shrugged. "He was high. It was past quitting time and he'd already had a hit."

"Willie was dipping into your product?" I asked.

"No," John said. "Willie wasn't dealing. Just me and Bart was. Willie was our friend from way back. We boosted cars together. That's all."

"If Willie was only a car boost," I asked, "then why did he go to prison for dealing?"

"He was in the club with us every night, and yeah, he might have handed someone a bag when we were really busy, but he didn't get paid for it. We sold him product at cost and took it out of our cut."

"So when the cops caught you boosting cars together," I said, "they assumed you were trying to leave town and took Willie down along with you."

John nodded and stared at the ground. "He was a good guy. I mean, yeah, he did too much drugs and all, but he didn't deserve to go to prison for it, and he damned sure didn't deserve to die."

"Okay, so if Willie hid the key in the Blazer, then why were you arrested boosting Escalades?"

"Willie forgot what vehicle he put the key in," John said.

"Jesus Christ," Big said, finally speaking. "My IQ has dropped just listening to this. Could someone be any more stupid?"

I shook my head. This was even more of a mess than I could have imagined. "This is your brain on drugs, gentlemen. So you three went up ten years for dealing. Why look for the evidence now? You've served your time."

"We needed money," John said. "We didn't know how much Gary left, but anything was more than we had."

"And we wanted to know," Bart said, breaking his silence. "We wanted to know who set us up."

"You wanted revenge," I said.

Bart shrugged. "So?"

He might not be bright, and he didn't fall into the decent guy category and probably never would, but I didn't blame him. I would have wanted to know too, and I was honest enough to admit that revenge would have been one of my top goals.

"Willie knew Hot Rod had bought the SUV," I said. "How did he find out?"

"He saw an auction paper with the SUV on it," John said.

I raised my eyebrows. "So the SUV that he couldn't remember ten years before suddenly stood out on a sheet of paper with a bunch of other vehicles on it?"

John nodded. "There was something about the grille. He said when he saw it, he knew immediately that was the right one. He still had some contacts in the business and found out Hot Rod bought the SUV."

"So Willie broke into Hot Rod's place," I said.

"Yeah, but not Sunday night," John said. "It must have been before then."

"How can you be certain of that?" Ida Belle asked.

I looked at the pained expression on the brothers' faces. "Because Willie was already dead, right?"

John looked down at the floor and nodded. "We had a message from him Sunday that he'd broken into Hot Rod's shop the night before. The SUV was gone but he knew who had bought it. He wanted us to come over that night and work out a plan to boost it."

"But someone else decided to chat with him first," I said. "Then why didn't that person go straight to Ida Belle's house and steal the SUV? Why go back to Hot Rod's place when the SUV wasn't there any longer?"

"I don't know," John said. "All we could figure was that Willie lied and told them the SUV was still at Hot Rod's place."

I nodded. "Thinking it would buy you time to steal the right vehicle. Willie didn't count on being killed."

I stepped closer to them and leaned down a bit. "Then if you two didn't shoot Willie and attempt to kill Hot Rod, who did?"

They glanced at each other, then back at me, and I could tell they didn't have an answer. Not a concrete one. Finally, John spoke.

"I guess whoever set us up," he said. "I mean, no one else would care, right?"

"I don't know. What happened to Gary Thibodeaux?" I asked.

John shook his head. "I guess he left like he told Willie."

I looked over at Big. "Can we speak for a minute outside?"

He nodded and everyone not duct-taped to a chair trailed outside the storage unit far enough away so that we wouldn't be overheard.

"Do you believe all of that?" Gertie asked.

"I think I do," I said, and looked over at Big and Little, who both nodded.

"Let's assume this Patrick Marion was looking into drug trafficking in the French Quarter, and one or more of the major players invited him to back off," I said. "Assuming he refused, killing his kid is one way to change his mind. Most people have more than one loved one to lose, and when they find out just how serious the warning was, they usually take heed."

"Filthy animals," Big said. "It's why we hate drug traffickers. They have no code."

"Family, especially children," Little said, "should never be made part of business, but unfortunately, the scenario you set forward is entirely plausible and likely exactly what happened."

"It had to be their supplier, right?" Ida Belle asked. "He's taking heat from the cop, and the brothers were expendable."

Big nodded. "That makes the most sense."

"Maybe," I said, "but there's also the cop. If he thought there was a chance the brothers were telling the truth and it was a setup, he'd also have a vested interest in knowing who the real killer was."

"But would a cop do that sort of thing?" Gertie asked.

"Cops go rogue," Ida Belle said. "Having your kid killed is enough to do it."

Little tapped on his phone. "Doesn't appear to be a lot on Marion on the Internet, but I can make some calls tomorrow and see if I can find out anything." He turned his phone around to us. "It's an old picture, but here he is."

We leaned forward to look at the image, and I frowned. The guy in the picture was around forty and completely average-looking, but I couldn't shake the feeling that I'd seen him somewhere before. I started rolling through the events since Monday morning and gasped.

"That's the deputy," I said. "The one from Mudbug who was guarding Hot Rod's place."

Everyone stared at me.

"You're sure?" Big asked.

"Yeah," I said. "He's older now, of course, but that was him. I'm certain."

Big shook his head. "Convenient that he just happened to be on location."

"Not convenient," I said. "Carter said this guy called and offered help in case they needed some extra hands. The local law enforcement likes to avoid calling in the state if they can help it."

"But if he's the one who broke in the night before," Gertie asked, "why would he come back to the scene of the crime?"

"He didn't find what he was looking for," I said. "Or he wanted a solid reason for his DNA to be at the scene."

Little nodded. "And if he wasn't the one who broke in before, he might have been hoping to find evidence of who did."

"So now there are two," Ida Belle said. "The cop and the supplier."

"Then let's find out who the supplier was," I said.

We all trailed back into the storage unit. The brothers had moved beyond looking uneasy and were drifting toward panic. They probably thought we were outside discussing whether or not to kill them.

"Who was the supplier?" I asked.

John shook his head. "We don't know."

"You have to know," I said. "Someone gave you drugs in return for cash."

"We only dealt with Gary," John said. "He didn't want to work the crowd, so he hired us to do it."

More likely Gary wanted his own plausible deniability if the brothers were busted. If the cops couldn't find anyone who bought drugs directly from Gary, it would be his word against the brothers if there was an arrest.

"You never saw anyone?" I asked. "Gary never mentioned a name?"

"I saw a guy once," John said, "and asked who he was, but Gary said he was just a delivery boy. Honestly, I don't think he wanted to know that kind of stuff. He always said the less everybody knew, the better."

I frowned. It was certainly possible that Gary didn't know who was ultimately running the show, especially since it appeared he had a desire to keep his own hands clean. Maybe being framed for murder had caused him to take a closer look into things he should have long before. Maybe that's why he had evidence to hide.

"Okay," I said, "let's just say we take your story at face value for now. The only way we keep believing it is if we catch the real killer. That means we need the evidence that Gary hid. So what's the name on the crypt?"

"We don't know," John said. "If we knew that, we would have

just broken the lock on it. We figure Gary told Willie when he gave him the key, but..."

"Willie forgot." I sighed.

"Do you at least know what cemetery?" I asked.

John nodded. "Metairie."

Ida Belle shook her head. "It had to be one of the biggest."

"Yeah," John said, "between that and the name...I mean, do you know how many Thibodeaux are buried there? We started hunting down the Thibodeaux crypts and breaking in but on the second night someone took a couple shots at us."

I looked over at Ida Belle and Gertie. "Does that cemetery have night patrol?"

"I don't think so," Ida Belle said. "But I haven't been out there in at least a decade."

"Who was doing the shooting?" I asked.

"I don't know," John said, "but we wasn't sticking around to find out. We figured if we found the key then we could go proper-like during the day."

I struggled a bit to keep from laughing at the use of the word "proper." There was absolutely nothing proper about any of this. If anything it was a campaign for anti-proper.

I looked back at Big. "Well?"

"You're the producer of this show," Big said. "How would you like to proceed?"

He didn't have to ask me twice. I already knew what I was doing, and a hundred bucks said Gertie and Ida Belle were right there with me.

"I think that if you're willing to host these two for a bit longer, a trip to Metairie cemetery is in order. This ten-year-old mystery ends now."

CHAPTER TWENTY-ONE

I awakened far earlier than I should have, especially given that I hadn't gone to bed until almost 4:00 a.m. By the time I finished questioning the Seal brothers and making plans with Big for our journey to Metairie cemetery, hours had passed. Fortunately, we'd gotten back into the house without incident and it didn't appear that Carter was aware we'd ever been gone.

I took a quick shower and headed downstairs for much-needed coffee. Despite the fact that it was only 8:00 a.m., Gertie and Ida Belle were both sitting in the kitchen, looking the way I felt. Given the amount of ground we had to cover, literally, it wasn't a good sign. I lifted a hand and headed for the coffeepot, then plopped into my chair with a full mug.

"So," I said after I'd had my first few sips. "Who's looking forward to walking miles through a cemetery?"

Gertie grimaced. "My knees just cringed. Both of them."

"Well, you better load up on Ace bandages and Aleve," Ida Belle said. "Either that or consider sitting this one out."

"No way!" Gertie said.

"I didn't figure," Ida Belle said. "You know there could be

shooting, right? The Seal brothers said someone took shots at them."

"Which is why we're going in daylight," Gertie said. "And with backup. Ohhhhhh, maybe we should go in disguise."

"What kind of disguise does one wear to the cemetery?" I asked.

"Nuns would be good," Gertie said. "You can carry all kinds of weapons under those robes."

"Absolutely not," Ida Belle said. "Remember what happened the last time you tried to run when you were dressed as a nun?"

"That could have happened to anyone," Gertie said.

"No costumes," I said. "Ida Belle's right. They inhibit running. We need to dress for speed. I'm hoping it doesn't come to that, but we know better than to assume. So everyone needs to wear their most comfortable and coolest attire and best running shoes."

"But what about the weapons part?" Gertie asked.

"We have no need to bring an armory," I said. "We've got Mannie."

"That's true," Gertie said. "He's sorta like having a tank along with you."

Ida Belle's phone rang, and she looked down at it and frowned. "It's Myrtle. She should be in bed asleep."

Myrtle had worked the four to midnight shift the day before, so if she was calling this early, something was wrong. I watched Ida Belle's expression shift from puzzled to concerned and prayed that whatever it was didn't interfere with our scheduled trip. So far, the Heberts had made good on their word not to harm the Seal brothers until we could sort everything out, but if left to their own devices for too long, I worried about the brothers' outlook.

Ida Belle disconnected the call and put her phone down on the table. "Ralph committed suicide."

"What?"

"Oh my God!"

Gertie and I spoke at the same time.

"Why? How?" Gertie asked. "Did it happen last night? Is that why Myrtle knows?"

"The temp they have filling in days was sick," Ida Belle said, "so Myrtle had to cover this morning. Apparently, Lucinda was trying to get a hold of Ralph but he wouldn't return her calls. She got worried and went over. She has a key."

"Oh no," Gertie said. "Lucinda found him?"

Ida Belle nodded. "Gunshot to the temple, sitting in his office chair."

Gertie shook her head. "Myrtle told me last week that she overheard Ralph on his cell phone talking to someone about an audit. She said he sounded worried. I wonder if that had something to do with it?"

I frowned. "Did Myrtle say how long he'd been dead?"

Ida Belle looked at me. "No. Why?"

I shrugged. "Maybe nothing."

"With you, it's never nothing," Ida Belle said. "Out with it."

"I don't have anything concrete," I said. "It just feels a little strange, the timing of it all. The Seal brothers get out of prison, ask Ralph for money, and then Ralph kills himself? I mean, I've met the guy for twenty seconds, so you'd have to tell me if you think this sounds in line with what you know about him."

Ida Belle frowned and looked at Gertie, whose brow was scrunched in concentration.

"I suppose you don't ever really know a person," Ida Belle said, "but if you'd asked me before today if I thought Ralph was the type who'd kill himself, I would have said absolutely not."

Gertie nodded. "He's never struck me as unstable. A bore, absolutely, but most people don't kill themselves because others find them boring. But what about the audit? I'm no accountant, but could something be so wrong that he pulled the trigger?"

"Maybe," I said. "People have definitely lost their minds over the IRS, but what's the worst thing that can happen—he goes to jail for doing hinky things on people's taxes? Shouldn't he wait for a conviction before he goes the ultimate checkout route?"

"You don't think the Seal brothers killed him, do you?" Ida Belle asked.

"They're desperate," I said, "and not very smart, but I think they're capable of killing someone, especially if they feel they're backed into a corner."

Ida Belle nodded, her expression grim. "Then maybe we should have a visit with Lucinda before we head to the cemetery."

———

IDA BELLE KNOCKED TWICE before we heard movement inside Lucinda's house. The door opened slowly and she peered out at us, her eyes red, her face puffy.

"We heard what happened," Ida Belle said. "I'm so sorry."

Lucinda nodded. "Thank you. Do you want to come in? I just made a fresh pot of coffee."

"Just for a minute," Ida Belle said. "We don't want to be in your way."

Lucinda stepped back and allowed us in, and we followed her back to the kitchen.

"You sit down," Gertie said. "I'll get the coffee."

Lucinda moved to the chair like a zombie and sank down into it. "I appreciate you checking on me. Carter, God bless him, offered to stay with me, but the boy's got a job to do. He said he was going to send his mama over when she got back from a doctor's appointment in New Orleans."

"He's a good deputy," Gertie said as she placed the coffee on the table. "And a good man."

Lucinda nodded. "I guess I'm still in shock. I mean, I know what I saw, but I can't reconcile it in my head."

"Of course you can't," Ida Belle said. "Anyone who knew Ralph would never expect something like this. He's just not the type."

Lucinda nodded. "I think that's why I'm having such a hard time with it."

Gertie finished serving and took a seat next to Lucinda. "I heard through the grapevine that Ralph was worried about an audit. Could that have had something to do with it?"

"Carter asked me the same thing," Lucinda said, "but I don't know anything about an audit. Besides which, Ralph's been dealing with that sort of thing for over thirty years. I'd think if he was going to collapse over it, it would have happened before now."

"You don't think..." I looked over at Ida Belle and Gertie, then back at Lucinda. "I mean, you were saying the other day how his nephews wanted money and he wouldn't give them any..."

Lucinda's eyes widened. "I hadn't even thought. Carter said there was no sign of forced entry and the gun was right there beside him on the floor, but I suppose..."

She shook her head. "No. I'm not going to think that. Carter will do his investigation and maybe whatever was wrong will come out. Maybe Ralph had an aneurysm and didn't know what he was doing. I saw something like that on the news once."

"Did Carter say when it might have happened?" I asked.

Lucinda shook her head. "I called him yesterday morning asking if he'd take a look at the outlet in my bathroom. Ralph is—was—handy with that sort of thing. I thought it strange that he never called me back, but sometimes he gets busy with client work. But when he didn't answer again this morning, I decided to check on him. Past a certain age, you never know...heart and all."

Gertie patted her hand. "You did everything you could. Chances are, he was already gone before you called the first time."

Lucinda nodded and wiped her nose with a tissue. "I know you're probably right, but I just keep thinking if I'd gone over sooner, I could have done something."

"That's a natural thing to think," Ida Belle said. "But I don't think there's anything you could have done. Please don't stress over it."

"You're all too kind," Lucinda said. "I really appreciate the clear thinking. It makes me feel a little better."

"Well," Ida Belle said, "if you don't need us for anything, we're going to get out of here and let you get some rest. You look exhausted."

Lucinda nodded. "I don't feel so great."

"If we can do anything to help with the arrangements," Gertie said, "please let us know. I'll bake that chicken casserole you like and bring it over."

"Thank you," Lucinda said. "Thank you so much."

We headed out of the house and climbed in my Jeep. As I pulled away from the curb, I looked over at Ida Belle. "Well?" I asked.

"I was about to ask you the same thing," she said.

"This is what I think," I said. "I think Ralph was already dead yesterday morning when Lucinda called because he doesn't strike me as the type of guy who would ignore a call from his cousin for an entire day, especially an older female cousin living alone."

"I think you're right on that," Ida Belle said.

"If he was already dead yesterday morning," Gertie said, "that means the Seal brothers could have done it."

"No sign of forced entry," Ida Belle reminded her.

"He would have let them in the house," Gertie said. "It would have never occurred to Ralph that he'd be in any physical danger from the brothers. He just didn't think that way."

"That's probably true enough," Ida Belle said. "So where does that leave us?"

I shook my head. "I don't know. I have a feeling it would be a waste of time to ask the brothers if they popped their uncle, but I'd also like to see their reaction. Let's keep this under our hat for now and we'll address it when we get back from the cemetery."

Ida Belle nodded. "I hope we find that crypt and this all ends today. The body count is rising too fast for my taste."

"Mine too," I agreed.

I wanted to believe that the logical line of thought was the way things had gone down, but there was an unsettling feeling I had that I couldn't get rid of. Finally, I pulled the Jeep over to the curb and yanked my cell phone out of my pocket. Before I could change my mind, I sent a text.

Ida Belle and Gertie were both staring at me with somewhat surprised expressions.

I handed Ida Belle my phone, and she read out loud the text I'd sent to Little Hebert to Gertie.

Can you do an asset check on Ralph Lynch?

Their eyes widened.

"You don't think?" Ida Belle asked.

"I think there's more to it than we can see," I said. "Maybe Ralph is only some boring accountant caught up in a shitstorm with his troubled nephews. That's probably the case, but I'd like to be sure."

"Or maybe there's more to that audit rumor than Lucinda thinks," Gertie said. "Only it wasn't about a client."

I nodded. "Exactly. Either way, I'd like to know if Ralph had a good reason to check out or if it's more likely someone checked him out."

CHAPTER TWENTY-TWO

It was almost eleven before we arrived at the cemetery, and the party was a bit bigger than I'd originally planned for. In addition to Mannie, Big and Little had both decided to join us, although Big was quick to say that he would be waiting in the Hummer, performing lookout duties. Ida Belle and I tried to convince Gertie to remain behind with him, but she was insistent that her knees were better and she wanted to be there when we found the goods.

I just hoped that if we located the crypt, there was something inside to find.

So many things could have happened in ten years. Gary could have changed his mind and removed the evidence. Someone else could have entered the crypt and found it. A storm could have taken out the crypt and the evidence along with it.

Mannie had printed a layout of the cemetery and mapped the most efficient route through the maze of crypts. We were just about to head out when Big received a phone call and signaled for us to hold up. When he hung up, he looked at me and smiled.

"One day," he said, "you're going to have to tell me your secret. Your friend Ralph had an interest in several real estate holding companies. Buried in a maze of ownership structure, of course, but my people were able to get through it. The properties were bought and sold over ten years ago, but the estimated value of them today is about ten million."

"Holy crap!" Gertie said. "That's some serious assets for a small-town accountant."

Big nodded. "Apparently, the IRS thinks so as well, especially since he only reported a couple hundred thousand in profit from the sales."

I didn't even bother to wonder how Big had gotten information from the IRS. Clearly he had sources everywhere.

"So it looks like the audit story might have held some truth," I said.

"Yes," Ida Belle said, "but the bigger question is where he got the money to buy the properties to begin with."

Big nodded. "Indeed. It might also interest you to know that Ralph is the accountant of record for a man rumored to be running the drug trade for one of the families in New Orleans."

"Do you think the brothers knew that?" Gertie asked.

"I'm going to guess that they didn't," I said. "Or they would have tried to get Ralph to use his connection to get them out of the country before they went to trial."

Little nodded. "I can't imagine that Ralph would offer up the names of his questionable clientele, especially to the brothers, but that doesn't mean they couldn't have found out at some point. Prison is filled with all sorts of interesting information."

I shook my head. It just kept getting messier. "All of this cannot be coincidence."

"No," Big agreed. "It's all tied together somehow."

"Maybe the simplest explanation is the correct one," Little said. "That the Seal brothers are behind it all. Maybe the only thing hidden in that crypt is a pile of money and the rest is an elaborate story to throw us off track."

"Time to find out," I said.

"I will watch all incoming traffic and alert you to anyone entering the cemetery," Big said. "But I wouldn't count on the parties we seek strolling in through the front gate. It goes without saying that you should watch your back."

Big headed for the Hummer and we separated into three groups. Ida Belle, Gertie, and I went first, scanning the crypts. I'd originally figured we would move at a deliberate but unrushed pace and maybe even take some pictures as we went so that we looked like tourists, but given the heat and humidity, the place was empty. Besides, if someone other than the Seal brothers was behind some of this mess, they probably already knew who Ida Belle was. And then there was the fact that Little, in his dress pants and button-up shirt, and Mannie, who resembled a cage fighter in both physique and dress, didn't exactly blend.

But ultimately, it didn't matter. The bottom line was that if someone wanted to take us out, it was five against one or two. At least, I hoped it wasn't more than two. I had no doubts about my ability or Mannie's, but I didn't want anyone else getting caught in the cross fire.

The slowest part of the process was the actual walking. Gertie was doing a decent job keeping up with Ida Belle and me. Quite frankly, better than I'd anticipated, but the cemetery was huge and the heat rose with every step we took. I glanced back occasionally and spotted Mannie some distance behind us, but within sight and definitely within firing range. Little had ventured onto the next row and was keeping pace with us there.

In the first two hours of walking, I tried the key in fifteen different Thibodeaux crypts, but so far, had come up empty. But we kept marching along, me clutching the key and Ida Belle a small can of WD-40 to grease up old locks. I had just suggested a water break when Little walked in between two crypts and approached us.

"We have a problem," he said. "The vehicle transporting the

brothers from the storage unit to the warehouse hit a deer. I'm afraid they've escaped."

"Escaped?" Ida Belle said. "I'm surprised your guys didn't just shoot them."

"They were both knocked unconscious in the wreck," Little said, looking aggravated. "I tell them to wear their seat belts but no one listens. Now it will be policy and I won't get any argument."

"Okay," I said. "Let's not panic. How long ago did it happen?"

"About an hour ago," he said.

"And how far away were they from somewhere that they could boost a car?" I asked.

"A couple miles," he said. "Their hands were still duct-taped, but the tape on their feet was removed in order to get them into the vehicle. I'm afraid they also lifted two pistols off of my drivers."

"Jesus," I said. "They know where we are, so we can bet they're headed this way and they're both armed."

"It's still two against five," Gertie said.

"Which in an open battle would be great odds," I said, "but given how easy it is to sneak around here unseen, it wouldn't be hard for them to come up on us and pick a couple of people off to help level the playing field."

Little nodded. "I'm really sorry about this. I feel we've failed you. How would you like to proceed? We can call the entire thing off until we've acquired the brothers again."

I shook my head. "We'd be looking over our shoulders every second anyway since they've probably guessed we have the key. I'd rather get it over with now. But anyone who is not completely on board with that plan is free to leave now. Gertie? You're an easy target with those bad knees."

"Actually," Gertie said, "I'm probably no target at all. They'll see me as no threat and go for the bigger players."

"She's right," Little said, "assuming the brothers use any fore-thought before they open fire, but that's questionable."

"I don't care," Gertie said. "I'm seeing this to the end."

"Me too," Ida Belle said.

Little nodded. "Mannie and I will maintain position as we have the past two hours. Big has arranged for more backup and it's on the way. Everyone needs to keep a close watch, and if you see anything, yell. If Mannie or I yell, find cover."

Little retreated back a row over and we continued our search of the crypts, the water break completely abandoned. The urgency we'd felt before was now multiplied by a thousand. I was certain the brothers were desperate and had no doubt about their ability to use the weapons they'd acquired. The slower, more deliberate walking was abandoned. I walked near one line of crypts and Ida Belle on the other side, scanning the names as we went. Gertie walked down the middle of the row, playing lookout. Fifteen minutes later, I spotted a crypt with "Thibodeaux" etched on the door. I signaled to Ida Belle, who came over to spray the ancient lock with WD-40, then I stuck the key in, expecting the same result as before.

But this time, it turned.

"This is it," I said.

Gertie waved at Little, who started toward us. I leaned against the stone door and gave it a shove. It barely moved, so I put some more back into it and tried again. This time the door pushed open. Little appeared behind me, gun drawn.

"Check it out," he said. "I'll stand guard."

I stepped inside the crypt, followed by Ida Belle and Gertie. The sunlight from outside streamed in, illuminating part of the small structure, but the back of it was still too dim to see every-thing. I pulled a penlight out of my pocket and shone it on the back of the crypt.

"There," Ida Belle said, pointing to the left rear corner.

I directed the light to the corner and saw a small duffel bag on a shelf in the corner. We hurried over, and I handed Ida Belle the penlight. I opened it and we peered down at the stacks of bundled hundreds.

"Holy crap," Gertie said. "There must be twenty thousand dollars in there."

"Anything else?" Ida Belle said.

I located a zippered pocket on the side and was just about to open it when I heard gunfire. The first shot sounded as though it was some distance from us, but it could have been muffled by the stone sides of the crypt. The second shot, however, ricocheted off the side of the crypt, sending Little scrambling inside.

He pulled out his phone, then cursed. It was the first time I'd ever seen the highly composed and polished Little lose his cool.

"The stone is blocking cell signal," he said.

"Surely Mannie is on the way," Gertie said.

"There are two shooters," I said. "The first shot was probably fired at Mannie."

Little nodded. "I think it hit him in the leg. I saw him go down and was trying to locate the shooter when the second shot came. No way the same person fired both shots. There's no line of sight for both of them."

"What do we do?" Ida Belle said.

I blew out a breath. With only one way out of the crypt, we were sitting ducks. The shooters could simply position themselves at the edge of a couple of nearby crypts and pick us off when we stepped outside. But on the flip side, no one could enter the crypt without us taking them out. It was officially a standoff.

"Get as close to the front wall as possible," I said. "Two on each side, next to each other. If someone steps in, identify and open fire if it's not one of our party. Do not shift your position to the side or you risk shooting the person next to you."

If Little was surprised by my handing out orders like a military commando, he didn't show it. I grabbed the bag and moved to the side next to Gertie and put the bag in front of her. "Give me your gun and check the inside pocket," I said.

Gertie handed me her pistol and crouched down to unzip the pocket. She dug around for a bit, then pulled out a USB. "Pay dirt," she said. "Maybe they were telling the truth."

"Maybe," I said.

I handed her gun back to her and took the USB, tucking it in my jeans pocket. Assuming it was the Seal brothers outside, maybe they would be happy to take the money and leave, thinking the evidence was still inside the bag. All we needed was a small window of opportunity to escape the crypt.

"We know you're inside," John Seal's voice sounded outside the crypt. "If you come out, we'll shoot. We've already shot one of your guys."

Little's jaw clenched and I knew he was worried about Mannie. So was I, but the quickest way to help him was to get out of here alive and get help.

I stepped to the edge of the crypt door. "What do you want?" I asked.

"Throw the money outside and to the left of crypt," John said. "Lean just far enough out to toss it. If we see a gun, we open fire."

"What if there hadn't been any money?" Gertie asked.

"Then we'd have been in a world of hurt," I said, and reached over to zip up the bag.

Gertie's eyes widened. "You're not going to give it to them, are you?"

"That's exactly what I'm going to do," I said. "The only way they're leaving is with this bag. If they leave without engaging, we can get out of here and get help for Mannie. Otherwise it's a shoot-out, and I don't like our odds."

I picked up the bag and stood at the edge of the doorway. Little moved up beside me, his pistol in the ready position.

"I'm about to step into the doorway to throw the bag," I yelled as I shoved my pistol in my waistband.

"Just do what I said," John said, "and no one else gets hurt."

Praying he was telling the truth, I stepped into the doorway and swung the duffel bag back, then slung it out of the crypt as far as I could. The instant the bag left my hand, I ducked back inside the crypt and pulled my pistol out.

A couple seconds later, I heard footsteps outside the crypt, then they grew more faint. I counted to ten and listened again, but this time, it was silent.

"Do you think they're gone?" Ida Belle asked.

"There's only one way to find out," I said.

CHAPTER TWENTY-THREE

I pulled my gun up to ready position and swung around the doorway, ready to fire. I scanned the aisle and the nearby crypts but didn't see any sign of movement. The duffel bag was gone and not even so much as a leaf stirred in the heat.

I turned around and looked at them. "Go find Mannie and get him help."

"Where are you going?" Gertie asked.

"After the Seal brothers," I said.

"Why?" Gertie asked. "You have the USB."

I nodded. "And when they don't find any evidence in that bag, they might come looking for it. I really don't want to play hide-and-seek with them any longer."

"I'm coming with you," Ida Belle said.

"Fine," I said, "but Gertie, you go with Little. He might need help."

I took off in the direction I'd heard the footsteps go, Ida Belle right behind. A couple crypts away from where I'd thrown the duffel bag, I spotted a shoe print in the dirt.

"This way," I said, and slipped in between the crypts to move to another row. When I got to the end of the crypt, I paused and peered around it. About fifty yards away, at the end of the row, I saw John Seal round the corner with the duffel bag.

"I see him," I said. "Come on."

I took off at a dead run for the end of the row and could hear Ida Belle behind me. When I got to the end of the row, I slid to a stop and looked around the last crypt as Ida Belle ran up beside me.

"The fence runs as far as I can see," I said, "but there's a gate about twenty yards up. I don't see him anywhere, so I'm guessing that's where he went, but there's a tall hedge blocking my view of what's on the other side of the fence."

Ida Belle nodded. "What about Bart?"

"No sign of him, but he might be ahead. Keep your eyes and ears open."

I slipped around the crypt and hurried to the gate. I looked over the gate and saw a small parking lot and the Seal brothers standing next to what was likely another stolen car. Two other cars occupied the lot but both were empty. I took all of this in with a single glance and whirled back around behind the hedge, signaling Ida Belle next to me.

"They're about twenty feet away," I said. "It's a parking lot."

"You got the money?" Bart said.

I heard the zipper on the duffel and a couple seconds later, John said, "Yeah, it's here."

"How much?" Bart asked.

"Enough to get out of here," John said. "It has to be."

"What about the evidence?" Bart asked.

"I don't know," John said. "We'll look later. It doesn't matter anymore. There's too many people after us and if we don't get out of here, we're going right back to prison because they'll pin Willie and Hot Rod on us."

I looked at Ida Belle and lifted one eyebrow. She knew exactly what I was asking. If the Seal brothers were going to take the money and run, maybe we just let them go. I didn't think they'd killed Willie or attacked Hot Rod, and we were safer if they left. I could find a way to get the evidence to the proper authorities, and if a story broke, maybe they'd see it on television and wouldn't come back. If not, maybe the threat of the Heberts looking for them would be enough. They *had* shot Mannie.

Which was a whole other problem.

"What about Big?" I whispered.

"You're a librarian. I'm a senior citizen. They got away."

It suddenly occurred to me that she was right. Granted, the Heberts had seen me somewhat in action and knew I was more capable than the average person, but they didn't know the extent of my ability and they didn't know anything at all about Ida Belle's military past.

But it bothered me. Could I just let them walk away? Yeah, they'd gone to prison for ten years, probably for something they didn't do, but they were drug dealers and generally all-around useless people. That wasn't likely to change. I pulled my pistol out. I couldn't do it. Ida Belle shook her head and smiled, and I felt my heart tug. She was the best friend a girl could ask for.

I was just about to burst through the gate when I heard a voice I hadn't expected to hear. One that had me frozen in my tracks.

"I'm afraid I'm going to have to take that bag," Lucinda said.

I looked over at Ida Belle, who was doing her own statue impression, her eyes wide.

"Mom?" John said.

Mom!?

I looked at Ida Belle. What the hell was going on here? Just when we thought we had most of it straightened out, the entire world turned upside down. I couldn't risk looking through the gate again. I was completely exposed that way, so instead, I reached into the bushes and tried to push some of the branches aside so that I could see where Lucinda was standing, but no matter how many ways I moved the thick green leaves, I couldn't see through the dense foliage.

"I tried so hard with you boys," Lucinda said, "but you've been more trouble than you were ever worth. All those years I did so well in the business, but you two didn't inherit one ounce of my ability. I'm not going to let you take me down. I've waited too long for certain things and just when they were falling in line, you two showed up, looking for that damned key again."

"*You* set us up?" John asked.

"How could you?" Bart asked.

"To save myself, of course," Lucinda said. "You shouldn't have drawn attention to yourselves with the drugs. You don't have the skill set for what you were attempting. If you'd kept boosting cars, things might have been different. Now drop your guns and kick them to the side. Careful now. You know I'm quick with the trigger."

I heard the guns hit the ground, and Ida Belle whispered, "Can you get a shot?"

I shook my head. "Can't see through the bushes. I'll have to chance it over the gate."

No way was Lucinda getting away with this. She was the one who'd stolen the vehicles from Hot Rod's place, and I'd bet anything Ralph had been her accomplice. The brothers had probably told their uncle and mother about the evidence Gary left for them, thinking they would help find the key. They had no idea they were feeding information to the enemy.

When I had some time to reflect, I would be properly sickened and outraged over the entire thing, but now, I had to take Lucinda down before she killed the brothers and left them on the hook for even more crimes she'd committed. I clenched my pistol and nodded at Ida Belle, then eased to the very edge of the bushes and started the countdown.

One. Two.

I never got to three.

Two shots rang out and I whirled around the gate, gun leveled and ready to fire at Lucinda, but she was on the ground, blood seeping from her chest and a hole in the middle of her forehead. The Seal brothers were staring in shock, hands empty, so I scanned the parking lot, figuring one of the Hebert clan had flanked them.

But it was Patrick Marion who appeared over the hood of a parked vehicle, leveling a pistol at the brothers. I spun back around, hoping that Marion had been concentrating on the brothers and hadn't seen me, but I didn't hold out much hope. The last thing I needed was a deputy putting me in his report. Especially this report. A scandal was going to be big news, and I was willing to bet that there was so much more to this one that we didn't know.

"You know who I am?" Marion asked.

"You're that cop," John said. "The one whose kid died. We told you we was set up."

"And I believed you, but I had no proof," Marion said. "Ms. Morrow and company, I know you're there behind the bushes. I followed you here. I'm not interested in anyone else getting hurt or quite frankly, in arresting anyone. All I want is the evidence."

"It's supposed to be in the bag," John said.

"What do you think?" Ida Belle whispered.

"I think we're screwed regardless," I said. "He's a cop. He can show up to arrest us at any time."

I shoved my pistol in my waistband and stepped out from behind the bushes and into clear view. "They don't have the evidence," I said. "I removed a USB from the bag before I gave it to them. I was going to turn it over to law enforcement so the people looking for it stopped targeting my friend."

Marion nodded. "I figured as much, especially with you bundled up with Deputy LeBlanc. Did you know my boy never did drugs before that night? Hair tests proved it. They found GHB in his system."

I shook my head. "Someone drugged him, then shot him up with bad heroin to make it look like an OD."

"Yes," Marion said. "To the cops it looked like any other drunk college student tragedy, but I knew better. I'd received the threats, but I didn't listen, and my son paid for it. I couldn't risk the rest of my family. Not with nothing else to go on."

"So you stopped your investigation," I said.

"And left the New Orleans PD. Moved to a small town and ran herd over drunks, wondering for ten years if that evidence really existed. If these two were telling the truth about being set up."

"Now you know," I said. "I'm going to remove the USB from my pocket."

He nodded, and I pulled it out and placed it on top of the gatepost.

"Get out of here," he said. "You don't want to be caught up in this mess. It would take over your lives for a long time."

"What are you going to do with them?" I asked.

He stared at them for several uncomfortable seconds.

"Nothing," he said finally. "They served more time than they were due for their actual crimes." He looked at the brothers. "Take the bag and get in your car and leave. I don't ever want to see you anywhere in Louisiana again."

The brothers' eyes widened in surprise. "You don't have to worry about that," John said. "Once we get out, we ain't ever setting foot here again."

John moved forward hesitantly and grabbed the bag of money. He hurried back to the car and they climbed inside, their expressions clearly showing their disbelief at this unexpected good fortune. He started the car and burned rubber leaving the parking lot.

When they were out of sight, Marion looked at me again. "I meant what I said. Get out of here. I don't want to file a report including civilians, and I'm going to guess you don't want to be in a report that includes information about you consorting with the

Heberts. Nor do I want people to know that I just let the Seal brothers go."

"What do I tell people if they ask?" I asked.

"Whatever you want to tell them," he said. "But as far as I'm concerned, we never met."

I nodded and whirled around, pulling Ida Belle's arm. "Let's get out of here before the cavalry shows up."

"What are we going to tell the Heberts?" she asked.

"You're going to tell them that you couldn't keep up and lost me."

"What about you? Little knew you had the USB."

"The Heberts don't care about the USB or what it contained."

"They care that Bart Seal shot Mannie."

"I'll figure it out. Come on, hustle before the police show up. All this gunfire is bound to bring law enforcement, and I don't want to have to give a statement, even one that says I didn't see anything."

We ran all the way back to the main parking lot. It was a good half mile, but neither of us slowed until we reached my Jeep. The Hummer was gone, and we figured they'd taken Mannie for help. I tore out of the parking lot and my cell phone buzzed as soon as we pulled onto the highway. It was Gertie.

"Where are you?" she asked.

"Just got on the interstate. How's Mannie?"

"Fine," she said. "Bart is a lousy shot, thank God. The bullet grazed his thigh but he hit his head on a crypt when he fell. He was just coming to when Little and I got there. Did you get the Seal brothers?"

"They got away," I said, and looked over at Ida Belle. "I'll tell you about it when I see you. Are you going to the warehouse?"

"Yes, we're halfway there. See you soon."

I disconnected and put the phone in the cup holder. I pressed the accelerator a little harder, anxious to get my conversation with the Heberts over with. I was contemplating lying to people who lied for a living. Granted, I'd done it all the time during missions, but that was always to people I didn't like. Targets. I was actually kind of fond of Big and Little, even though it probably wasn't in my best interest to be.

"You can pull this off," Ida Belle said, cluing in to my thoughts.

"I hope so."

———

LITTLE LET us into the warehouse and we went straight upstairs to Big's office. Mannie was lying on a couch, his leg wrapped up and an ice pack on his head. He smiled and waved when we came in, so I guessed he was feeling all right, considering. Little motioned us to our usual seats, where Gertie was already perched and drinking a double serving of whiskey.

"I'll have what she's having," Ida Belle said as she dropped into the chair.

"Me too," I said.

Little poured the drinks and Big looked across the desk at us. "I understand the Seal brothers got away?"

I took a drink of the whiskey and nodded. I'd already decided that the best thing to do was to tell the truth. The Heberts might not be happy about the Seal brothers getting away, but surely they would understand why I wasn't interested in getting in a shoot-out with a cop.

"I caught up to them at a parking lot," I said. "I lost Ida Belle somewhere along the way."

"I couldn't keep up," Ida Belle said. "Maybe thirty years ago…"

Big nodded. "I understand completely. So what happened?"

I started filling them in on everything, Lucinda, Marion, his story about his son, and how he'd followed us to the cemetery hoping for the evidence.

"You gave him the USB?" Little asked.

"I couldn't see any reason not to," I said. "We didn't need it and he did, especially to prove why he shot Lucinda. Just saying she had a gun wouldn't be enough to get him off, and although I think the cops will eventually uncover everything, it will probably take a while."

Little nodded. "So you think Lucinda was behind killing Willie and attacking Hot Rod?"

"Yes. The brothers were shocked that Lucinda set them up," I said. "That was apparent."

"And she was their mother?" Gertie asked. "What about Carol?"

"I have no idea," I said. "But I'm sure it will all come out eventually."

"So this cop let the Seal brothers go," Big mused. "Why?"

"He said because they'd already served more time than their crimes called for," I said. "I don't know. Maybe he felt a little sorry for them that their own mother had set them up. I have to admit, I felt a little horror and a lot of repulsion myself."

Big shook his head. "It's an amazing twist, and one that I'll admit I never saw coming."

"Me either," Little said. "And I'm usually pretty good at spotting such things."

"I'm sorry they got away," I said to Big. "I know you want to address them shooting Mannie and shooting at Little, but I didn't feel I had much of an option."

"You didn't have any option," Big said, "unless you were crazy enough to exchange gunfire with a cop. You're a risk taker, but not stupid. Besides, I tend to agree with Marion. The brothers have probably suffered enough, and Mannie will recover quickly from his injury."

Relief coursed through me. It was over.

We'd gotten away with it all. Again.

CHAPTER TWENTY-FOUR

Three days later, I was reading a book in my hammock and hoping to get in a nap when Carter walked into my backyard and took a seat in the lawn chair. Since the showdown in the cemetery, things had gotten crazy. Marion had gone public with his story, and the video contained on the USB had featured Lucinda and Ralph discussing how they planned to kill Marion's son and frame John and Bart. How Gary Thibodeaux had gotten the footage would probably remain a mystery, as all attempts to locate him had still proved unsuccessful. I wondered if the club owner had been intercepted by Lucinda before he could escape.

So far, Marion had kept his promise and neither my name nor Ida Belle's had popped up during the investigation. As far as Carter knew, I'd never set foot in that cemetery nor had I ever had the USB in my possession. We'd simply left Big's office and returned to my house, pretending we knew nothing until Carter showed up on my doorstep to tell us it was officially over. We'd waited a day before retrieving Ida Belle's SUV from the storage facility, then Ida Belle and Gertie had returned to their homes; everything was back to normal.

Sort of. Carter and I were still sidestepping the big issues between us, but at least we were talking again without arguing about every sentence spoken. It helped that there were plenty of other things to talk about. It allowed us to easily avoid the harder stuff.

"How's the discovery going?" I asked.

Marion had officially apologized to Carter for using him to gain access to Hot Rod's shop under the guise of helping. Given the situation with Marion's son, Carter hadn't been holding a grudge anyway, but the apology hadn't hurt, and when Marion had asked for his help uncovering the web of deceit that Lucinda and Ralph had designed, he was happy to assist.

"It's incredible," he said. "I thought I'd seen things, especially lately, but this is a doozy."

"Can you tell me anything?"

He nodded. "Marion is releasing everything to the press as we uncover it. With Lucinda and Ralph both dead, there's no trial to secure the evidence for."

"So?"

"Well, for starters, Lucinda isn't Lucinda. She's Carol."

"What?"

"Carol Seal was a dedicated employee of the tax assessor's office by day and a drug supplier for one of the local mobsters by night. When Marion started getting too close, she issued the threat and took out his son. Unfortunately, it appears that the family she worked for was afraid she was too exposed and put out a hit on her."

"So she faked her own death," I said.

Carter nodded. "Ralph identified the body, and Carol became Lucinda and disappeared to Sinful."

"Didn't you say Ralph was the accountant for some drug dealer in New Orleans years ago? Wasn't it risky relocating Carol to Sinful?"

"I'm sure Ralph met with all his questionable clients in New Orleans. Neither party would want to be seen together in Sinful.

Too much talk. Besides, it appears he parted ways with that client shortly after Carol's 'death.'"

I nodded. Hiding in plain sight, sort of. It made sense. "So who was the woman in the car?"

"Probably some unfortunate junkie who resembled Carol enough to avoid a red flag with the coroner. They're going to exhume the body to get DNA. Maybe they'll find a match to a missing persons case."

"How does Ralph fit into all of this now? If he wasn't still in the hinky accounting business why all the worry over an audit?"

"Ralph and Carol had a property scheme going. It was their retirement plan. Ralph used the money they made from their drug-related pursuits to buy and sell real estate during the hurricane rebuilding. Then Carol changed the purchase and sales amounts in the tax assessor's computer system."

"That way the IRS was never alerted to large profits so they didn't question lifestyle versus income claims," I said. "That's genius. But they must have figured it out somehow since Ralph was worried about an audit."

"The tax assessor's office began implementing a new system a couple months ago. While converting the historical data, the techs noticed some discrepancies and turned the information over to the IRS."

"So if they made all this money, why didn't they just skip town with it? I mean, I figure Carol had to lie low for a while because she didn't want the family she dealt for to catch her walking around alive somewhere. But ten years is a lot of aging to wait for."

Carter nodded. "For years, Ralph has been in the process of shifting everything to offshore accounts for shell corporations, but changes to banking laws have made it hard to move a lot of money without sending up red flags. It's a slow process if you want to get away clean."

"And technically speaking, Carol wasn't at risk of losing

anything but the money because as far as the IRS was concerned, she was already dead. Which left Ralph on the hook for everything. So I guess he *did* commit suicide."

"I don't think so. The coroner's report came in. Ralph had GHB in his system. There was gunpowder residue on his hand, but she could have held the gun in his hand and pulled the trigger. Maybe he really was panicking over the audit. Carol might have decided he was a liability like everyone else."

I shook my head. It was so fantastic, more like a movie than real life. "What about the Seal brothers?"

"We got a video from border patrol showing them crossing into Mexico."

"Are you going to look for them?"

"Not my jurisdiction. My guess is New Orleans PD will issue a warrant for parole violation and that will be the end of it unless they get stupid."

I nodded. I hoped they used the money to get their lives together and keep those lives south of the border. I had a bit of hope for the second item. I didn't have much for the first.

"We went to visit Hot Rod this morning," I said. "He's looking great. I mean, considering."

Carter nodded. "I saw him yesterday evening. I like a happy ending."

The best news to come out of all of this was that Hot Rod had regained consciousness and it looked as though he was going to make a full recovery. When he'd woken up, he'd immediately started yelling for a phone to call Ida Belle, and it took two orderlies to hold him down while Shonda and the evening news convinced him that Ida Belle was safe and it was all over. The two people who'd broken in his shop had worn ski masks, but I had no doubt it was Carol and Ralph. Hot Rod had been shocked to hear what had happened while he was sleeping and thrilled to find out that Ida Belle was all right and the entire mess was over.

Carter rose from his chair. "I've got to get back to the office for a while. I'm still trying to wrap up all the paperwork from this. I'm hoping to finish everything today. If I do, I'm taking a day off tomorrow. I thought maybe we could talk."

"Okay," I said. It probably wouldn't be pleasant, but it was necessary. I was tired of all the unspoken words between us. It was time to get everything out into the open. Once and for all.

I watched him walk away and wondered again how much compromise I was willing to make to have a future with him. Definitely some, but not all. I just hoped he could meet somewhere that worked for both of us.

My cell phone rang and I checked the display, then popped upright. It was Harrison.

"Redding," Harrison said when I answered. "We have Ahmad on radar in Miami. The takedown will happen in two days. Do you want in?"

"Do you have to ask?"

Will Fortune finally be free of Ahmad and the CIA?

Find out in CHANGE OF FORTUNE, coming the end of 2017. To receive notice of new releases by Jana DeLeon, please sign up for her newsletter.